ULYSSES

VOLUME THREE OF THREE

Ulysses

Joyce, James 1882 – 1941
First Published by Sylvia Beach in 1922

Text set in 18 point Helvetica.
Chapter headings set in Helvetica Neue.

ISBN: 978-1-83412-425-4 Volume One
ISBN: 978-1-83412-426-1 Volume Two
ISBN: 978-1-83412-427-8 Volume Three

ULYSSES

VOLUME THREE OF THREE

JAMES JOYCE

GRAND TYPE CLASSICS

CONTENTS

Part Three

CHAPTER SIXTEEN

PREPARATORY to anything else Mr Bloom brushed off the greater bulk of the shavings and handed Stephen the hat and ashplant and bucked him up generally in orthodox Samaritan fashion which he very badly needed. His (Stephen's) mind was not exactly what you would call wandering but a bit unsteady and on his expressed desire for some beverage to drink Mr Bloom in view of the hour it was and there being no pump of Vartry water available for their ablutions let alone drinking purposes hit upon an expedient by suggesting, off the reel, the propriety of the cabman's shelter, as it was called, hardly a stonesthrow away near Butt bridge where they might hit upon some drinkables in the shape of a milk and soda or a mineral. But how to get there was the rub. For the nonce he was rather nonplussed but inasmuch as the duty plainly devolved upon him to take some measures on the subject he pondered suitable ways and means during which Stephen repeatedly yawned. So far as he could see he was rather pale in the face so that it occurred to him as highly advisable to get a conveyance of some description which would answer in their then condition, both of them being e.d.ed, particularly Stephen, always assuming that there was such a thing to be found. Accordingly after a few such preliminaries as brushing, in spite of his having forgotten to take up his rather soapsuddy handkerchief after it had done yeoman service in the shaving line, they both walked together along Beaver street or, more properly, lane as far as the farrier's and the distinctly fetid atmosphere of the livery stables at the corner of Montgomery street where they made tracks to the left from thence debouching into Amiens street round by the corner of Dan Bergin's. But as he confidently anticipated there was not a sign of a Jehu plying for hire anywhere to be seen except a fourwheeler, probably engaged by some fellows inside on the spree, outside the North Star hotel and there was no symptom of its budging a quarter of an inch when Mr Bloom, who was anything but a professional whistler, endeavoured to hail it by emitting a kind of a whistle, holding his arms arched over his head, twice.

This was a quandary but, bringing common sense to bear on it, evidently there was nothing for it but put a good face on the matter and foot it which they accordingly did.

So, bevelling around by Mullett's and the Signal House which they shortly reached, they proceeded perforce in the direction of Amiens street railway terminus, Mr Bloom being handicapped by the circumstance that one of the back buttons of his trousers had, to vary the timehonoured adage, gone the way of all buttons though, entering thoroughly into the spirit of the thing, he heroically made light of the mischance. So as neither of them were particularly pressed for time, as it happened, and the temperature refreshing since it cleared up after the recent visitation of Jupiter Pluvius, they dandered along past by where the empty vehicle was waiting without a fare or a jarvey. As it so happened a Dublin United Tramways Company's sandstrewer happened to be returning and the elder man recounted to his companion à propos of the incident his own truly miraculous escape of some little while back. They passed the main entrance of the Great Northern railway station, the starting point for Belfast, where of course all traffic was suspended at that late hour and passing the backdoor of the morgue (a not very enticing locality, not to say gruesome to a degree, more especially at night) ultimately gained the Dock Tavern and in due course turned into Store street, famous for its C division police station. Between this point and the high at present unlit warehouses of Beresford place Stephen thought to think of Ibsen, associated with Baird›s the stonecutter›s in his mind somehow in Talbot place, first turning on the right, while the other who was acting as his **fidus Achates** inhaled with internal satisfaction the smell of James Rourke's city bakery, situated quite close to where they were, the very palatable odour indeed of our daily bread, of all commodities of the public the primary and most indispensable. Bread, the staff of life, earn your bread, O tell me where is fancy bread, at Rourke's the baker's it is said.

En route to his taciturn and, not to put

too fine a point on it, not yet perfectly sober companion Mr Bloom who at all events was in complete possession of his faculties, never more so, in fact disgustingly sober, spoke a word of caution re the dangers of nighttown, women of ill fame and swell mobsmen, which, barely permissible once in a while though not as a habitual practice, was of the nature of a regular deathtrap for young fellows of his age particularly if they had acquired drinking habits under the influence of liquor unless you knew a little jiujitsu for every contingency as even a fellow on the broad of his back could administer a nasty kick if you didn't look out. Highly providential was the appearance on the scene of Corny Kelleher when Stephen was blissfully unconscious but for that man in the gap turning up at the eleventh hour the finis might have been that he might have been a candidate for the accident ward or, failing that, the bridewell and an appearance in the court next day before Mr Tobias or, he being the solicitor rather, old Wall, he meant to say, or Mahony which simply spelt ruin for a chap when it got bruited about. The reason he mentioned the fact was that a lot of those policemen, whom he cordially disliked, were admittedly unscrupulous in the service of the Crown and, as Mr Bloom put it, recalling a case or two in the A division in Clanbrassil street, prepared to swear a hole through a ten gallon pot. Never on the spot when wanted but in quiet parts of the city, Pembroke road for example, the guardians of the law were well in evidence, the obvious reason being they were paid to protect the upper classes. Another thing he commented on was equipping soldiers with firearms or sidearms of any description liable to go off at any time which was tantamount to inciting them against civilians should by any chance they fall out over anything. You frittered away your time, he very sensibly maintained, and health and also character besides which, the squandermania of the thing, fast women of the **demimonde** ran away with a lot of £. s. d. into the bargain and the greatest danger of all was who you got drunk with though, touching the much vexed question of stimulants, he relished a glass of choice old wine in season as both nourishing and bloodmaking and possessing aperient virtues (notably a good burgundy which he was a staunch believer in) still never beyond a certain point where he invariably drew the line as it simply led to trouble all round to say nothing of your being at the tender mercy of others practically. Most of all he commented adversely on the desertion of Stephen by all his pubhunting **confrères** but one, a most glaring piece of ratting on the part of his brother medicos under all the circs.

– And that one was Judas, Stephen said, who up to then had said nothing whatsoever of any kind.

Discussing these and kindred topics they made a beeline across the back of the

Customhouse and passed under the Loop Line bridge where a brazier of coke burning in front of a sentrybox or something like one attracted their rather lagging footsteps. Stephen of his own accord stopped for no special reason to look at the heap of barren cobblestones and by the light emanating from the brazier he could just make out the darker figure of the corporation watchman inside the gloom of the sentrybox. He began to remember that this had happened or had been mentioned as having happened before but it cost him no small effort before he remembered that he recognised in the sentry a quondam friend of his father's, Gumley. To avoid a meeting he drew nearer to the pillars of the railway bridge.

– Someone saluted you, Mr Bloom said.

A figure of middle height on the prowl evidently under the arches saluted again, calling:

– **Night!**

Stephen of course started rather dizzily

and stopped to return the compliment. Mr Bloom actuated by motives of inherent delicacy inasmuch as he always believed in minding his own business moved off but nevertheless remained on the **qui vive** with just a shade of anxiety though not funkyish in the least. Though unusual in the Dublin area he knew that it was not by any means unknown for desperadoes who had next to nothing to live on to be abroad waylaying and generally terrorising peaceable pedestrians by placing a pistol at their head in some secluded spot outside the city proper, famished loiterers of the Thames embankment category they might be hanging about there or simply marauders ready to decamp with whatever boodle they could in one fell swoop at a moment's notice, your money or your life, leaving you there to point a moral, gagged and garrotted.

Stephen, that is when the accosting figure came to close quarters, though he was not in an over sober state himself recognised

Corley's breath redolent of rotten cornjuice. Lord John Corley some called him and his genealogy came about in this wise. He was the eldest son of inspector Corley of the G division, lately deceased, who had married a certain Katherine Brophy, the daughter of a Louth farmer. His grandfather Patrick Michael Corley of New Ross had married the widow of a publican there whose maiden name had been Katherine (also) Talbot. Rumour had it (though not proved) that she descended from the house of the lords Talbot de Malahide in whose mansion, really an unquestionably fine residence of its kind and well worth seeing, her mother or aunt or some relative, a woman, as the tale went, of extreme beauty, had enjoyed the distinction of being in service in the washkitchen. This therefore was the reason why the still comparatively young though dissolute man who now addressed Stephen was spoken of by some with facetious proclivities as Lord John Corley.

Taking Stephen on one side he had the

customary doleful ditty to tell. Not as much as a farthing to purchase a night's lodgings. His friends had all deserted him. Furthermore he had a row with Lenehan and called him to Stephen a mean bloody swab with a sprinkling of a number of other uncalledfor expressions. He was out of a job and implored of Stephen to tell him where on God's earth he could get something, anything at all, to do. No, it was the daughter of the mother in the washkitchen that was fostersister to the heir of the house or else they were connected through the mother in some way, both occurrences happening at the same time if the whole thing wasn't a complete fabrication from start to finish. Anyhow he was all in.

– I wouldn't ask you only, pursued he, on my solemn oath and God knows I'm on the rocks.

– There'll be a job tomorrow or next day, Stephen told him, in a boys' school at Dalkey for a gentleman usher. Mr Garrett Deasy.

Try it. You may mention my name.

– Ah, God, Corley replied, sure I couldn't teach in a school, man. I was never one of your bright ones, he added with a half laugh. I got stuck twice in the junior at the christian brothers.

– I have no place to sleep myself, Stephen informed him.

Corley at the first go-off was inclined to suspect it was something to do with Stephen being fired out of his digs for bringing in a bloody tart off the street. There was a dosshouse in Marlborough street, Mrs Maloney's, but it was only a tanner touch and full of undesirables but M'Conachie told him you got a decent enough do in the Brazen Head over in Winetavern street (which was distantly suggestive to the person addressed of friar Bacon) for a bob. He was starving too though he hadn't said a word about it.

Though this sort of thing went on every other night or very near it still Stephen's feelings got the better of him in a sense though he knew that Corley's brandnew rigmarole on a par with the others was hardly deserving of much credence. However **haud ignarus malorum miseris succurrere disco** etcetera as the Latin poet remarks especially as luck would have it he got paid his screw after every middle of the month on the sixteenth which was the date of the month as a matter of fact though a good bit of the wherewithal was demolished. But the cream of the joke was nothing would get it out of Corley's head that he was living in affluence and hadn't a thing to do but hand out the needful. Whereas. He put his hand in a pocket anyhow not with the idea of finding any food there but thinking he might lend him anything up to a bob or so in lieu so that he might endeavour at all events and get sufficient to eat but the result was in the negative for, to his chagrin, he found his cash missing. A few broken biscuits were all the result of his investigation. He tried his hardest to recollect for the moment whether he had lost as well he might have or left because in that contingency it was not a pleasant lookout, very much the reverse in fact. He was altogether too fagged out to institute a thorough search though he tried to recollect. About biscuits he dimly remembered. Who now exactly gave them he wondered or where was or did he buy. However in another pocket he came across what he surmised in the dark were pennies, erroneously however, as it turned out.

– Those are halfcrowns, man, Corley corrected him.

And so in point of fact they turned out to be. Stephen anyhow lent him one of them.

– Thanks, Corley answered, you're a gentleman. I'll pay you back one time. Who's that with you? I saw him a few times in the Bleeding Horse in Camden street with Boylan, the billsticker. You might put in a good word for us to get me taken on there. I'd carry a sandwichboard only the girl in the office told me they're full up for the next three weeks, man. God, you've to book ahead, man, you'd think it was for the Carl Rosa. I don't give a shite anyway so long as I get a job, even as a crossing sweeper.

Subsequently being not quite so down in the mouth after the two and six he got he informed Stephen about a fellow by the name of Bags Comisky that he said Stephen knew well out of Fullam's, the shipchandler's, bookkeeper there that used to be often round in Nagle's back with O'Mara and a little chap with a stutter the name of Tighe. Anyhow he was lagged the night before last and fined ten bob for a drunk and disorderly and refusing to go with the constable.

210

Mr Bloom in the meanwhile kept dodging about in the vicinity of the cobblestones near the brazier of coke in front of the corporation watchman's sentrybox who evidently a glutton for work, it struck him, was having a quiet forty winks for all intents and purposes on his own private account while Dublin slept. He threw an odd eye at the same time now and then at Stephen's anything but immaculately attired interlocutor as if he had seen that nobleman somewhere or other though where he was not in a position to truthfully state nor had he the remotest idea when. Being a levelheaded individual who could give points to not a few in point of shrewd observation he also remarked on his very dilapidated hat and slouchy wearing apparel generally testifying to a chronic impecuniosity. Palpably he was one of his hangerson but for the matter of that it was merely a question of one preying on his nextdoor neighbour all round, in every deep, so to put it, a deeper depth and for the matter of that if the man in the street chanced to be in the dock himself penal servitude with or without the option of a fine would be a very rara avis altogether. In any case he had a consummate amount of cool assurance intercepting people at that hour of the night or morning. Pretty thick that was certainly.

The pair parted company and Stephen

rejoined Mr Bloom who, with his practised eye, was not without perceiving that he had succumbed to the blandiloquence of the other parasite. Alluding to the encounter he said, laughingly, Stephen, that is:

– He is down on his luck. He asked me to ask you to ask somebody named Boylan, a billsticker, to give him a job as a sandwichman.

At this intelligence, in which he seemingly evinced little interest, Mr Bloom gazed abstractedly for the space of a half a second or so in the direction of a bucketdredger, rejoicing in the farfamed name of Eblana, moored alongside Customhouse quay and quite possibly out of repair, whereupon he observed evasively:

– Everybody gets their own ration of luck, they say. Now you mention it his face was familiar to me. But, leaving that for the moment, how much did you part with, he queried, if I am not too inquisitive?

– Half a crown, Stephen responded. I

daresay he needs it to sleep somewhere.

– Needs! Mr Bloom ejaculated, professing not the least surprise at the intelligence, I can quite credit the assertion and I guarantee he invariably does. Everyone according to his needs or everyone according to his deeds. But, talking about things in general, where, added he with a smile, will you sleep yourself? Walking to Sandycove is out of the question. And even supposing you did you won't get in after what occurred at Westland Row station. Simply fag out there for nothing. I don't mean to presume to dictate to you in the slightest degree but why did you leave your father's house?

– To seek misfortune, was Stephen's answer.

– I met your respected father on a recent occasion, Mr Bloom diplomatically returned, today in fact, or to be strictly accurate, on yesterday. Where does he live at present? I gathered in the course of conversation that he had moved.

– I believe he is in Dublin somewhere, Stephen answered unconcernedly. Why?

– A gifted man, Mr Bloom said of Mr Dedalus senior, in more respects than one and a born **raconteur** if ever there was one. He takes great pride, quite legitimate, out of you. You could go back perhaps, he hasarded, still thinking of the very unpleasant scene at Westland Row terminus when it was perfectly evident that the other two, Mulligan, that is, and that English tourist friend of his, who eventually euchred their third companion, were patently trying as if the whole bally station belonged to them to give Stephen the slip in the confusion, which they did.

There was no response forthcoming to the suggestion however, such as it was, Stephen's mind's eye being too busily engaged in repicturing his family hearth the last time he saw it with his sister Dilly sitting by the ingle, her hair hanging down, waiting for some weak Trinidad shell cocoa that was in the sootcoated kettle to be done so that she and he could drink it with the oatmealwater for milk after the Friday herrings they had eaten at two a penny with an egg apiece for Maggy, Boody and Katey, the cat meanwhile under the mangle devouring a mess of eggshells and charred fish heads and bones on a square of brown paper, in accordance with the third precept of the church to fast and abstain on the days commanded, it being quarter tense or if not, ember days or something like that.

– No, Mr Bloom repeated again, I wouldn't personally repose much trust in that boon companion of yours who contributes the humorous element, Dr Mulligan, as a guide, philosopher and friend if I were in your shoes. He knows which side his bread is buttered on though in all probability he never realised what it is to be without regular meals. Of course you didn't notice as much as I did. But it wouldn't occasion me the least surprise to learn that a pinch of tobacco or some narcotic was put in your drink for some ulterior object.

He understood however from all he heard that Dr Mulligan was a versatile allround man, by no means confined to medicine only, who was rapidly coming to the fore in his line and, if the report was verified, bade fair to enjoy a flourishing practice in the not too distant future as a tony medical practitioner drawing a handsome fee for his services in addition to which professional status his rescue of that man from certain drowning by artificial respiration and what they call first aid at Skerries, or Malahide was it?, was, he was bound to admit, an exceedingly plucky deed which he could not too highly praise, so that frankly he was utterly at a loss to fathom what earthly reason could be at the back of it except he put it down to sheer cussedness or jealousy, pure and simple.

– Except it simply amounts to one thing and he is what they call picking your brains, he ventured to throw out.

The guarded glance of half solicitude half

curiosity augmented by friendliness which he gave at Stephen's at present morose expression of features did not throw a flood of light, none at all in fact on the problem as to whether he had let himself be badly bamboozled to judge by two or three lowspirited remarks he let drop or the other way about saw through the affair and for some reason or other best known to himself allowed matters to more or less. Grinding poverty did have that effect and he more than conjectured that, high educational abilities though he possessed, he experienced no little difficulty in making both ends meet.

Adjacent to the men's public urinal they perceived an icecream car round which a group of presumably Italians in heated altercation were getting rid of voluble expressions in their vivacious language in a particularly animated way, there being some little differences between the parties.

– **Puttana madonna, che ci dia i quattrini! Ho ragione? Culo rotto!**

– Intendiamoci. Mezzo sovrano piu...
– Dice lui, pero!
– Mezzo.
– Farabutto! Mortacci sui!
– Ma ascolta! Cinque la testa piu...

Mr Bloom and Stephen entered the cabman's shelter, an unpretentious wooden structure, where, prior to then, he had rarely if ever been before, the former having previously whispered to the latter a few hints anent the keeper of it said to be the once famous Skin-the-Goat Fitzharris, the invincible, though he could not vouch for the actual facts which quite possibly there was not one vestige of truth in. A few moments later saw our two noctambules safely seated in a discreet corner only to be greeted by stares from the decidedly miscellaneous collection of waifs and strays and other nondescript specimens of the genus **homo** already there engaged in eating and drinking diversified by conversation for whom they seemingly formed an object of marked curiosity.

– Now touching a cup of coffee, Mr Bloom ventured to plausibly suggest to break the ice, it occurs to me you ought to sample something in the shape of solid food, say, a roll of some description.

Accordingly his first act was with characteristic **sangfroid** to order these commodities quietly. The **hoi polloi** of jarvies or stevedores or whatever they were after a cursory examination turned their eyes apparently dissatisfied, away though one redbearded bibulous individual portion of whose hair was greyish, a sailor probably, still stared for some appreciable time before transferring his rapt attention to the floor. Mr Bloom, availing himself of the right of free speech, he having just a bowing acquaintance with the language in dispute, though, to be sure, rather in a quandary over **voglio**, remarked to his **protégé** in an audible tone of voice **a propos** of the battle royal in the street which was still raging fast and furious:

– A beautiful language. I mean for singing purposes. Why do you not write your poetry in that language? **Bella Poetria**! It is so melodious and full. **Belladonna. Voglio.**

Stephen, who was trying his dead best to yawn if he could, suffering from lassitude generally, replied:

– To fill the ear of a cow elephant. They were haggling over money.

– Is that so? Mr Bloom asked. Of course, he subjoined pensively, at the inward reflection of there being more languages to start with than were absolutely necessary, it may be only the southern glamour that surrounds it.

The keeper of the shelter in the middle of this **tête-â-tête** put a boiling swimming cup of a choice concoction labelled coffee on the table and a rather antediluvian specimen of a bun, or so it seemed. After which he beat a retreat to his counter, Mr Bloom determining to have a good square look at him later on so as not to appear to. For which reason he encouraged Stephen to proceed with his eyes while he did the honours by surreptitiously pushing the cup of what was temporarily supposed to be called coffee gradually nearer him.

– Sounds are impostures, Stephen said after a pause of some little time, like names. Cicero, Podmore. Napoleon, Mr Goodbody. Jesus, Mr Doyle. Shakespeares were as common as Murphies. What's in a name?

– Yes, to be sure, Mr Bloom unaffectedly concurred. Of course. Our name was changed too, he added, pushing the socalled roll across.

The redbearded sailor who had his weather eye on the newcomers boarded Stephen, whom he had singled out for attention in particular, squarely by asking:

– And what might your name be?

Just in the nick of time Mr Bloom touched his companion's boot but Stephen, apparently disregarding the warm pressure from an unexpected quarter, answered:

– Dedalus.

The sailor stared at him heavily from a pair of drowsy baggy eyes, rather bunged up from excessive use of boose, preferably good old Hollands and water.

– You know Simon Dedalus? he asked at length.

– I've heard of him, Stephen said.

Mr Bloom was all at sea for a moment, seeing the others evidently eavesdropping too.

– He's Irish, the seaman bold affirmed, staring still in much the same way and nodding. All Irish.

– All too Irish, Stephen rejoined.

As for Mr Bloom he could neither make head or tail of the whole business and he was just asking himself what possible connection when the sailor of his own accord turned to the other occupants of the shelter with the remark:

– I seen him shoot two eggs off two bottles

at fifty yards over his shoulder. The lefthand dead shot.

Though he was slightly hampered by an occasional stammer and his gestures being also clumsy as it was still he did his best to explain.

– Bottles out there, say. Fifty yards measured. Eggs on the bottles. Cocks his gun over his shoulder. Aims.

He turned his body half round, shut up his right eye completely. Then he screwed his features up someway sideways and glared out into the night with an unprepossessing cast of countenance.

– Pom! he then shouted once.

The entire audience waited, anticipating an additional detonation, there being still a further egg.

– Pom! he shouted twice.

Egg two evidently demolished, he nodded and winked, adding bloodthirstily:

– Buffalo Bill shoots to kill, Never missed nor he never will.

A silence ensued till Mr Bloom for agreeableness' sake just felt like asking him whether it was for a marksmanship competition like the Bisley.

– Beg pardon, the sailor said.

– Long ago? Mr Bloom pursued without flinching a hairsbreadth.

– Why, the sailor replied, relaxing to a certain extent under the magic influence of diamond cut diamond, it might be a matter of ten years. He toured the wide world with Hengler's Royal Circus. I seen him do that in Stockholm.

– Curious coincidence, Mr Bloom confided to Stephen unobtrusively.

– Murphy's my name, the sailor continued. D. B. Murphy of Carrigaloe. Know where that is?

– Queenstown harbour, Stephen replied.

– That's right, the sailor said. Fort Camden and Fort Carlisle. That's where I hails from. I belongs there. That's where I hails from. My little woman's down there. She's waiting for me, I know. **For England, home and beauty**. She's my own true wife I haven't seen for seven years now, sailing about.

Mr Bloom could easily picture his advent on this scene, the homecoming to the mariner's roadside shieling after having diddled Davy Jones, a rainy night with a blind moon. Across the world for a wife. Quite a number of stories there were on that particular Alice Ben Bolt topic, Enoch Arden and Rip van Winkle and does anybody hereabouts remember Caoc O'Leary, a favourite and most trying declamation piece by the way of poor John Casey and a bit of perfect poetry in its own small way. Never about the runaway wife coming back, however much devoted to the absentee. The face at the window! Judge of his astonishment when he finally did breast the tape and the awful truth dawned upon him anent his better half, wrecked in his affections. You little expected me but I've come to stay and make a fresh start. There she sits, a grasswidow, at the selfsame fireside. Believes me dead, rocked in the cradle of the deep. And there sits uncle Chubb or Tomkin, as the case might be, the publican of the Crown and Anchor, in shirtsleeves, eating rumpsteak and onions. No chair for father. Broo! The wind! Her brandnew arrival is on her knee, **post mortem** child. With a high ro! and a randy ro! and my galloping tearing tandy, O! Bow to the inevitable. Grin and bear it. I remain with much love your brokenhearted husband D B Murphy.

The sailor, who scarcely seemed to be a Dublin resident, turned to one of the jarvies with the request:

– You don't happen to have such a thing as a spare chaw about you?

The jarvey addressed as it happened had not but the keeper took a die of plug from his good jacket hanging on a nail and the desired object was passed from hand to hand.

– Thank you, the sailor said.

He deposited the quid in his gob and, chewing and with some slow stammers, proceeded:

– We come up this morning eleven o'clock. The threemaster **Rosevean** from Bridgwater with bricks. I shipped to get over. Paid off this afternoon. There's my discharge. See? D. B. Murphy. A. B. S.

In confirmation of which statement he extricated from an inside pocket and handed to his neighbour a not very cleanlooking folded document.

– You must have seen a fair share of the world, the keeper remarked, leaning on the counter.

– Why, the sailor answered upon reflection upon it, I've circumnavigated a bit since I first joined on. I was in the Red Sea. I was in China and North America and South America. We was chased by pirates one voyage. I seen icebergs plenty, growlers. I was in Stockholm and the Black Sea, the Dardanelles under Captain Dalton, the best bloody man that ever scuttled a ship. I seen Russia. **Gospodi pomilyou**. That's how the Russians prays.

– You seen queer sights, don't be talking, put in a jarvey.

– Why, the sailor said, shifting his partially chewed plug. I seen queer things too, ups and downs. I seen a crocodile bite the fluke of an anchor same as I chew that quid.

He took out of his mouth the pulpy quid and, lodging it between his teeth, bit ferociously:

– Khaan! Like that. And I seen maneaters in Peru that eats corpses and the livers of horses. Look here. Here they are. A friend of mine sent me.

He fumbled out a picture postcard from his inside pocket which seemed to be in its way a species of repository and pushed it along the table. The printed matter on it stated: **Choza de Indios. Beni, Bolivia.**

All focussed their attention at the scene exhibited, a group of savage women in striped loincloths, squatted, blinking, suckling, frowning, sleeping amid a swarm of infants (there must have been quite a score of them) outside some primitive shanties of osier.

– Chews coca all day, the communicative tarpaulin added. Stomachs like breadgraters. Cuts off their diddies when they can't bear no more children.

See them sitting there stark ballocknaked eating a dead horse's liver raw.

His postcard proved a centre of attraction for Messrs the greenhorns for several minutes if not more.

– Know how to keep them off? he inquired generally.

Nobody volunteering a statement he winked, saying:

– Glass. That boggles 'em. Glass.

Mr Bloom, without evincing surprise, unostentatiously turned over the card to peruse the partially obliterated address and postmark. It ran as follows: **Tarjeta Postal, Señor A Boudin, Galeria Becche,**

Santiago, Chile. There was no message evidently, as he took particular notice. Though not an implicit believer in the lurid story narrated (or the eggsniping transaction for that matter despite William Tell and the Lazarillo-Don Cesar de Bazan incident depicted in **Maritana** on which occasion the former's ball passed through the latter's hat) having detected a discrepancy between his name (assuming he was the person he represented himself to be and not sailing under false colours after having boxed the compass on the strict q.t. somewhere) and the fictitious addressee of the missive which made him nourish some suspicions of our friend's **bona fides** nevertheless it reminded him in a way of a longcherished plan he meant to one day realise some Wednesday or Saturday of travelling to London via long sea not to say that he had ever travelled extensively to any great extent but he was at heart a born adventurer though by a trick of fate he had consistently remained a landlubber except you call going to Holyhead which was his longest. Martin Cunningham frequently said he would work a pass through Egan but some deuced hitch or other eternally cropped up with the net result that the scheme fell through. But even suppose it did come to planking down the needful and breaking Boyd's heart it was not so dear, purse permitting, a few guineas at the outside considering the fare to Mullingar where he figured on going was five and six, there and back. The trip would benefit health on account of the bracing ozone and be in every way thoroughly pleasurable, especially for a chap whose liver was out of order, seeing the different places along the route, Plymouth, Falmouth, Southampton and so on culminating in an instructive tour of the sights of the great metropolis, the spectacle of our modern Babylon where doubtless he would see the greatest improvement, tower, abbey, wealth of Park lane to renew acquaintance with. Another thing just struck him as a by no means bad notion was he might have a gaze around on the spot to see about trying to make arrangements about a concert tour of summer music embracing the most prominent pleasure resorts, Margate with mixed bathing and firstrate hydros and spas, Eastbourne, Scarborough, Margate and so on, beautiful Bournemouth, the Channel islands and similar bijou spots, which might prove highly remunerative. Not, of course, with a hole and corner scratch company or local ladies on the job, witness Mrs C P M'Coy type lend me your valise and I'll post you the ticket. No, something top notch, an all star Irish caste, the Tweedy-Flower grand opera company with his own legal consort as leading lady as a sort of counterblast to the Elster Grimes and Moody-Manners, perfectly simple matter and he was quite sanguine of success, providing puffs in the local papers could be managed by some fellow with a bit of bounce who could pull the indispensable wires and thus combine business with pleasure. But who? That was the rub. Also, without being actually positive, it struck him a great field was to be opened up in the line of opening up new routes to keep pace with the times **apropos** of the Fishguard-Rosslare route which, it was mooted, was once more on the **tapis** in the circumlocution departments with the usual quantity of red tape and dillydallying of effete fogeydom and dunderheads generally. A great opportunity there certainly was for push and enterprise to meet the travelling needs of the public at large, the average man, i.e. Brown, Robinson and Co.

It was a subject of regret and absurd as well on the face of it and no small blame to our vaunted society that the man in the street, when the system really needed toning up, for the matter of a couple of paltry pounds was debarred from seeing more of the world they lived in instead of being always and ever cooped up since my old stick-in-the-mud took me for a wife. After all, hang it, they had their eleven and more humdrum months of it and merited a radical change of **venue** after the grind of city life in the summertime for choice when dame Nature is at her spectacular best constituting nothing short of a new lease of life. There were equally excellent opportunities for vacationists in the home island, delightful sylvan spots for rejuvenation, offering a plethora of attractions as well as a bracing tonic for the system in and around Dublin and its picturesque environs even, Poulaphouca to which there was a steamtram, but also farther away from the madding crowd in Wicklow, rightly termed the garden of Ireland, an ideal neighbourhood for elderly wheelmen so long as it didn't come down, and in the wilds of Donegal where if report spoke true the **coup d'œil** was exceedingly grand though the lastnamed locality was not easily getatable so that the influx of visitors was not as yet all that it might be considering the signal benefits to be derived from it while Howth with its historic associations and otherwise, Silken Thomas, Grace O'Malley, George IV, rhododendrons several hundred feet above sealevel was a favourite haunt with all sorts and conditions of men especially in the spring when young men's fancy, though it had its own toll of deaths by falling off the cliffs by design or accidentally, usually, by the way, on their left leg, it being only about three quarters of an hour's run from the pillar. Because of course uptodate tourist travelling was as yet merely in its infancy, so to speak, and the accommodation left much to be desired. Interesting to fathom it seemed to him from a motive of curiosity, pure and simple, was whether it was the traffic that created the route or viceversa or the two sides in fact. He turned back the other side of the card, picture, and passed it along to Stephen.

– I seen a Chinese one time, related the doughty narrator, that had little pills like putty and he put them in the water and they opened and every pill was something different. One was a ship, another was a house, another was a flower. Cooks rats in your soup, he appetisingly added, the chinks does.

Possibly perceiving an expression of dubiosity on their faces the globetrotter went on, adhering to his adventures.

– And I seen a man killed in Trieste by an Italian chap. Knife in his back. Knife like that.

Whilst speaking he produced a dangerouslooking claspknife quite in keeping with his character and held it in the striking position.

– In a knockingshop it was count of a tryon between two smugglers. Fellow hid behind a door, come up behind him. Like that. **Prepare to meet your God**, says he. Chuk! It went into his back up to the butt.

His heavy glance drowsily roaming about kind of defied their further questions even should they by any chance want to.

– That's a good bit of steel, repeated he, examining his formidable **stiletto**.

After which harrowing **dénouement** sufficient to appal the stoutest he snapped the blade to and stowed the weapon in question away as before in his chamber of horrors, otherwise pocket.

–They're great for the cold steel, somebody who was evidently quite in the dark said for the benefit of them all. That was why they thought the park murders of the invincibles was done by foreigners on account of them using knives.

At this remark passed obviously in the spirit of **where ignorance is bliss** Mr B. and Stephen, each in his own particular way, both instinctively exchanged meaning glances, in a religious silence of the strictly **entre nous** variety however, towards where Skin-the-Goat, **alias** the keeper, not turning a hair, was drawing spurts of liquid from his boiler affair. His inscrutable face which was really a work of art, a perfect study in itself, beggaring description, conveyed the impression that he didn't understand one jot of what was going on. Funny, very!

There ensued a somewhat lengthy pause. One man was reading in fits and starts a stained by coffee evening journal, another the card with the natives **choza de**, another the seaman's discharge. Mr Bloom, so far as he was personally concerned, was just pondering in pensive mood. He vividly recollected when the occurrence alluded to took place as well as yesterday, roughly some score of years previously in the days of the land troubles, when it took the civilised world by storm, figuratively speaking, early in the eighties, eightyone to be correct, when he was just turned fifteen.

– Ay, boss, the sailor broke in. Give us back them papers.

The request being complied with he clawed them up with a scrape.

– Have you seen the rock of Gibraltar? Mr Bloom inquired.

The sailor grimaced, chewing, in a way that might be read as yes, ay or no.

– Ah, you've touched there too, Mr Bloom said, Europa point, thinking he had, in the hope that the rover might possibly by some reminiscences but he failed to do so, simply letting spirt a jet of spew into the sawdust, and shook his head with a sort of lazy scorn.

– What year would that be about? Mr B interrogated. Can you recall the boats?

Our **soi-disant** sailor munched heavily awhile hungrily before answering:

– I'm tired of all them rocks in the sea, he said, and boats and ships. Salt junk all the time.

Tired seemingly, he ceased. His questioner perceiving that he was not likely to get a great deal of change out of such a wily old customer, fell to woolgathering on the enormous dimensions of the water about the globe, suffice it to say that, as a casual glance at the map revealed, it covered fully three fourths of it and he fully realised accordingly what it meant to rule the waves. On more than one occasion, a dozen at the lowest, near the North Bull at Dollymount he had remarked a superannuated old salt, evidently derelict, seated habitually near the not particularly redolent sea on the wall, staring quite obliviously at it and it at him, dreaming of fresh woods and pastures new as someone somewhere sings. And it left him wondering why. Possibly he had tried to find out the secret for himself, floundering up and down the antipodes and all that sort of thing and over and under, well, not exactly under, tempting the fates. And the odds were twenty to nil there was really no secret about it at all. Nevertheless, without going into the **minutiae** of the business, the eloquent fact remained that the sea was there in all its glory and in the natural course of things somebody or other had to sail on it and fly in the face of providence though it merely went to show how people usually contrived to load that sort of onus on to the other fellow like the hell idea and the lottery and insurance which were run on identically the same lines so that for that very reason if no other lifeboat Sunday was a highly laudable institution to which the public at large, no matter where living inland or seaside, as the case might be, having it brought home to them like that should extend its gratitude also to the harbourmasters and coastguard service who had to man the rigging and push off and out amid the elements whatever the season when duty called **Ireland expects that every man** and so on and sometimes had a terrible time of it in the wintertime not forgetting the Irish lights, Kish and others, liable to capsize at any moment, rounding which he once with his daughter had experienced some remarkably choppy, not to say stormy, weather.

– There was a fellow sailed with me in the Rover, the old seadog, himself a rover, proceeded, went ashore and took up a soft job as gentleman's valet at six quid a month.

Them are his trousers I've on me and he gave me an oilskin and that jackknife. I'm game for that job, shaving and brushup. I hate roaming about. There's my son now, Danny, run off to sea and his mother got him took in a draper's in Cork where he could be drawing easy money.

– What age is he? queried one hearer who, by the way, seen from the side, bore a distant resemblance to Henry Campbell, the townclerk, away from the carking cares of office, unwashed of course and in a seedy getup and a strong suspicion of nosepaint about the nasal appendage.

– Why, the sailor answered with a slow puzzled utterance, my son, Danny? He'd be about eighteen now, way I figure it.

The Skibbereen father hereupon tore open his grey or unclean anyhow shirt with his two hands and scratched away at his chest on which was to be seen an image tattooed in blue Chinese ink intended to represent an anchor.

– There was lice in that bunk in Bridgwater, he remarked, sure as nuts. I must get a wash tomorrow or next day. It's them black lads I objects to. I hate those buggers. Suck your blood dry, they does.

Seeing they were all looking at his chest he accommodatingly dragged his shirt more open so that on top of the timehonoured symbol of the mariner's hope and rest they had a full view of the figure 16 and a young man's sideface looking frowningly rather.

– Tattoo, the exhibitor explained. That was done when we were lying becalmed off Odessa in the Black Sea under Captain Dalton. Fellow, the name of Antonio, done that. There he is himself, a Greek.

– Did it hurt much doing it? one asked the sailor.

That worthy, however, was busily engaged in collecting round the. Someway in his. Squeezing or.

– See here, he said, showing Antonio. There he is cursing the mate. And there he is now, he added, the same fellow, pulling the skin with his fingers, some special knack evidently, and he laughing at a yarn.

And in point of fact the young man named Antonio's livid face did actually look like forced smiling and the curious effect excited the unreserved admiration of everybody including Skin-the-Goat, who this time stretched over.

– Ay, ay, sighed the sailor, looking down on his manly chest. He's gone too. Ate by sharks after. Ay, ay.

He let go of the skin so that the profile resumed the normal expression of before.

– Neat bit of work, one longshoreman said.

– And what's the number for? loafer number two queried.

– Eaten alive? a third asked the sailor.

–Ay, ay, sighed again the latter personage, more cheerily this time with some sort of a half smile for a brief duration only in the direction of the questioner about the number. Ate. A Greek he was.

And then he added with rather gallowsbird humour considering his alleged end:

– **As bad as old Antonio, For he left me on my ownio.**

The face of a streetwalker glazed and haggard under a black straw hat peered askew round the door of the shelter palpably reconnoitring on her own with the object of bringing more grist to her mill. Mr Bloom, scarcely knowing which way to look, turned away on the moment flusterfied but outwardly calm, and, picking up from the table the pink sheet of the Abbey street organ which the jarvey, if such he was, had laid aside, he picked it up and looked at the pink of the paper though why pink. His reason for so doing was he recognised on the moment round the door the same face he had caught a fleeting glimpse of that afternoon on Ormond quay, the partially idiotic female, namely, of the lane who knew the lady in the brown costume does be with you (Mrs

B.) and begged the chance of his washing. Also why washing which seemed rather vague than not, your washing. Still candour compelled him to admit he had washed his wife's undergarments when soiled in Holles street and women would and did too a man's similar garments initialled with Bewley and Draper's marking ink (hers were, that is) if they really loved him, that is to say, love me, love my dirty shirt. Still just then, being on tenterhooks, he desired the female's room more than her company so it came as a genuine relief when the keeper made her a rude sign to take herself off. Round the side of the Evening Telegraph he just caught a fleeting glimpse of her face round the side of the door with a kind of demented glassy grin showing that she was not exactly all there, viewing with evident amusement the group of gazers round skipper Murphy's nautical chest and then there was no more of her.

– The gunboat, the keeper said.

– It beats me, Mr Bloom confided to

Stephen, medically I am speaking, how a wretched creature like that from the Lock hospital reeking with disease can be barefaced enough to solicit or how any man in his sober senses, if he values his health in the least. Unfortunate creature! Of course I suppose some man is ultimately responsible for her condition. Still no matter what the cause is from...

Stephen had not noticed her and shrugged his shoulders, merely remarking:

– In this country people sell much more than she ever had and do a roaring trade. Fear not them that sell the body but have not power to buy the soul. She is a bad merchant. She buys dear and sells cheap.

The elder man, though not by any manner of means an old maid or a prude, said it was nothing short of a crying scandal that ought to be put a stop to **instanter** to say that women of that stamp (quite apart from any oldmaidish squeamishness on the subject), a necessary evil, w ere not licensed and medically inspected by the proper authorities, a thing, he could truthfully state, he, as a **paterfamilias**, was a stalwart advocate of from the very first start. Whoever embarked on a policy of the sort, he said, and ventilated the matter thoroughly would confer a lasting boon on everybody concerned.

– You as a good catholic, he observed, talking of body and soul, believe in the soul. Or do you mean the intelligence, the brainpower as such, as distinct from any outside object, the table, let us say, that cup. I believe in that myself because it has been explained by competent men as the convolutions of the grey matter. Otherwise we would never have such inventions as X rays, for instance. Do you?

Thus cornered, Stephen had to make a superhuman effort of memory to try and concentrate and remember before he could say:

– They tell me on the best authority it is a

simple substance and therefore incorruptible. It would be immortal, I understand, but for the possibility of its annihilation by its First Cause Who, from all I can hear, is quite capable of adding that to the number of His other practical jokes, **corruptio per se** and **corruptio per accidens** both being excluded by court etiquette.

Mr Bloom thoroughly acquiesced in the general gist of this though the mystical finesse involved was a bit out of his sublunary depth still he felt bound to enter a demurrer on the head of simple, promptly rejoining:

– Simple? I shouldn't think that is the proper word. Of course, I grant you, to concede a point, you do knock across a simple soul once in a blue moon. But what I am anxious to arrive at is it is one thing for instance to invent those rays Röntgen did or the telescope like Edison, though I believe it was before his time Galileo was the man, I mean, and the same applies to the laws, for example, of a farreaching natural phenomenon such as electricity but it's a horse of quite another colour to say you believe in the existence of a supernatural God.

– O that, Stephen expostulated, has been proved conclusively by several of the bestknown passages in Holy Writ, apart from circumstantial evidence.

On this knotty point however the views of the pair, poles apart as they were both in schooling and everything else with the marked difference in their respective ages, clashed.

– Has been? the more experienced of the two objected, sticking to his original point with a smile of unbelief. I'm not so sure about that. That's a matter for everyman's opinion and, without dragging in the sectarian side of the business, I beg to differ with you **in toto** there. My belief is, to tell you the candid truth, that those bits were genuine forgeries all of them put in by monks most probably or it's the big question of our national poet over again, who precisely wrote them like **Hamlet** and Bacon, as, you who know your Shakespeare infinitely better than I, of course I needn't tell you. Can't you drink that coffee, by the way? Let me stir it. And take a piece of that bun. It's like one of our skipper's bricks disguised. Still no-one can give what he hasn't got. Try a bit.

– Couldn't, Stephen contrived to get out, his mental organs for the moment refusing to dictate further.

Faultfinding being a proverbially bad hat Mr Bloom thought well to stir or try to the clotted sugar from the bottom and reflected with something approaching acrimony on the Coffee Palace and its temperance (and lucrative) work. To be sure it was a legitimate object and beyond yea or nay did a world of good, shelters such as the present one they were in run on teetotal lines for vagrants at night, concerts, dramatic evenings and useful lectures (admittance free) by qualified men for the lower orders. On the other hand he had a distinct and painful recollection they paid his wife, Madam Marion Tweedy who had been prominently associated with it at one time, a very modest remuneration indeed for her pianoplaying. The idea, he was strongly inclined to believe, was to do good and net a profit, there being no competition to speak of. Sulphate of copper poison SO4 or something in some dried peas he remembered reading of in a cheap eatinghouse somewhere but he couldn't remember when it was or where. Anyhow inspection, medical inspection, of all eatables seemed to him more than ever necessary which possibly accounted for the vogue of Dr Tibble's Vi-Cocoa on account of the medical analysis involved.

– Have a shot at it now, he ventured to say of the coffee after being stirred.

Thus prevailed on to at any rate taste it Stephen lifted the heavy mug from the brown puddle it clopped out of when taken up by the handle and took a sip of the offending beverage.

– Still it's solid food, his good genius urged, I'm a stickler for solid food, his one and only reason being not gormandising in the least but regular meals as the **sine qua non** for any kind of proper work, mental or manual. You ought to eat more solid food. You would feel a different man.

– Liquids I can eat, Stephen said. But O, oblige me by taking away that knife. I can't look at the point of it. It reminds me of Roman history.

Mr Bloom promptly did as suggested and removed the incriminated article, a blunt hornhandled ordinary knife with nothing particularly Roman or antique about it to the lay eye, observing that the point was the least conspicuous point about it.

– Our mutual friend's stories are like himself, Mr Bloom **apropos** of knives remarked to his **confidante sotto voce**. Do you think they are genuine? He could spin those yarns for hours on end all night long and lie like old boots. Look at him.

Yet still though his eyes were thick with sleep and sea air life was full of a host of things and coincidences of a terrible nature and it was quite within the bounds of possibility that it was not an entire fabrication though at first blush there was not much inherent probability in all the spoof he got off his chest being strictly accurate gospel.

He had been meantime taking stock of the individual in front of him and Sherlockholmesing him up ever since he clapped eyes on him. Though a wellpreserved man of no little stamina, if a trifle prone to baldness, there was something spurious in the cut of his jib that suggested a jail delivery and it required no violent stretch of imagination to associate such a weirdlooking specimen with the oakum and treadmill fraternity. He might even have done for his man supposing it was his own case he told, as people often did about others, namely, that he killed him himself and had served his four or five goodlooking years in durance vile to say nothing of the Antonio personage (no relation to the dramatic personage of identical name who sprang from the pen of our national poet) who expiated his crimes in the melodramatic manner above described. On the other hand he might be only bluffing, a pardonable weakness because meeting unmistakable mugs, Dublin residents, like those jarvies waiting news from abroad would tempt any ancient mariner who sailed the ocean seas to draw the long bow about the schooner **Hesperus** and etcetera. And when all was said and done the lies a fellow told about himself couldn't probably hold a proverbial candle to the wholesale whoppers other fellows coined about him.

– Mind you, I'm not saying that it's all a pure invention, he resumed. Analogous scenes are occasionally, if not often, met with. Giants, though that is rather a far cry, you see once in a way, Marcella the midget queen. In those waxworks in Henry street I myself saw some Aztecs, as they are called, sitting bowlegged, they couldn't straighten their legs if you paid them because the muscles here, you see, he proceeded, indicating on his companion the brief outline of the sinews or whatever you like to call them behind the right knee, were utterly powerless from sitting that way so long cramped up, being adored as gods. There's an example again of simple souls.

However reverting to friend Sinbad and his horrifying adventures (who reminded him a bit of Ludwig, **alias** Ledwidge, when he occupied the boards of the Gaiety when Michael Gunn was identified with the management in the **Flying Dutchman**, a stupendous success, and his host of admirers came in large numbers, everyone simply flocking to hear him though ships of any sort, phantom or the reverse, on the stage usually fell a bit flat as also did trains) there was nothing intrinsically incompatible about it, he conceded. On the contrary that stab in the back touch was quite in keeping with those italianos though candidly he was none the less free to admit those icecreamers and friers in the fish way not to mention the chip potato variety and so forth over in little Italy there near the Coombe were sober thrifty hardworking fellows except perhaps a bit too given to pothunting the harmless necessary animal of the feline persuasion of others at night so as to have a good old succulent tuckin with garlic **de rigueur** off him or her next day on the quiet and, he added, on the cheap.

– Spaniards, for instance, he continued, passionate temperaments like that, impetuous as Old Nick, are given to taking the law into their own hands and give you your quietus doublequick with those poignards they carry in the abdomen. It comes from the great heat, climate generally. My wife is, so to speak, Spanish, half that is. Point of fact she could actually claim Spanish nationality if she wanted, having been born in (technically) Spain, i.e. Gibraltar. She has the Spanish type. Quite dark, regular brunette, black. I for one certainly believe climate accounts for character. That's why I asked you if you wrote your poetry in Italian.

– The temperaments at the door, Stephen interposed with, were very passionate about ten shillings. **Roberto ruba roba sua**.

– Quite so, Mr Bloom dittoed.

– Then, Stephen said staring and rambling on to himself or some unknown listener somewhere, we have the impetuosity of Dante and the isosceles triangle miss Portinari he fell in love with and Leonardo and san Tommaso Mastino.

– It's in the blood, Mr Bloom acceded at once. All are washed in the blood of the sun. Coincidence I just happened to be in the Kildare street museum 890 today, shortly prior to our meeting if I can so call it, and I was just looking at those antique statues there. The splendid proportions of hips, bosom. You simply don't knock against those kind of women here. An exception here and there. Handsome yes, pretty in a way you find but what I'm talking about is the female form. Besides they have so little taste in dress, most of them, which greatly enhances a woman's natural beauty, no matter what you say. Rumpled stockings, it may be, possibly is, a foible of mine but still it's a thing I simply hate to see.

Interest, however, was starting to flag somewhat all round and then the others got on to talking about accidents at sea, ships lost in a fog, goo collisions with icebergs, all that sort of thing. Shipahoy of course had his own say to say. He had doubled the cape a few odd times and weathered a monsoon, a kind of wind, in the China seas and through all those perils of the deep there was one thing, he declared, stood to him or words to that effect, a pious medal he had that saved him.

So then after that they drifted on to the wreck off Daunt's rock, wreck of that illfated Norwegian barque nobody could think of her name for the moment till the jarvey who had really quite a look of Henry Campbell remembered it **Palme** on Booterstown strand. That was the talk of the town that year (Albert William Quill wrote a fine piece of original verse of 910 distinctive merit on the topic for the Irish **Times**), breakers running over her and crowds and crowds on the shore in commotion petrified with horror. Then someone said something about the case of the s. s. **Lady Cairns** of Swansea run into by the **Mona** which was on an opposite tack in rather muggyish weather and lost with all hands on deck. No aid was given. Her master, the **Mona's**, said he was afraid his collision bulkhead would give way. She had no water, it appears, in her hold.

At this stage an incident happened. It having become necessary for him to unfurl a reef the sailor vacated his seat.

– Let me cross your bows mate, he said to his neighbour who was just gently dropping off into a peaceful doze.

He made tracks heavily, slowly with a

dumpy sort of a gait to the door, stepped heavily down the one step there was out of the shelter and bore due left. While he was in the act of getting his bearings Mr Bloom who noticed when he stood up that he had two flasks of presumably ship's rum sticking one out of each pocket for the private consumption of his burning interior, saw him produce a bottle and uncork it or unscrew and, applying its nozz1e to his lips, take a good old delectable swig out of it with a gurgling noise. The irrepressible Bloom, who also had a shrewd suspicion that the old stager went out on a manoeuvre after the counterattraction in the shape of a female who however had disappeared to all intents and purposes, could by straining just perceive him, when duly refreshed by his rum puncheon exploit, gaping up at the piers and girders of the Loop line rather out of his depth as of course it was all radically altered since his last visit and greatly improved. Some person or persons invisible directed him to the male urinal erected by the cleansing committee all over the place for the purpose but after a brief space of time during which silence reigned supreme the sailor, evidently giving it a wide berth, eased himself closer at hand, the noise of his bilgewater some little time subsequently splashing on the ground where it apparently awoke a horse of the cabrank. A hoof scooped anyway for new foothold after sleep and harness jingled. Slightly disturbed in his sentrybox by the brazier of live coke the watcher of the corporation stones who, though now broken down and fast breaking up, was none other in stern reality than the Gumley aforesaid, now practically on the parish rates, given the temporary job by Pat Tobin in all human probability from dictates of humanity knowing him before shifted about and shuffled in his box before composing his limbs again in to the arms of Morpheus, a truly amazing piece of hard lines in its most virulent form on a fellow most respectably connected and familiarised with decent home comforts all his life who came in for a cool £ 100 a year at one time which of course the doublebarrelled ass proceeded to make general ducks and drakes of. And there he was at the end of his tether after having often painted the town tolerably pink without a beggarly stiver. He drank needless to be told and it pointed only once more a moral when he might quite easily be in a large way of business if – a big if, however – he had contrived to cure himself of his particular partiality.

All meantime were loudly lamenting the falling off in Irish shipping, coastwise and foreign as well, which was all part and parcel of the same thing. A Palgrave Murphy boat was put off the ways at Alexandra basin, the only launch that year. Right enough the harbours were there only no ships ever called.

There were wrecks and wreckers, the keeper said, who was evidently **au fait**.

What he wanted to ascertain was why that

ship ran bang against the only rock in Galway bay when the Galway harbour scheme was mooted by a Mr Worthington or some name like that, eh? Ask the then captain, he advised them, how much palmoil the British government gave him for that day's work, Captain John Lever of the Lever Line.

– Am I right, skipper? he queried of the sailor, now returning after his private potation and the rest of his exertions.

That worthy picking up the scent of the fagend of the song or words growled in wouldbe music but with great vim some kind of chanty or other in seconds or thirds. Mr Bloom's sharp ears heard him then expectorate the plug probably (which it was), so that he must have lodged it for the time being in his fist while he did the drinking and making water jobs and found it a bit sour after the liquid fire in question. Anyhow in he rolled after his successful libation-**cum**-potation, introducing an atmosphere of drink into the **soirée**, boisterously trolling, like a veritable son of a seacook:

– The biscuits was as hard as brass
And the beef as salt as Lot's wife's
arse.
O, Johnny Lever!
Johnny Lever, O!

After which effusion the redoubtable specimen duly arrived on the scene and regaining his seat he sank rather than sat heavily on the form provided. Skin-the-Goat, assuming he was he, evidently with an axe to grind, was airing his grievances in a forcible-feeble philippic anent the natural resources of Ireland or something of that sort which he described in his lengthy dissertation as the richest country bar none on the face of God's earth, far and away superior to England, with coal in large quantities, six million pounds worth of pork exported every year, ten millions between butter and eggs and all the riches drained out of it by England levying taxes on the poor people that paid through the nose always and gobbling up the best meat in the market and a lot more surplus steam in the same vein. Their conversation accordingly became general and all agreed that that was a fact. You could grow any mortal thing in Irish soil, he stated, and there was that colonel Everard down there in Navan growing tobacco. Where would you find anywhere the like of Irish bacon? But a day of reckoning, he stated **crescendo** with no uncertain voice, thoroughly monopolising all the conversation, was in store for mighty England, despite her power of pelf on account of her crimes. There would be a fall and the greatest fall in history. The Germans and the Japs were going to have their little lookin, he affirmed. The Boers were the beginning of the end. Brummagem England was toppling already and her downfall would be Ireland, her Achilles heel, which he explained to them about the vulnerable point of Achilles, the Greek hero, a point his auditors at once seized as he completely gripped their attention by showing the tendon referred to on his boot. His advice to every Irishman was: stay in the land of your birth and work for Ireland and live for Ireland. Ireland, Parnell said, could not spare a single one of her sons.

Silence all round marked the termination of his **finale**. The impervious navigator heard these lurid tidings, undismayed.

– Take a bit of doing, boss, retaliated that rough diamond palpably a bit peeved in response to the foregoing truism.

To which cold douche referring to downfall and so on the keeper concurred but nevertheless held to his main view.

– Who's the best troops in the army? the grizzled old veteran irately interrogated. And the best jumpers and racers? And the best admirals and generals we've got? Tell me that.

– The Irish, for choice, retorted the cabby

like Campbell, facial blemishes apart.

– That's right, the old tarpaulin corroborated. The Irish catholic peasant. He's the backbone of our empire. You know Jem Mullins?

While allowing him his individual opinions as everyman the keeper added he cared nothing for any empire, ours or his, and considered no Irishman worthy of his salt that served it. Then they began to have a few irascible words when it waxed hotter, both, needless to say, appealing to the listeners who followed the passage of arms with interest so long as they didn't indulge in recriminations and come to blows.

From inside information extending over a series of years Mr Bloom was rather inclined to poohpooh the suggestion as egregious balderdash for, pending that consummation devoutly to be or not to be wished for, he was fully cognisant of the fact that their neighbours across the channel, unless they were much bigger fools than he took them for, rather concealed their strength than the opposite. It was quite on a par with the quixotic idea in certain quarters that in a hundred million years the coal seam of the sister island would be played out and if, as time went on, that turned out to be how the cat jumped all he could personally say on the matter was that as a host of contingencies, equally relevant to the issue, might occur ere then it was highly advisable in the interim to try to make the most of both countries even though poles apart. Another little interesting point, the amours of whores and chummies, to put it in common parlance, reminded him Irish soldiers had as often fought for England as against her, more so, in fact. And now, why? So the scene between the pair of them, the licensee of the place rumoured to be or have been Fitzharris, the famous invincible, and the other, obviously bogus, reminded him forcibly as being on all fours with the confidence trick, supposing, that is, it was prearranged as the lookeron, a student of the human soul if anything, the others seeing least of the game. And as for the lessee or keeper, who probably wasn't the other person at all, he (B.) couldn't help feeling and most properly it was better to give people like that the goby unless you were a blithering idiot altogether and refuse to have anything to do with them as a golden rule in private life and their felonsetting, there always being the offchance of a Dannyman coming forward and turning queen's evidence or king's now like Denis or Peter Carey, an idea he utterly repudiated. Quite apart from that he disliked those careers of wrongdoing and crime on principle. Yet, though such criminal propensities had never been an inmate of his bosom in any shape or form, he certainly did feel and no denying it (while inwardly remaining what he was) a certain kind of admiration for a man who had actually brandished a knife, cold steel, with the courage of his political convictions (though, personally, he would never be a party to any such thing), off the same bat as those love vendettas of the south, have her or swing for her, when the husband frequently, after some words passed between the two concerning her relations with the other lucky mortal (he having had the pair watched), inflicted fatal injuries on his adored one as a result of an alternative postnuptial **liaison** by plunging his knife into her, until it just struck him that Fitz, nicknamed Skin-the-Goat, merely drove the car for the actual perpetrators of the outrage and so was not, if he was reliably informed, actually party to the ambush which, in point of fact, was the plea some legal luminary saved his skin on. In any case that was very ancient history by now and as for our friend, the pseudo Skin-the-etcetera, he had transparently outlived his welcome. He ought to have either died naturally or on the scaffold high. Like actresses, always farewell positively last performance then come up smiling again. Generous to a fault of course, temperamental, no economising or any idea of the sort, always snapping at the bone for the shadow. So similarly he had a very shrewd suspicion that Mr Johnny Lever got rid of some l s d. in the course of his perambulations round the docks in the congenial atmosphere of the **Old Ireland** tavern, come back to Erin and so on. Then as for the other he had heard not so long before the same identical lingo as he told Stephen how he simply but effectually silenced the offender.

– He took umbrage at something or other, that muchinjured but on the whole eventempered person declared, I let slip. He called me a jew and in a heated fashion offensively. So I without deviating from plain facts in the least told him his God, I mean Christ, was a jew too and all his family like me though in reality I'm not. That was one for him. A soft answer turns away wrath. He hadn't a word to say for himself as everyone saw. Am I not right?

He turned a long you are wrong gaze on

Stephen of timorous dark pride at the soft impeachment with a glance also of entreaty for he seemed to glean in a kind of a way that it wasn't all exactly.

– **Ex quibus**, Stephen mumbled in a noncommittal accent, their two or four eyes conversing, **Christus** or Bloom his name is or after all any other, **secundum carnem**.

– Of course, Mr B. proceeded to stipulate, you must look at both sides of the question. It is hard to lay down any hard and fast rules as to right and wrong but room for improvement all round there certainly is though every country, they say, our own distressful included, has the government it deserves. But with a little goodwill all round. It's all very fine to boast of mutual superiority but what about mutual equality. I resent violence and intolerance in any shape or form. It never reaches anything or stops anything. A revolution must come on the due instalments plan. It's a patent absurdity on the face of it to hate people because they live round the corner and speak another vernacular, in the next house so to speak.

– Memorable bloody bridge battle and seven minutes' war, Stephen assented, between Skinner's alley and Ormond market.

Yes, Mr Bloom thoroughly agreed, entirely endorsing the remark, that was overwhelmingly right. And the whole world was full of that sort of thing.

– You just took the words out of my mouth, he said. A hocuspocus of conflicting evidence that candidly you couldn't remotely...

All those wretched quarrels, in his humble opinion, stirring up bad blood, from some bump of combativeness or gland of some kind, erroneously supposed to be about a punctilio of honour and a flag, were very largely a question of the money question which was at the back of everything greed and jealousy, people never knowing when to stop.

– They accuse, remarked he audibly.

He turned away from the others who probably and spoke nearer to, so as the others in case they.

– Jews, he softly imparted in an aside in Stephen's ear, are accused of ruining. Not a vestige of truth in it, I can safely say. History, would you be surprised to learn, proves up to the hilt Spain decayed when the inquisition hounded the jews out and England prospered when Cromwell, an uncommonly able ruffian who in other respects has much to answer for, imported them. Why? Because they are imbued with the proper spirit. They are practical and are proved to be so. I don't want to indulge in any because you know the standard works on the subject and then orthodox as you are. But in the economic, not touching religion, domain the priest spells poverty. Spain again, you saw in the war, compared with goahead America. Turks. It's in the dogma. Because if they didn't believe they'd go straight to heaven when they die they'd try to live better, at least so I think. That's the juggle on which the p.p's raise the wind on false pretences. I'm, he resumed with dramatic force, as good an Irishman as that rude person I told you about at the outset and I want to see everyone, concluded he, all creeds and classes **pro rata** having a comfortable tidysized income, in no niggard fashion either, something in the neighbourhood of £ 300 per annum. That's the vital issue at stake and it's feasible and would be provocative of friendlier intercourse between man and man. At least that's my idea for what it's worth. I call that patriotism. **Ubi patria**, as we learned a smattering of in our classical days in **Alma Mater, vita bene**. Where you can live well, the sense is, if you work.

Over his untastable apology for a cup of coffee, listening to this synopsis of things in general, Stephen stared at nothing in particular. He could hear, of course, all kinds of words changing colour like those crabs about Ringsend in the morning burrowing quickly into all colours of different sorts of the same sand where they had a home somewhere beneath or seemed to. Then he looked up and saw the eyes that said or didn't say the words the voice he heard said, if you work.

– Count me out, he managed to remark, meaning work.

The eyes were surprised at this observation because as he, the person who owned them pro tem. observed or rather his voice speaking did, all must work, have to, together.

– I mean, of course, the other hastened to affirm, work in the widest possible sense. Also literary labour not merely for the kudos of the thing. Writing for the newspapers which is the readiest channel nowadays. That's work too. Important work. After all, from the little I know of you, after all the money expended on your education you are entitled to recoup yourself and command your price. You have every bit as much right to live by your pen in pursuit of your philosophy as the peasant has. What? You both belong to Ireland, the brain and the brawn. Each is equally important.

– You suspect, Stephen retorted with a sort of a half laugh, that I may be important because I belong to the **faubourg Saint Patrice** called Ireland for short.

– I would go a step farther, Mr Bloom insinuated.

– But I suspect, Stephen interrupted, that Ireland must be important because it belongs to me.

– What belongs, queried Mr Bloom bending, fancying he was perhaps under some misapprehension. Excuse me. Unfortunately, I didn't catch the latter portion. What was it you...?

Stephen, patently crosstempered, repeated and shoved aside his mug of coffee or whatever you like to call it none too politely, adding:

– We can't change the country. Let us change the subject.

At this pertinent suggestion Mr Bloom, to change the subject, looked down but in a quandary, as he couldn't tell exactly what construction to put on belongs to which sounded rather a far cry. The rebuke of some kind was clearer than the other part. Needless to say the fumes of his recent orgy spoke then with some asperity in a curious bitter way foreign to his sober state. Probably the homelife to which Mr B attached the utmost importance had not been all that was needful or he hadn't been familiarised with the right sort of people. With a touch of fear for the young man beside him whom he furtively scrutinised with an air of some consternation remembering he had just come back from Paris, the eyes more especially reminding him forcibly of father and sister, failing to throw much light on the subject, however, he brought to mind instances of cultured fellows that promised so brilliantly nipped in the bud of premature decay and nobody to blame but themselves. For instance there was the case of O'Callaghan, for one, the halfcrazy faddist, respectably connected though of inadequate means, with his mad vagaries among whose other gay doings when rotto and making himself a nuisance to everybody all round he was in the habit of ostentatiously sporting in public a suit of brown paper (a fact). And then the usual **dénouement** after the fun had gone on fast and furious he got 1190 landed into hot water and had to be spirited away by a few friends, after a strong hint to a blind horse from John Mallon of Lower Castle Yard, so as not to be made amenable under section two of the criminal law amendment act, certain names of those subpoenaed being handed in but not divulged for reasons which will occur to anyone with a pick of brains. Briefly, putting two and two together, six sixteen which he pointedly turned a deaf ear to, Antonio and so forth, jockeys and esthetes and the tattoo which was all the go in the seventies or thereabouts even in the house of lords because early in life the occupant of the throne, then heir apparent, the other members of the upper ten and other high personages simply following in the footsteps of the head of the state, he reflected about the errors of notorieties and crowned heads running counter to morality such as the Cornwall case a number of years before under their veneer in a way scarcely intended by nature, a thing good Mrs Grundy, as the law stands, was terribly down on though not for the reason they thought they were probably whatever it was except women chiefly who were always fiddling more or less at one another it being largely a matter of dress and all the rest of it. Ladies who like distinctive underclothing should, and every welltailored man must, trying to make the gap wider between them by innuendo and give more of a genuine filip to acts of impropriety between the two, she unbuttoned his and then he untied her, mind the pin, whereas savages in the cannibal islands, say, at ninety degrees in the shade not caring a continental. However, reverting to the original, there were on the other hand others who had forced their way to the top from the lowest rung by the aid of their bootstraps. Sheer force of natural genius, that. With brains, sir.

For which and further reasons he felt it was his interest and duty even to wait on and profit by the unlookedfor occasion though why he could not exactly tell being as it was already several shillings to the bad having in fact let himself in for it. Still to cultivate the acquaintance of someone of no uncommon calibre who could provide food for reflection would amply repay any small. Intellectual stimulation, as such, was, he felt, from time to time a firstrate tonic for the mind. Added to which was the coincidence of meeting, discussion, dance, row, old salt of the here today and gone tomorrow type, night loafers, the whole galaxy of events, all went to make up a miniature cameo of the world we live in especially as the lives of the submerged tenth, viz. coalminers, divers, scavengers etc., were very much under the microscope lately. To improve the shining hour he wondered whether he might meet with anything approaching the same luck as Mr Philip Beaufoy if taken down in writing suppose he were to pen something out of the common groove (as he fully intended doing) at the rate of one guinea per column. **My Experiences**, let us say, **in a Cabman's Shelter**.

The pink edition extra sporting of the **Telegraph** tell a graphic lie lay, as luck would have it, beside his elbow and as he was just puzzling again, far from satisfied, over a country belonging to him and the preceding rebus the vessel came from Bridgwater and the postcard was addressed A. Boudin find the captain's age, his eyes went aimlessly over the respective captions which came under his special province the allembracing give us this day our daily press. First he got a bit of a start but it turned out to be only something about somebody named H. du Boyes, agent for typewriters or something like that. Great battle, Tokio. Lovemaking in Irish, 200 pounds damages. Gordon Bennett. Emigration Swindle. Letter from His Grace. William. Ascot meeting, the Gold Cup. Victory of outsider **Throwaway** recalls Derby of '92 when Capt. Marshall's dark horse **Sir Hugo** captured the blue ribband at long odds. New York disaster. Thousand lives lost. Foot and Mouth. Funeral of the late Mr Patrick Dignam.

So to change the subject he read about Dignam R. I. P. which, he reflected, was anything but a gay sendoff. Or a change of address anyway.

– **This morning** (Hynes put it in of course) **the remains of the late Mr Patrick Dignam were removed from his residence, no 9 Newbridge Avenue, Sandymount, for**

interment in Glasnevin. The deceased gentleman was a most popular and genial personality in city life and his demise after a brief illness came as a great shock to citizens of all classes by whom he is deeply regretted. The obsequies, at which many friends of the deceased were present, were carried out (certainly Hynes wrote it with a nudge from Corny) **by Messrs H. J. O'Neill and Son, 164 North Strand Road. The mourners included: Patk. Dignam (son), Bernard Corrigan (brother-in-law), Jno. Henry Menton, solr, Martin Cunningham, John Power, eatondph 1/8 ador dorador douradora** (mustbewherehecalledMonksthedayfather about Keyes's ad) **Thomas Kernan, Simon Dedalus, Stephen Dedalus B.,4., Edw. J. Lambert, Cornelius T. Kelleher, Joseph M'C Hynes, L. Boom, CP M'Coy, – M'Intosh and several others**.

Nettled not a little by L. **Boom** (as it incorrectly stated) and the line of bitched type but tickled to death simultaneously by C. P. M'Coy and Stephen Dedalus B. A. who were conspicuous, needless to say, by their total absence (to say nothing of M'Intosh) L. Boom pointed it out to his companion B. A. engaged in stifling another yawn, half nervousness, not forgetting the usual crop of nonsensical howlers of misprints.

– Is that first epistle to the Hebrews, he asked as soon as his bottom jaw would let him, in? Text: open thy mouth and put thy foot in it.

– It is. Really, Mr Bloom said (though first he fancied he alluded to the archbishop till he added about foot and mouth with which there could be no possible connection) overjoyed to set his mind at rest and a bit flabbergasted at Myles Crawford's after all managing to. There.

While the other was reading it on page two Boom (to give him for the nonce his new misnomer) whiled away a few odd leisure moments in fits and starts with the account of the third event at Ascot on page three, his side. Value 1000 sovs with 3000 sovs in specie added. For entire colts and fillies. Mr F. Alexander's **Throwaway**, b. h. by **Rightaway**, 5 yrs, 9 st 4 lbs (W. Lane) 1, lord Howard de Walden's **Zinfandel** (M. Cannon) z, Mr W. Bass's **Sceptre** 3. Betting 5 to 4 on **Zinfandel**, 20 to 1 **Throwaway** (off). **Sceptre** a shade heavier, 5 to 4 on **Zinfandel**, 20 to 1 **Throwaway** (off). **Throwaway** and **Zinfandel** stood close order. It was anybody's race then the rank outsider drew to the fore, got long lead, beating lord Howard de Walden's chestnut colt and Mr W. Bass's bay filly Sceptre on a 2 1/2 mile course. Winner trained by Braime so that Lenehan's version of the business was all pure buncombe. Secured the verdict cleverly by a length. 1000 sovs with 3000 in specie. Also ran: J de Bremond's (French horse Bantam Lyons was anxiously inquiring after not in yet but expected any minute) **Maximum II**. Different ways of bringing off a coup. Lovemaking damages. Though that halfbaked Lyons ran off at a tangent in his impetuosity to get left. Of course gambling eminently lent itself to that sort of thing though as the event turned out the poor fool hadn't much reason to congratulate himself on his pick, the forlorn hope. Guesswork it reduced itself to eventually.

– There was every indication they would arrive at that, he, Bloom, said.

– Who? the other, whose hand by the way was hurt, said.

One morning you would open the paper, the cabman affirmed, and read: **Return of Parnell**. He bet them what they liked. A Dublin fusilier was in that shelter one night and said he saw him in South Africa. Pride it was killed him. He ought to have done away with himself or lain low for a time after committee room no 15 until he was his old self again with no-one to point a finger at him. Then they would all to a man have gone down on their marrowbones to him to come back when he had recovered his senses. Dead he wasn't. Simply absconded somewhere. The coffin they brought over was full of stones. He changed his name to De Wet, the Boer general. He made a mistake to fight the priests. And so forth and so on.

All the same Bloom (properly so dubbed) was rather surprised at their memories for in nine cases out of ten it was a case of tarbarrels and not singly but in their thousands and then complete oblivion because it was twenty odd years. Highly unlikely of course there was even a shadow of truth in the stones and, even supposing, he thought a return highly inadvisable, all things considered. Something evidently riled them in his death. Either he petered out too tamely of acute pneumonia just when his various different political arrangements were nearing completion or whether it transpired he owed his death to his having neglected to change his boots and clothes-after a wetting when a cold resulted and failing to consult a specialist he being confined to his room till he eventually died of it amid widespread regret before a fortnight was at an end or quite possibly they were distressed to find the job was taken out of their hands. Of course nobody being acquainted with his movements even before there was absolutely no clue as to his whereabouts which were decidedly of the **Alice, where art thou** order even prior to his starting to go under several aliases such as Fox and Stewart so the remark which emanated from friend cabby might be within the bounds of possibility. Naturally then it would prey on his mind as a born leader of men which undoubtedly he was and a commanding figure, a sixfooter or at any rate five feet ten or eleven in his stockinged feet, whereas Messrs So and So who, though they weren't even a patch on the former man, ruled the roost after their redeeming features were very few and far between. It certainly pointed a moral, the idol with feet of clay, and then seventytwo of his trusty henchmen rounding on him with mutual mudslinging. And the identical same with murderers. You had to come back. That haunting sense kind of drew you. To show the understudy in the title **rôle** how to. He saw him once on the auspicious occasion when they broke up the type in the **Insuppressible** or was it **United Ireland**, a privilege he keenly appreciated, and, in point of fact, handed him his silk hat when it was knocked off and he said **Thank you**, excited as he undoubtedly was under his frigid exterior notwithstanding the little misadventure mentioned between the cup and the lip: what's bred in the bone. Still as regards return. You were a lucky dog if they didn't set the terrier at you directly you got back. Then a lot of shillyshally usually followed, Tom for and Dick and Harry against. And then, number one, you came up against the man in possession and had to produce your credentials like the claimant in the Tichborne case, Roger Charles

Tichborne, **Bella** was the boat's name to the best of his recollection he, the heir, went down in as the evidence went to show and there was a tattoo mark too in Indian ink, lord Bellew was it, as he might very easily have picked up the details from some pal on board ship and then, when got up to tally with the description given, introduce himself with: **Excuse me, my name is So and So** or some such commonplace remark. A more prudent course, as Bloom said to the not over effusive, in fact like the distinguished personage under discussion beside him, would have been to sound the lie of the land first.

– That bitch, that English whore, did for him, the shebeen proprietor commented. She put the first nail in his coffin.

– Fine lump of a woman all the same, the **soi-disant** townclerk Henry Campbell remarked, and plenty of her. She loosened many a man's thighs. I seen her picture in a barber's. The husband was a captain or an officer.

– Ay, Skin-the-Goat amusingly added, he was and a cottonball one.

This gratuitous contribution of a humorous character occasioned a fair amount of laughter among his **entourage**. As regards Bloom he, without the faintest suspicion of a smile, merely gazed in the direction of the door and reflected upon the historic story which had aroused extraordinary interest at the time when the facts, to make matters worse, were made public with the usual affectionate letters that passed between them full of sweet nothings. First it was strictly Platonic till nature intervened and an attachment sprang up between them till bit by bit matters came to a climax and the matter became the talk of the town till the staggering blow came as a welcome intelligence to not a few evildisposed, however, who were resolved upon encompassing his downfall though the thing was public property all along though not to anything like the sensational extent that it subsequently blossomed into. Since their names were coupled, though, since he was her declared favourite, where was the particular necessity to proclaim it to the rank and file from the housetops, the fact, namely, that he had shared her bedroom which came out in the witnessbox on oath when a thrill went through the packed court literally electrifying everybody in the shape of witnesses swearing to having witnessed him on such and such a particular date in the act of scrambling out of an upstairs apartment with the assistance of a ladder in night apparel, having gained admittance in the same fashion, a fact the weeklies, addicted to the lubric a little, simply coined shoals of money out of. Whereas the simple fact of the case was it was simply a case of the husband not being up to the scratch, with nothing in common between them beyond the name, and then a real man arriving on the scene, strong to the verge of weakness, falling a victim to her siren charms and forgetting home ties, the usual sequel, to bask in the loved one's smiles. The eternal question of the life connubial, needless to say, cropped up. Can real love, supposing there happens to be another chap in the case, exist between married folk? Poser. Though it was no concern of theirs absolutely if he regarded her with affection, carried away by a wave of folly. A magnificent specimen of manhood he was truly augmented obviously by gifts of a high order, as compared with the other military supernumerary that is (who was just the usual everyday **farewell, my gallant captain** kind of an individual in the light dragoons, the 18th hussars to be accurate) and inflammable doubtless (the fallen leader, that is, not the other) in his own peculiar way which she of course, woman, quickly perceived as highly likely to carve his way to fame which he almost bid fair to do till the priests and ministers of the gospel as a whole, his erstwhile staunch adherents, and his beloved evicted tenants for whom he had done yeoman service in the rural parts of the country by taking up the cudgels on their behalf in a way that exceeded their most sanguine expectations, very effectually cooked his matrimonial goose, thereby heaping coals of fire on his head much in the same way as the fabled ass's kick. Looking back now in a retrospective kind of arrangement all seemed a kind of dream. And then coming back was the worst thing you ever did because it went without saying you would feel out of place as things always moved with the times. Why, as he reflected, Irishtown strand, a locality he had not been in for quite a number of years looked different somehow since, as it happened, he went to reside on the north side. North or south, however, it was just the wellknown case of hot passion, pure and simple, upsetting the applecart with a vengeance and just bore out the very thing he was saying as she also was Spanish or half so, types that wouldn't do things by halves, passionate abandon of the south, casting every shred of decency to the winds.

– Just bears out what I was saying, he, with glowing bosom said to Stephen, about blood and the sun. And, if I don't greatly mistake she was Spanish too.

– The king of Spain's daughter, Stephen answered, adding something or other rather muddled about farewell and adieu to you Spanish onions and the first land called the Deadman and from Ramhead to Scilly was so and so many.

– Was she? Bloom ejaculated, surprised though not astonished by any means, I never heard that rumour before. Possible, especially there, it was as she lived there. So, Spain.

Carefully avoiding a book in his pocket **Sweets of**, which reminded him by the by of that Cap I street library book out of date, he took out his pocketbook and, turning over the various contents it contained rapidly finally he.

– Do you consider, by the by, he said, thoughtfully selecting a faded photo which he laid on the table, that a Spanish type?

Stephen, obviously addressed, looked down on the photo showing a large sized lady with her fleshy charms on evidence in an open fashion as she was in the full bloom of womanhood in evening dress cut ostentatiously low for the occasion to give a liberal display of bosom, with more than vision of breasts, her full lips parted and some perfect teeth, standing near, ostensibly with gravity, a piano on the rest of which was **In Old Madrid**, a ballad, pretty in its way, which was then all the vogue. Her (the lady's) eyes, dark, large, looked at Stephen, about to smile about something to be admired, Lafayette of Westmoreland street, Dublin's premier photographic artist, being responsible for the esthetic execution.

– Mrs Bloom, my wife the **prima donna** Madam Marion Tweedy, Bloom indicated. Taken a few years since. In or about ninety six. Very like her then.

Beside the young man he looked also at the photo of the lady now his legal wife who, he intimated, was the accomplished daughter of Major Brian Tweedy and displayed at an early age remarkable proficiency as a singer having even made her bow to the public when her years numbered barely sweet sixteen. As for the face it was a speaking likeness in expression but it did not do justice to her figure which came in for a lot of notice usually and which did not come out to the best advantage in that getup. She could without difficulty, he said, have posed for the ensemble, not to dwell on certain opulent curves of the. He dwelt, being a bit of an artist in his spare time, on the female form in general developmentally because, as it so happened, no later than that afternoon he had seen those Grecian statues, perfectly developed as works of art, in the National Museum. Marble could give the original, shoulders, back, all the symmetry, all the rest. Yes, puritanisme, it does though Saint Joseph's sovereign thievery alors (Bandez!) Figne toi trop. Whereas no photo could because it simply wasn't art in a word.

The spirit moving him he would much have liked to follow Jack Tar's good example and leave the likeness there for a very few minutes to speak for itself on the plea he so that the other could drink in the beauty for himself, her stage presence being, frankly, a treat in itself which the camera could not at all do justice to. But it was scarcely professional etiquette so. Though it was a warm pleasant sort of a night now yet wonderfully cool for the season considering, for sunshine after storm. And he did feel a kind of need there and then to follow suit like a kind of inward voice and satisfy a possible need by moving a motion. Nevertheless he sat tight just viewing the slightly soiled photo creased by opulent curves, none the worse for wear however, and looked away thoughtfully with the intention of not further increasing the other's possible embarrassment while gauging her symmetry of heaving **embonpoint**. In fact the slight soiling was only an added charm like the case of linen slightly soiled, good as new, much better in fact with the starch out. Suppose she was gone when he? I looked for the lamp which she told me came into his mind but merely as a passing fancy of his because he then recollected the morning littered bed etcetera and the book about Ruby with met him pike hoses (**sic**) in it which must have fell down sufficiently appropriately beside the domestic chamberpot with apologies to Lindley Murray.

The vicinity of the young man he certainly relished, educated, **distingué** and impulsive into the bargain, far and away the pick of the bunch though you wouldn't think he had it in him yet you would. Besides he said the picture was handsome which, say what you like, it was though at the moment she was distinctly stouter. And why not? An awful lot of makebelieve went on about that sort of thing involving a lifelong slur with the usual splash page of gutterpress about the same old matrimonial tangle alleging misconduct with professional golfer or the newest stage favourite instead of being honest and aboveboard about the whole business. How they were fated to meet and an attachment sprang up between the two so that their names were coupled in the public eye was told in court with letters containing the habitual mushy and compromising expressions leaving no loophole to show that they openly cohabited two or three times a week at some wellknown seaside hotel and relations, when the thing ran its normal course, became in due course intimate. Then the decree **nisi** and the King's proctor tries to show cause why and, he failing to quash it, **nisi** was made absolute. But as for that the two misdemeanants, wrapped up as they largely were in one another, could safely afford to ignore it as they very largely did till the matter was put in the hands of a solicitor who filed a petition for the party wronged in due course. He, B, enjoyed the distinction of being close to Erin's uncrowned king in the flesh when the thing occurred on the historic **fracas** when the fallen leader's, who notoriously stuck to his guns to the last drop even when clothed in the mantle of adultery, (leader's) trusty henchmen to the number of ten or a dozen or possibly even more than that penetrated into the printing works of the **Insuppressible** or no it was **United Ireland** (a by no means by the by appropriate appellative) and broke up the typecases with hammers or something like that all on account of some scurrilous effusions from the facile pens of the O'Brienite scribes at the usual mudslinging occupation reflecting on the erstwhile tribune's private morals. Though palpably a radically altered man he was still a commanding figure though carelessly garbed as usual with that look of settled purpose which went a long way with the shillyshallyers till they discovered to their vast discomfiture that their idol had feet of clay after placing him upon a pedestal which she, however, was the first to perceive. As those were particularly hot times in the general hullaballoo Bloom sustained a minor injury from a nasty prod of some chap's elbow in the crowd that of course congregated lodging some place about the pit of the stomach, fortunately not of a grave character. His hat (Parnell's) a silk one was inadvertently knocked off and, as a matter of strict history, Bloom was the man who picked it up in the crush after witnessing the occurrence meaning to return it to him (and return it to him he did with the utmost celerity) who panting and hatless and whose thoughts were miles away from his hat at the time all the same being a gentleman born with a stake in the country he, as a matter of fact, having gone into it more for the kudos of the thing than anything else, what's bred in the bone instilled into him in infancy at his mother's knee in the shape of knowing what good form was came out at once because he turned round to the donor and thanked him with perfect **aplomb**, saying: **Thank you, sir**, though in a very different tone of voice from the ornament of the legal profession whose headgear Bloom also set to rights earlier in the course of the day, history repeating itself with a difference, after the burial of a mutual friend when they had left him alone in his glory after the grim task of having committed his remains to the grave.

On the other hand what incensed him more inwardly was the blatant jokes of the cabman and so on who passed it all off as a jest, laughing immoderately, pretending to understand everything, the why and the wherefore, and in reality not knowing their own minds, it being a case for the two parties themselves unless it ensued that the legitimate husband happened to be a party to it owing to some anonymous letter from the usual boy Jones, who happened to come across them at the crucial moment in a loving position locked in one another's arms, drawing attention to their illicit proceedings and leading up to a domestic rumpus and the erring fair one begging forgiveness of her lord and master upon her knees and promising to sever the connection and not receive his visits any more if only the aggrieved husband would overlook the matter and let bygones be bygones with tears in her eyes though possibly with her tongue in her fair cheek at the same time as quite possibly there were several others. He personally, being of a sceptical bias, believed and didn't make the smallest bones about saying so either that man or men in the plural were always hanging around on the waiting list about a lady, even supposing she was the best wife in the world and they got on fairly well together for the sake of argument, when, neglecting her duties, she chose to be tired of wedded life and was on for a little flutter in polite debauchery to press their attentions on her with improper intent, the upshot being that her affections centred on another, the cause of many **liaisons** between still attractive married women getting on for fair and forty and younger men, no doubt as several famous cases of feminine infatuation proved up to the hilt.

It was a thousand pities a young fellow, blessed with an allowance of brains as his neighbour obviously was, should waste his valuable time with profligate women who might present him with a nice dose to last him his lifetime. In the nature of single blessedness he would one day take unto himself a wife when Miss Right came on the scene but in the interim ladies' society was a **conditio sine qua non** though he had the gravest possible doubts, not that he wanted in the smallest to pump Stephen about Miss Ferguson (who was very possibly the particular lodestar who brought him down to Irishtown so early in the morning), as to whether he would find much satisfaction basking in the boy and girl courtship idea and the company of smirking misses without a penny to their names bi or triweekly with the orthodox preliminary canter of complimentplaying and walking out leading up to fond lovers' ways and flowers and chocs. To think of him house and homeless, rooked by some landlady worse than any stepmother, was really too bad at his age. The queer suddenly things he popped out with attracted the elder man who was several years the other's senior or like his father but something substantial he certainly ought to eat even were it only an eggflip made on unadulterated maternal nutriment or, failing that, the homely Humpty Dumpty boiled.

– At what o'clock did you dine? he questioned of the slim form and tired though unwrinkled face.

– Some time yesterday, Stephen said.

– Yesterday! exclaimed Bloom till he remembered it was already tomorrow Friday. Ah, you mean it's after twelve!

– The day before yesterday, Stephen

said, improving on himself.

Literally astounded at this piece of intelligence Bloom reflected. Though they didn't see eye to eye in everything a certain analogy there somehow was as if both their minds were travelling, so to speak, in the one train of thought. At his age when dabbling in politics roughly some score of years previously when he had been a **quasi** aspirant to parliamentary honours in the Buckshot Foster days he too recollected in retrospect (which was a source of keen satisfaction in itself) he had a sneaking regard for those same ultra ideas. For instance when the evicted tenants question, then at its first inception, bulked largely in people's mind though, it goes without saying, not contributing a copper or pinning his faith absolutely to its dictums, some of which wouldn't exactly hold water, he at the outset in principle at all events was in thorough sympathy with peasant possession as voicing the trend of modern opinion (a partiality, however, which, realising his mistake, he was subsequently partially cured of) and even was twitted with going a step farther than Michael Davitt in the striking views he at one time inculcated as a backtothelander, which was one reason he strongly resented the innuendo put upon him in so barefaced a fashion by our friend at the gathering of the clans in Barney Kiernan's so that he, though often considerably misunderstood and the least pugnacious of mortals, be it repeated, departed from his customary habit to give him (metaphorically) one in the gizzard though, so far as politics themselves were concerned, he was only too conscious of the casualties invariably resulting from propaganda and displays of mutual animosity and the misery and suffering it entailed as a foregone conclusion on fine young fellows, chiefly, destruction of the fittest, in a word.

Anyhow upon weighing up the pros and cons, getting on for one, as it was, it was high time to be retiring for the night. The crux was it was a bit risky to bring him home as eventualitiesmightpossiblyensue(somebody having a temper of her own sometimes) and spoil the hash altogether as on the night he misguidedly brought home a dog (breed unknown) with a lame paw (not that the cases were either identical or the reverse though he had hurt his hand too) to Ontario Terrace as he very distinctly remembered, having been there, so to speak. On the other hand it was altogether far and away too late for the Sandymount or Sandycove suggestion so that he was in some perplexity as to which of the two alternatives. Everything pointed to the fact that it behoved him to avail himself to the full of the opportunity, all things considered. His initial impression was he was a shade standoffish or not over effusive but it grew on him someway. For one thing he mightn't what you call jump at the idea, if approached, and what mostly worried him was he didn't know how to lead up to it or word it exactly, supposing he did entertain the proposal, as it would afford him very great personal pleasure if he would allow him to help to put coin in his way or some wardrobe, if found suitable. At all events he wound up by concluding, eschewing for the nonce hidebound precedent, a cup of Epps's cocoa and a shakedown for the night plus the use of a rug or two and overcoat doubled into a pillow at least he would be in safe hands and as warm as a toast on a trivet he failed to perceive any very vast amount of harm in that always with the proviso no rumpus of any sort was kicked up. A move had to be made because that merry old soul, the grasswidower in question who appeared to be glued to the spot, didn't appear in any particular hurry to wend his way home to his dearly beloved Queenstown and it was highly likely some sponger's bawdyhouse of retired beauties where age was no bar off Sheriff street lower would be the best clue to that equivocal character's whereabouts for a few days to come, alternately racking their feelings (the mermaids') with sixchamber revolver anecdotes verging on the tropical calculated to freeze the marrow of anybody's bones and mauling their largesized charms betweenwhiles with rough and tumble gusto to the accompaniment of large potations of potheen and the usual blarney about himself for as to who he in reality was let x equal my right name and address, as Mr Algebra remarks **passim**. At the same time he inwardly chuckled over his gentle repartee to the blood and ouns champion about his god being a jew. People could put up with being bitten by a wolf but what properly riled them was a bite from a sheep. The most vulnerable point too of tender Achilles. Your god was a jew. Because mostly they appeared to imagine he came from Carrick-on-Shannon or somewhereabouts in the county Sligo.

– I propose, our hero eventually suggested after mature reflection while prudently pocketing her photo, as it's rather stuffy here you just come home with me and talk things over. My diggings are quite close in the vicinity. You can't drink that stuff. Do you like cocoa? Wait. I'll just pay this lot.

The best plan clearly being to clear out, the remainder being plain sailing, he beckoned, while prudently pocketing the photo, to the keeper of the shanty who didn't seem to.

– Yes, that's the best, he assured Stephen to whom for the matter of that Brazen Head or him or anywhere else was all more or less.

All kinds of Utopian plans were flashing through his (B's) busy brain, education (the genuine article), literature, journalism, prize titbits, up to date billing, concert tours in English watering resorts packed with hydros and seaside theatres, turning money away, duets in Italian with the accent perfectly true to nature and a quantity of other things, no necessity, of course, to tell the world and his wife from the housetops about it, and a slice of luck. An opening was all was wanted. Because he more than suspected he had his father's voice to bank his hopes on which it was quite on the cards he had so it would be just as well, by the way no harm, to trail the conversation in the direction of that particular red herring just to.

The cabby read out of the paper he had got hold of that the former viceroy, earl Cadogan, had presided at the cabdrivers' association dinner in London somewhere. Silence with a yawn or two accompanied this thrilling announcement. Then the old specimen in the corner who appeared to have some spark of vitality left read out that sir Anthony MacDonnell had left Euston for the chief secretary's lodge or words to that effect. To which absorbing piece of intelligence echo answered why.

– Give us a squint at that literature, grandfather, the ancient mariner put in, manifesting some natural impatience.

– And welcome, answered the elderly party thus addressed.

The sailor lugged out from a case he had

a pair of greenish goggles which he very slowly hooked over his nose and both ears.

–Are you bad in the eyes? the sympathetic personage like the townclerk queried.

– Why, answered the seafarer with the tartan beard, who seemingly was a bit of a literary cove in his own small way, staring out of seagreen portholes as you might well describe them as, I uses goggles reading. Sand in the Red Sea done that. One time I could read a book in the dark, manner of speaking. **The Arabian Nights Entertainment** was my favourite and **Red as a Rose is She.**

Hereupon he pawed the journal open and pored upon Lord only knows what, found drowned or the exploits of King Willow, Iremonger having made a hundred and something second wicket not out for Notts, during which time (completely regardless of Ire) the keeper was intensely occupied loosening an apparently new or secondhand boot which manifestly pinched him as he muttered against whoever it was sold it, all of them who were sufficiently awake enough to be picked out by their facial expressions, that is to say, either simply looking on glumly or passing a trivial remark.

To cut a long story short Bloom, grasping the situation, was the first to rise from his seat so as not to outstay their welcome having first and foremost, being as good as his word that he would foot the bill for the occasion, taken the wise precaution to unobtrusively motion to mine host as a parting shot a scarcely perceptible sign when the others were not looking to the effect that the amount due was forthcoming, making a grand total of fourpence (the amount he deposited unobtrusively in four coppers, literally the last of the Mohicans), he having previously spotted on the printed pricelist for all who ran to read opposite him in unmistakable figures, coffee 2d, confectionery do, and honestly well worth twice the money once in a way, as Wetherup used to remark.

– Come, he counselled to close the **séance**.

Seeing that the ruse worked and the coast was clear they left the shelter or shanty together and the élite society of oilskin and company whom nothing short of an earthquake would move out of their **dolce far niente**. Stephen, who confessed to still feeling poorly and fagged out, paused at the, for a moment, the door.

– One thing I never understood, he said to be original on the spur of the moment. Why they put tables upside down at night, I mean chairs upside down, on the tables in cafés. To which impromptu the neverfailing Bloom replied without a moment's hesitation, saying straight off:

– To sweep the floor in the morning.

So saying he skipped around, nimbly considering, frankly at the same time apologetic to get on his companion's right, a habit of his, by the bye, his right side being, in classical idiom, his tender Achilles. The night air was certainly now a treat to breathe though Stephen was a bit weak on his pins.

– It will (the air) do you good, Bloom said, meaning also the walk, in a moment. The only thing is to walk then you'll feel a different man. Come. It's not far. Lean on me.

Accordingly he passed his left arm in Stephen's right and led him on accordingly.

– Yes, Stephen said uncertainly because he thought he felt a strange kind of flesh of a different man approach him, sinewless and wobbly and all that.

Anyhow they passed the sentrybox with stones, brazier etc. where the municipal supernumerary, ex Gumley, was still to all intents and purposes wrapped in the arms of Murphy, as the adage has it, dreaming of fresh fields and pastures new. And **apropos** of coffin of stones the analogy was not at all bad as it was in fact a stoning to death on the part of seventytwo out of eighty odd constituencies that ratted at the time of the split and chiefly the belauded peasant class, probably the selfsame evicted tenants he had put in their holdings.

So they turned on to chatting about music, a form of art for which Bloom, as a pure amateur, possessed the greatest love, as they made tracks arm in arm across Beresford place. Wagnerian music, though confessedly grand in its way, was a bit too heavy for Bloom and hard to follow at the first go-off but the music of Mercadante's **Huguenots**, Meyerbeer's **Seven Last Words on the Cross** and Mozart's **Twelfth Mass** he simply revelled in, the **Gloria** in that being, to his mind, the acme of first class music as such, literally knocking everything else into a cocked hat. He infinitely preferred the sacred music of the catholic church to anything the opposite shop could offer in that line such as those Moody and Sankey hymns or **Bid me to live and i will live thy protestant to be**. He also yielded to none in his admiration of Rossini's **Stabat Mater**, a work simply abounding in immortal numbers, in which his wife, Madam Marion Tweedy, made a hit, a veritable sensation, he might safely say, greatly adding to her other laureis and putting the others totally in the shade, in the jesuit fathers' church in upper Gardiner street, the sacred edifice being thronged to the doors to hear her with virtuosos, or **virtuosi** rather. There was the unanimous opinion that there was none to come up to her and suffice it to say in a place of worship for music of a sacred character there was a generally voiced desire for an encore. On the whole though favouring preferably light opera of the **Don Giovanni** description and **Martha**, a gem in its line, he had a **penchant**, though with only a surface knowledge, for the severe classical school such as Mendelssohn. And talking of that, taking it for granted he knew all about the old favourites, he mentioned **par excellence** Lionel's air in **Martha, M'appari**, which, curiously enough, he had heard or overheard, to be more accurate, on yesterday, a privilege he keenly appreciated, from the lips of Stephen's respected father, sung to perfection, a study of the number, in fact, which made all the others take a back seat. Stephen, in reply to a politely put query, said he didn't sing it but launched out into praises of Shakespeare's songs, at least of in or about that period, the lutenist Dowland who lived in Fetter lane near Gerard the herbalist, who **anno ludendo hausi, Doulandus**, an instrument he was contemplating purchasing from Mr Arnold Dolmetsch, whom B. did not quite recall though the name certainly sounded familiar, for sixtyfive guineas and Farnaby and son with their **dux** and **comes** conceits and Byrd (William) who played the virginals, he said, in the Queen's chapel or anywhere else he found them and one Tomkins who made toys or airs and John Bull.

On the roadway which they were approaching whilst still speaking beyond the swingchains a horse, dragging a sweeper, paced on the paven ground, brushing a long swathe of mire up so that with the noise Bloom was not perfectly certain whether he had caught aright the allusion to sixtyfive guineas and John Bull. He inquired if it was John Bull the political celebrity of that ilk, as it struck him, the two identical names, as a striking coincidence.

By the chains the horse slowly swerved to turn, which perceiving, Bloom, who was keeping a sharp lookout as usual, plucked the other's sleeve gently, jocosely remarking:

– Our lives are in peril tonight. Beware of the steamroller.

They thereupon stopped. Bloom looked at the head of a horse not worth anything like sixtyfive guineas, suddenly in evidence in the dark quite near so that it seemed new, a different grouping of bones and even flesh because palpably it was a fourwalker, a hipshaker, a blackbuttocker, a taildangler, a headhanger putting his hind foot foremost the while the lord of his creation sat on the perch, busy with his thoughts. But such a good poor brute he was sorry he hadn't a lump of sugar but, as he wisely reflected, you could scarcely be prepared for every emergency that might crop up. He was just a big nervous foolish noodly kind of a horse, without a second care in the world. But even a dog, he reflected, take that mongrel in Barney Kiernan's, of the same size, would be a holy horror to face. But it was no animal's fault in particular if he was built that way like the camel, ship of the desert, distilling grapes into potheen in his hump. Nine tenths of them all could be caged or trained, nothing beyond the art of man barring the bees. Whale with a harpoon hairpin, alligator tickle the small of his back and he sees the joke, chalk a circle for a rooster, tiger my eagle eye. These timely reflections anent the brutes of the field occupied his mind somewhat distracted from Stephen's words while the ship of the street was manoeuvring and Stephen went on about the highly interesting old.

– What's this I was saying? Ah, yes! My wife, he intimated, plunging **in medias res**, would have the greatest of pleasure in making your acquaintance as she is passionately attached to music of any kind.

He looked sideways in a friendly fashion at the sideface of Stephen, image of his mother, which was not quite the same as the usual handsome blackguard type they unquestionably had an insatiable hankering after as he was perhaps not that way built.

Still, supposing he had his father's gift as he more than suspected, it opened up new vistas in his mind such as Lady Fingall's Irish industries, concert on the preceding Monday, and aristocracy in general.

Exquisite variations he was now describing on an air **Youth here has End** by Jans Pieter Sweelinck, a Dutchman of Amsterdam where the frows come from. Even more he liked an old German song of **Johannes**

Jeep about the clear sea and the voices of sirens, sweet murderers of men, which boggled Bloom a bit:

> **Von der Sirenen Listigkeit**
> **Tun die Poeten dichten.**

These opening bars he sang and translated **extempore**. Bloom, nodding, said he perfectly understood and begged him to go on by all means which he did.

A phenomenally beautiful tenor voice like that, the rarest of boons, which Bloom appreciated at the very first note he got out, could easily, if properly handled by some recognised authority on voice production such as Barraclough and being able to read music into the bargain, command its own price where baritones were ten a penny and procure for its fortunate possessor in the near future an **entrée** into fashionable houses in the best residential quarters of financial magnates in a large way of business and titled people where with his university degree of B. A. (a huge ad in its way) and gentlemanly bearing to all the more influence the good impression he would infallibly score a distinct success, being blessed with brains which also could be utilised for the purpose and other requisites, if his clothes were properly attended to so as to the better worm his way into their good graces as he, a youthful tyro in – society's sartorial niceties, hardly understood how a little thing like that could militate against you. It was in fact only a matter of months and he could easily foresee him participating in their musical and artistic **conversaziones** during the festivities of the Christmas season, for choice, causing a slight flutter in the dovecotes of the fair sex and being made a lot of by ladies out for sensation, cases of which, as he happened to know, were on record – in fact, without giving the show away, he himself once upon a time, if he cared to, could easily have. Added to which of course would be the pecuniary emolument by no means to be sneezed at, going hand in hand with his tuition fees. Not, he parenthesised, that for the sake of filthy lucre he need necessarily embrace the lyric platform as a walk in life for any lengthy space of time. But a step in the required direction it was beyond yea or nay and both monetarily and mentally it contained no reflection on his dignity in the smallest and it often turned in uncommonly handy to be handed a cheque at a muchneeded moment when every little helped. Besides, though taste latterly had deteriorated to a degree, original music like that, different from the conventional rut, would rapidly have a great vogue as it would be a decided novelty for Dublin's musical world after the usual hackneyed run of catchy tenor solos foisted on a confiding public by Ivan St Austell and Hilton St Just and their **genus omne**. Yes, beyond a shadow of a doubt he could with all the cards in his hand and he had a capital opening to make a name for himself and win a high place in the city's esteem where he could command a stiff figure and, booking ahead, give a grand concert for the patrons of the King street house, given a backerup, if one were forthcoming to kick him upstairs, so to speak, a big **if**, however, with some impetus of the goahead sort to obviate the inevitable procrastination which often tripped-up a too much fêted prince of good fellows. And it need not detract from the other by one iota as, being his own master, he would have heaps of time to practise literature in his spare moments when desirous of so doing without its clashing with his vocal career or containing anything derogatory whatsoever as it was a matter for himself alone. In fact, he had the ball at his feet and that was the very reason why the other, possessed of a remarkably sharp nose for smelling a rat of any sort, hung on to him at all.

The horse was just then. And later on

at a propitious opportunity he purposed (Bloom did), without anyway prying into his private affairs on the **fools step in where angels** principle, advising him to sever his connection with a certain budding practitioner who, he noticed, was prone to disparage and even to a slight extent with some hilarious pretext when not present, deprecate him, or whatever you like to call it which in Bloom's humble opinion threw a nasty sidelight on that side of a person's character, no pun intended.

The horse having reached the end of his tether, so to speak, halted and, rearing high a proud feathering tail, added his quota by letting fall on the floor which the brush would soon brush up and polish, three smoking globes of turds. Slowly three times, one after another, from a full crupper he mired. And humanely his driver waited till he (or she) had ended, patient in his scythed car.

Side by side Bloom, profiting by the **contretemps**, with Stephen passed through the gap of the chains, divided by the upright, and, stepping over a strand of mire, went across towards Gardiner street lower, Stephen singing more boldly, but not loudly, the end of the ballad.

Und alle Schiffe brücken.

The driver never said a word, good, bad or indifferent, but merely watched the two figures, as he sat on his lowbacked car, both black, one full, one lean, walk towards the railway bridge, **to be married by Father Maher**. As they walked they at times stopped and walked again continuing their **tête-à-tête** (which, of course, he was utterly out of) about sirens enemies of man's reason, mingled with a number of other topics of the same category, usurpers, historical cases of the kind while the man in the sweeper car or you might as well call it in the sleeper car who in any case couldn't possibly hear because they were too far simply sat in his seat near the end of lower Gardiner street **and looked after their lowbacked car**.

CHAPTER SEVENTEEN

WHAT PARALLEL COURSES did Bloom and Stephen follow returning?

Starting united both at normal walking pace from Beresford place they followed in the order named Lower and Middle Gardiner streets and Mountjoy square, west: then, at reduced pace, each bearing left, Gardiner's place by an inadvertence as far as the farther corner of Temple street: then, at reduced pace with interruptions of halt, bearing right, Temple street, north, as far as Hardwicke place. Approaching, disparate, at relaxed walking pace they crossed both the circus before George's church diametrically, the chord in any circle being less than the arc which it subtends.

Of what did the duumvirate deliberate during their itinerary?

Music, literature, Ireland, Dublin, Paris, friendship, woman, prostitution, diet, the influence of gaslight or the light of arc and glowlamps on the growth of adjoining paraheliotropic trees, exposed corporation emergency dustbuckets, the Roman catholic church, ecclesiastical celibacy, the Irish nation, jesuit education, careers, the study of medicine, the past day, the maleficent influence of the presabbath, Stephen's collapse.

Did Bloom discover common factors of similarity between their respective like and unlike reactions to experience?

Both were sensitive to artistic impressions, musical in preference to plastic or pictorial.

Both preferred a continental to an insular manner of life, a cisatlantic to a transatlantic place of residence. Both indurated by early domestic training and an inherited tenacity of heterodox resistance professed their disbelief in many orthodox religious, national, social and ethical doctrines. Both admitted the alternately stimulating and obtunding influence of heterosexual magnetism.

Were their views on some points divergent?

Stephen dissented openly from Bloom's views on the importance of dietary and civic selfhelp while Bloom dissented tacitly from Stephen's views on the eternal affirmation of the spirit of man in literature. Bloom assented covertly to Stephen's rectification of the anachronism involved in assigning the date of the conversion of the Irish nation to christianity from druidism by Patrick son of Calpornus, son of Potitus, son of Odyssus, sent by pope Celestine I in the year 432 in the reign of Leary to the year 260 or thereabouts in the reign of Cormac MacArt († 266 A.D.), suffocated by imperfect deglutition of aliment at Sletty and interred at Rossnaree. The collapse which Bloom ascribed to gastric inanition and certain chemical compounds of varying degrees of adulteration and alcoholic strength, accelerated by mental exertion and the velocity of rapid circular motion in a relaxing atmosphere, Stephen attributed to the reapparition of a matutinal cloud (perceived by both from two different points of observation Sandycove and Dublin) at first no bigger than a woman's hand.

Was there one point on which their views were equal and negative?

The influence of gaslight or electric light on the growth of adjoining paraheliotropic trees.

Had Bloom discussed similar subjects during nocturnal perambulations in the past?

In 1884 with Owen Goldberg and Cecil Turnbull at night on public thoroughfares between Longwood avenue and Leonard's corner and Leonard's corner and Synge street and Synge street and Bloomfield avenue.

In 1885 with Percy Apjohn in the evenings, reclined against the wall between Gibraltar villa and Bloomfield house in Crumlin, barony of Uppercross. In 1886 occasionally with casual acquaintances and prospective purchasers on doorsteps, in front parlours, in third class railway carriages of suburban lines. In 1888 frequently with major Brian Tweedy and his daughter Miss Marion Tweedy, together and separately on the lounge in Matthew Dillon's house in Roundtown. Once in 1892 and once in 1893 with Julius (Juda) Mastiansky, on both occasions in the parlour of his (Bloom's) house in Lombard street, west.

What reflection concerning the irregular sequence of dates 1884, 1885, 1886, 1888, 1892, 1893, 1904 did Bloom make before their arrival at their destination?

He reflected that the progressive extension

of the field of individual development and experience was regressively accompanied by a restriction of the converse domain of interindividual relations.

As in what ways?

From inexistence to existence he came to many and was as one received: existence with existence he was with any as any with any: from existence to nonexistence gone he would be by all as none perceived.

What act did Bloom make on their arrival at their destination?

At the housesteps of the 4th Of the equidifferent uneven numbers, number 7 Eccles street, he inserted his hand mechanically into the back pocket of his trousers to obtain his latchkey.

Was it there?

It was in the corresponding pocket of the trousers which he had worn on the day but one preceding.

Why was he doubly irritated?

Because he had forgotten and because he

remembered that he had reminded himself twice not to forget.

What were then the alternatives before the, premeditatedly (respectively) and inadvertently, keyless couple?

To enter or not to enter. To knock or not to knock.

Bloom's decision?

A stratagem. Resting his feet on the dwarf wall, he climbed over the area railings, compressed his hat on his head, grasped two points at the lower union of rails and stiles, lowered his body gradually by its length of five feet nine inches and a half to within two feet ten inches of the area pavement and allowed his body to move freely in space by separating himself from the railings and crouching in preparation for the impact of the fall.

Did he fall?

By his body's known weight of eleven stone and four pounds in avoirdupois measure, as certified by the graduated machine for periodical selfweighing in the premises of Francis Froedman, pharmaceutical chemist of 19 Frederick street, north, on the last feast of the Ascension, to wit, the twelfth day of May of the bissextile year one thousand nine hundred and four of the christian era (jewish era five thousand six hundred and sixtyfour, mohammadan era one thousand three hundred and twentytwo), golden number 5, epact 13, solar cycle 9, dominical letters C B, Roman indiction 2, Julian period 6617, MCMIV.

Did he rise uninjured by concussion?

Regaining new stable equilibrium he rose uninjured though concussed by the impact, raised the latch of the area door by the exertion of force at its freely moving flange and by leverage of the first kind applied at its fulcrum, gained retarded access to the kitchen through the subadjacent scullery, ignited a lucifer match by friction, set free inflammable coal gas by turningon the ventcock, lit a high flame which, by regulating, he reduced to quiescent candescence and lit finally a portable candle.

What discrete succession of images did Stephen meanwhile perceive?

Reclined against the area railings he perceived through the transparent kitchen panes a man regulating a gasflame of 14 CP, a man lighting a candle of 1 CP, a man removing in turn each of his two boots, a man leaving the kitchen holding a candle.

Did the man reappear elsewhere?

After a lapse of four minutes the glimmer of his candle was discernible through the semitransparent semicircular glass fanlight over the halldoor. The halldoor turned gradually on its hinges. In the open space of the doorway the man reappeared without his hat, with his candle.

Did Stephen obey his sign?

Yes, entering softly, he helped to close and chain the door and followed softly along the hallway the man's back and listed feet and lighted candle past a lighted crevice of doorway on the left and carefully down a turning staircase of more than five steps into the kitchen of Bloom's house.

What did Bloom do?

He extinguished the candle by a sharp expiration of breath upon its flame, drew two spoonseat deal chairs to the hearthstone, one for Stephen with its back to the area window, the other for himself when necessary, knelt on one knee, composed in the grate a pyre of crosslaid resintipped sticks and various coloured papers and irregular polygons of best Abram coal at twentyone shillings a ton from the yard of Messrs Flower and M'Donald of 14 D'Olier street, kindled it at three projecting points of paper with one ignited lucifer match, thereby releasing the potential energy contained in the fuel by allowing its carbon and hydrogen elements to enter into free union with the oxygen of the air.

Of what similar apparitions did Stephen think?

Of others elsewhere in other times who, kneeling on one knee or on two, had kindled fires for him, of Brother Michael in the infirmary of the college of the Society of Jesus at Clongowes Wood, Sallins, in the county of Kildare: of his father, Simon Dedalus, in an unfurnished room of his first residence in Dublin, number thirteen Fitzgibbon street: of his godmother Miss Kate Morkan in the house of her dying sister Miss Julia Morkan at 15 Usher's Island: of his aunt Sara, wife of Richie (Richard) Goulding, in the kitchen of their lodgings at 62 Clanbrassil street: of his mother Mary, wife of Simon Dedalus, in the kitchen of number twelve North Richmond street on the morning of the feast of Saint Francis Xavier 1898: of the dean of studies, Father Butt, in the physics' theatre of university College, 16 Stephen's Green, north: of his sister Dilly (Delia) in his father's house in Cabra.

What did Stephen see on raising his gaze

to the height of a yard from the fire towards the opposite wall?

Under a row of five coiled spring housebells a curvilinear rope, stretched between two holdfasts athwart across the recess beside the chimney pier, from which hung four smallsized square handkerchiefs folded unattached consecutively in adjacent rectangles and one pair of ladies' grey hose with Lisle suspender tops and feet in their habitual position clamped by three erect wooden pegs two at their outer extremities and the third at their point of junction.

What did Bloom see on the range?

On the right (smaller) hob a blue enamelled saucepan: on the left (larger) hob a black iron kettle.

What did Bloom do at the range?

He removed the saucepan to the left hob, rose and carried the iron kettle to the sink in order to tap the current by turning the faucet to let it flow.

Did it flow?

Yes. From Roundwood reservoir in county Wicklow of a cubic capacity of 2400 million gallons, percolating through a subterranean aqueduct of filter mains of single and double pipeage constructed at an initial plant cost of £ 5 per linear yard by way of the Dargle, Rathdown, Glen of the Downs and Callowhill to the 26 acre reservoir at Stillorgan, a distance of 22 statute miles, and thence, through a system of relieving tanks, by a gradient of 250 feet to the city boundary at Eustace bridge, upper Leeson street, though from prolonged summer drouth and daily supply of 12 1/2 million gallons the water had fallen below the sill of the overflow weir for which reason the borough surveyor and waterworks engineer, Mr Spencer Harty, C. E., on the instructions of the waterworks committee had prohibited the use of municipal water for purposes other than those of consumption (envisaging the possibility of recourse being had to the impotable water of the Grand and Royal canals as in 1893) particularly as the

South Dublin Guardians, notwithstanding their ration of 15 gallons per day per pauper supplied through a 6 inch meter, had been convicted of a wastage of 20,000 gallons per night by a reading of their meter on the affirmation of the law agent of the corporation, Mr Ignatius Rice, solicitor, thereby acting to the detriment of another section of the public, selfsupporting taxpayers, solvent, sound.

What in water did Bloom, waterlover, drawer of water, watercarrier, returning to the range, admire?

Its universality: its democratic equality and constancy to its nature in seeking its own level: its vastness in the ocean of Mercator's projection: its unplumbed profundity in the Sundam trench of the Pacific exceeding 8000 fathoms: the restlessness of its waves and surface particles visiting in turn all points of its seaboard: the independence of its units: the variability of states of sea: its hydrostatic quiescence in calm: its hydrokinetic turgidity in neap and spring tides: its subsidence after devastation: its sterility in the circumpolar icecaps, arctic and antarctic: its climatic and commercial significance: its preponderance of 3 to 1 over the dry land of the globe: its indisputable hegemony extending in square leagues over all the region below the subequatorial tropic of Capricorn: the multisecular stability of its primeval basin: its luteofulvous bed: its capacity to dissolve and hold in solution all soluble substances including millions of tons of the most precious metals: its slow erosions of peninsulas and islands, its persistent formation of homothetic islands, peninsulas and downwardtending promontories: its alluvial deposits: its weight and volume and density: its imperturbability in lagoons and highland tarns: its gradation of colours in the torrid and temperate and frigid zones: its vehicular ramifications in continental lakecontained streams and confluent oceanflowing rivers with their tributaries and transoceanic currents, gulfstream, north and south equatorial courses: its violence in seaquakes, waterspouts, Artesian wells, eruptions, torrents, eddies, freshets, spates, groundswells, watersheds, waterpartings, geysers, cataracts, whirlpools, maelstroms, inundations, deluges, cloudbursts: its vast circumterrestrial ahorizontal curve: its secrecy in springs and latent humidity, revealed by rhabdomantic or hygrometric instruments and exemplified by the well by the hole in the wall at Ashtown gate, saturation of air, distillation of dew: the simplicity of its composition, two constituent parts of hydrogen with one constituent part of oxygen: its healing virtues: its buoyancy in the waters of the Dead Sea: its persevering penetrativeness in runnels, gullies, inadequate dams, leaks on shipboard: its properties for cleansing, quenching thirst and fire, nourishing vegetation: its infallibility as paradigm and paragon: its metamorphoses as vapour, mist, cloud, rain, sleet, snow, hail: its strength in rigid hydrants: its variety of forms in loughs and bays and gulfs and bights and guts and lagoons and atolls and archipelagos and sounds and fjords and minches and tidal estuaries and arms of sea: its solidity in glaciers, icebergs, icefloes: its docility in working hydraulic millwheels, turbines, dynamos, electric power stations, bleachworks, tanneries, scutchmills: its utility in canals, rivers, if navigable, floating and graving docks: its potentiality derivable from harnessed tides or watercourses falling from level to level: its submarine fauna and flora (anacoustic, photophobe), numerically, if not literally, the inhabitants of the globe: its ubiquity as constituting 90 percent of the human body: the noxiousness of its effluvia in lacustrine marshes, pestilential fens, faded flowerwater, stagnant pools in the waning moon.

Having set the halffilled kettle on the now burning coals, why did he return to the stillflowing tap?

To wash his soiled hands with a

partially consumed tablet of Barrington's lemonflavoured soap, to which paper still adhered, (bought thirteen hours previously for fourpence and still unpaid for), in fresh cold neverchanging everchanging water and dry them, face and hands, in a long redbordered holland cloth passed over a wooden revolving roller.

What reason did Stephen give for declining Bloom's offer?

That he was hydrophobe, hating partial contact by immersion or total by submersion in cold water, (his last bath having taken place in the month of October of the preceding year), disliking the aqueous substances of glass and crystal, distrusting aquacities of thought and language.

What impeded Bloom from giving Stephen counsels of hygiene and prophylactic to which should be added suggestions concerning a preliminary wetting of the head and contraction of the muscles with rapid splashing of the face and neck and thoracic and epigastric region in case of sea or river bathing, the parts of the human anatomy most sensitive to cold being the nape, stomach and thenar or sole of foot?

The incompatibility of aquacity with the erratic originality of genius.

What additional didactic counsels did he similarly repress?

Dietary: concerning the respective percentage of protein and caloric energy in bacon, salt ling and butter, the absence of the former in the lastnamed and the abundance of the latter in the firstnamed.

Which seemed to the host to be the predominant qualities of his guest?

Confidence in himself, an equal and opposite power of abandonment and recuperation.

What concomitant phenomenon took place in the vessel of liquid by the agency of fire?

The phenomenon of ebullition. Fanned by a constant updraught of ventilation between the kitchen and the chimneyflue, ignition was communicated from the faggots of precombustible fuel to polyhedral masses of bituminous coal, containing in compressed mineral form the foliated fossilised decidua of primeval forests which had in turn derived their vegetative existence from the sun, primal source of heat (radiant), transmitted through omnipresent luminiferous diathermanous ether. Heat (convected), a mode of motion developed by such combustion, was constantly and increasingly conveyed from the source of calorification to the liquid contained in the vessel, being radiated through the uneven unpolished dark surface of the metal iron, in part reflected, in part absorbed, in part transmitted, gradually raising the temperature of the water from normal to boiling point, a rise in temperature expressible as the result of an expenditure of 72 thermal units needed to raise 1 pound of water from 50 degrees to 212 degrees

Fahrenheit.

What announced the accomplishment of this rise in temperature?

A double falciform ejection of water vapour from under the kettlelid at both sides simultaneously.

For what personal purpose could Bloom have applied the water so boiled?

To shave himself.

What advantages attended shaving by night?

A softer beard: a softer brush if intentionally allowed to remain from shave to shave in its agglutinated lather: a softer skin if unexpectedly encountering female acquaintances in remote places at incustomary hours: quiet reflections upon the course of the day: a cleaner sensation when awaking after a fresher sleep since matutinal noises, premonitions and perturbations, a clattered milkcan, a postman's double knock, a paper read, reread while lathering, relathering the same spot, a shock, a shoot, with thought of aught he sought though fraught with nought might cause a faster rate of shaving and a nick on which incision plaster with precision cut and humected and applied adhered: which was to be done.

Why did absence of light disturb him less than presence of noise?

Because of the surety of the sense of touch in his firm full masculine feminine passive active hand.

What quality did it (his hand) possess but with what counteracting influence?

The operative surgical quality but that he was reluctant to shed human blood even when the end justified the means, preferring, in their natural order, heliotherapy, psychophysicotherapeutics, osteopathic surgery.

What lay under exposure on the lower, middle and upper shelves of the kitchen dresser, opened by Bloom?

On the lower shelf five vertical breakfast plates, six horizontal breakfast saucers on which rested inverted breakfast cups, a moustachecup, uninverted, and saucer of Crown Derby, four white goldrimmed eggcups, an open shammy purse displaying coins, mostly copper, and a phial of aromatic (violet) comfits. On the middle shelf a chipped eggcup containing pepper, a drum of table salt, four conglomerated black olives in oleaginous paper, an empty pot of Plumtree's potted meat, an oval wicker basket bedded with fibre and containing one Jersey pear, a halfempty bottle of William Gilbey and Co's white invalid port, half disrobed of its swathe of coralpink tissue paper, a packet of Epps's soluble cocoa, five ounces of Anne Lynch's choice tea at 2/- per lb in a crinkled leadpaper bag, a cylindrical canister containing the best crystallised lump sugar, two onions, one, the larger, Spanish, entire, the other, smaller, Irish, bisected with augmented surface and more redolent, a jar of Irish Model Dairy's cream, a jug of brown crockery containing a naggin and a quarter of soured adulterated milk, converted by heat into water, acidulous serum and semisolidified curds, which added to the quantity subtracted for Mr Bloom's and Mrs Fleming's breakfasts, made one imperial pint, the total quantity originally delivered, two cloves, a halfpenny and a small dish containing a slice of fresh ribsteak. On the upper shelf a battery of jamjars (empty) of various sizes and proveniences.

What attracted his attention lying on the apron of the dresser?

Four polygonal fragments of two lacerated scarlet betting tickets, numbered 8 87, 88 6.

What reminiscences temporarily corrugated his brow?

Reminiscences of coincidences, truth stranger than fiction, preindicative of the result of the Gold Cup flat handicap, the official and definitive result of which he had read in the **Evening Telegraph**, late pink edition, in the cabman's shelter, at Butt bridge.

Where had previous intimations of the result, effected or projected, been received by him?

In Bernard Kiernan's licensed premises 8, 9 and 10 little Britain street: in David Byrne's licensed premises, 14 Duke street: in O'Connell street lower, outside Graham Lemon's when a dark man had placed in his hand a throwaway (subsequently thrown away), advertising Elijah, restorer of the church in Zion: in Lincoln place outside the premises of F. W. Sweny and Co (Limited), dispensing chemists, when, when Frederick M. (Bantam) Lyons had rapidly and successively requested, perused and restituted the copy of the current issue of the **Freeman's Journal and National Press** which he had been about to throw away (subsequently thrown away), he had proceeded towards the oriental edifice of the Turkish and Warm Baths, 11 Leinster street, with the light of inspiration shining in his countenance and bearing in his arms the secret of the race, graven in the language of prediction.

What qualifying considerations allayed his perturbations?

The difficulties of interpretation since the significance of any event followed its occurrence as variably as the acoustic report followed the electrical discharge and of counterestimating against an actual loss by failure to interpret the total sum of possible losses proceeding originally from a successful interpretation.

His mood?

He had not risked, he did not expect, he had not been disappointed, he was satisfied.

What satisfied him?

To have sustained no positive loss. To have brought a positive gain to others. Light to the gentiles.

How did Bloom prepare a collation for a gentile?

He poured into two teacups two level

spoonfuls, four in all, of Epps's soluble cocoa and proceeded according to the directions for use printed on the label, to each adding after sufficient time for infusion the prescribed ingredients for diffusion in the manner and in the quantity prescribed.

What supererogatory marks of special hospitality did the host show his guest?

Relinquishing his symposiarchal right to the moustache cup of imitation Crown Derby presented to him by his only daughter, Millicent (Milly), he substituted a cup identical with that of his guest and served extraordinarily to his guest and, in reduced measure, to himself the viscous cream ordinarily reserved for the breakfast of his wife Marion (Molly).

Was the guest conscious of and did he acknowledge these marks of hospitality?

His attention was directed to them by his host jocosely, and he accepted them seriously as they drank in jocoserious silence Epps's massproduct, the creature cocoa.

Were there marks of hospitality which he contemplated but suppressed, reserving them for another and for himself on future occasions to complete the act begun?

The reparation of a fissure of the length of 1 1/2 inches in the right side of his guest's jacket. A gift to his guest of one of the four lady's handkerchiefs, if and when ascertained to be in a presentable condition.

Who drank more quickly?

Bloom, having the advantage of ten seconds at the initiation and taking, from the concave surface of a spoon along the handle of which a steady flow of heat was conducted, three sips to his opponent's one, six to two, nine to three.

What cerebration accompanied his frequentative act?

Concluding by inspection but erroneously that his silent companion was engaged in mental composition he reflected on the pleasures derived from literature of instruction rather than of amusement as he himself had applied to the works of William Shakespeare more than once for the solution of difficult problems in imaginary or real life.

Had he found their solution?

In spite of careful and repeated reading of certain classical passages, aided by a glossary, he had derived imperfect conviction from the text, the answers not bearing in all points.

What lines concluded his first piece of original verse written by him, potential poet, at the age of 11 in 1877 on the occasion of the offering of three prizes of 10/-, 5/- and 2/6 respectively for competition by the **Shamrock**, a weekly newspaper?

An ambition to squint
At my verses in print
Makes me hope that for these you'll find room?.
If you so condescend
Then please place at the end

The name of yours truly, L. Bloom.

Did he find four separating forces between his temporary guest and him?

Name, age, race, creed.

What anagrams had he made on his name in youth?

Leopold Bloom
Ellpodbomool
Molldopeloob
Bollopedoom
Old Ollebo, M. P.

What acrostic upon the abbreviation of his first name had he (kinetic poet) sent to Miss Marion (Molly) Tweedy on the 14 February 1888?

Poets oft have sung in rhyme
Of music sweet their praise divine.
Let them hymn it nine times nine.
Dearer far than song or wine.

You are mine. The world is mine.

What had prevented him from completing a topical song (music by R. G. Johnston) on the events of the past, or fixtures for the actual, years, entitled **If Brian Boru could but come back and see old Dublin now**, commissioned by Michael Gunn, lessee of the Gaiety Theatre, 46, 47, 48, 49 South King street, and to be introduced into the sixth scene, the valley of diamonds, of the second edition (30 January 1893) of the grand annual Christmas pantomime **Sinbad the Sailor** (produced by R Shelton 26 December 1892, written by Greenleaf Whittier, scenery by George A. Jackson and Cecil Hicks, costumes by Mrs and Miss Whelan under the personal supervision of Mrs Michael Gunn, ballets by Jessie Noir, harlequinade by Thomas Otto) and sung by Nelly Bouverist, principal girl?

Firstly, oscillation between events of imperial and of local interest, the anticipated diamond jubilee of Queen Victoria (born 1820, acceded 1837) and the posticipated opening of the new municipal fish market: secondly, apprehension of opposition from extreme circles on the questions of the respective visits of Their Royal Highnesses the duke and duchess of York (real) and of His Majesty King Brian Boru (imaginary): thirdly, a conflict between professional etiquette and professional emulation concerning the recent erections of the Grand Lyric Hall on Burgh Quay and the Theatre Royal in Hawkins street: fourthly, distraction resultant from compassion for Nelly Bouverist's non-intellectual, non-political, non-topical expression of countenance and concupiscence caused by Nelly Bouverist's revelations of white articles of non-intellectual, non-political, non-topical underclothing while she (Nelly Bouverist) was in the articles: fifthly, the difficulties of the selection of appropriate music and humorous allusions from

Everybody's Book of Jokes (1000 pages and a laugh in every one): sixthly, the rhymes, homophonous and cacophonous, associated with the names of the new lord mayor, Daniel Tallon, the new high sheriff, Thomas Pile and the new solicitorgeneral, Dunbar Plunket Barton.

What relation existed between their ages?

16 years before in 1888 when Bloom was of Stephen's present age Stephen was 6. 16 years after in 1920 when Stephen would be of Bloom's present age Bloom would be 54. In 1936 when Bloom would be 70 and Stephen 54 their ages initially in the ratio of 16 to 0 would be as 17 1/2 to 13 1/2, the proportion increasing and the disparity diminishing according as arbitrary future years were added, for if the proportion existing in 1883 had continued immutable, conceiving that to be possible, till then 1904 when Stephen was 22 Bloom would be 374 and in 1920 when Stephen would be 38, as Bloom then was, Bloom would be 646 while

in 1952 when Stephen would have attained the maximum postdiluvian age of 70 Bloom, being 1190 years alive having been born in the year 714, would have surpassed by 221 years the maximum antediluvian age, that of Methusalah, 969 years, while, if Stephen would continue to live until he would attain that age in the year 3072 A.D., Bloom would have been obliged to have been alive 83,300 years, having been obliged to have been born in the year 81,396 B.C.

What events might nullify these calculations?

The cessation of existence of both or either, the inauguration of a new era or calendar, the annihilation of the world and consequent extermination of the human species, inevitable but impredictable.

How many previous encounters proved their preexisting acquaintance?

Two. The first in the lilacgarden of Matthew Dillon's house, Medina Villa, Kimmage road, Roundtown, in 1887, in the company of Stephen's mother, Stephen being then of the age of 5 and reluctant to give his hand in salutation. The second in the coffeeroom of Breslin's hotel on a rainy Sunday in the January of 1892, in the company of Stephen's father and Stephen's granduncle, Stephen being then 5 years older.

Did Bloom accept the invitation to dinner given then by the son and afterwards seconded by the father?

Very gratefully, with grateful appreciation, with sincere appreciative gratitude, in appreciatively grateful sincerity of regret, he declined.

Did their conversation on the subject of these reminiscences reveal a third connecting link between them?

Mrs Riordan (Dante), a widow of independent means, had resided in the house of Stephen's parents from 1 September 1888 to 29 December 1891 and had also resided during the years 1892, 1893 and 1894 in the City Arms Hotel owned by Elizabeth O'Dowd of 54 Prussia street where, during parts of the years 1893 and 1894, she had been a constant informant of Bloom who resided also in the same hotel, being at that time a clerk in the employment of Joseph Cuffe of 5 Smithfield for the superintendence of sales in the adjacent Dublin Cattle market on the North Circular road.

Had he performed any special corporal work of mercy for her?

He had sometimes propelled her on warm summer evenings, an infirm widow of independent, if limited, means, in her convalescent bathchair with slow revolutions of its wheels as far as the corner of the North Circular road opposite Mr Gavin Low's place of business where she had remained for a certain time scanning through his onelensed binocular fieldglasses unrecognisable citizens on tramcars, roadster bicycles equipped with inflated pneumatic tyres, hackney carriages, tandems, private and hired landaus, dogcarts, ponytraps and brakes passing from the city to the Phoenix Park and vice versa.

Why could he then support that his vigil with the greater equanimity?

Because in middle youth he had often sat observing through a rondel of bossed glass of a multicoloured pane the spectacle offered with continual changes of the thoroughfare without, pedestrians, quadrupeds, velocipedes, vehicles, passing slowly, quickly, evenly, round and round and round the rim of a round and round precipitous globe.

What distinct different memories had each of her now eight years deceased?

The older, her bezique cards and counters, her Skye terrier, her suppositious wealth, her lapses of responsiveness and incipient catarrhal deafness: the younger, her lamp of colza oil before the statue of the Immaculate Conception, her green and maroon brushes for Charles Stewart Parnell and for Michael

Davitt, her tissue papers.

Were there no means still remaining to him to achieve the rejuvenation which these reminiscences divulged to a younger companion rendered the more desirable?

The indoor exercises, formerly intermittently practised, subsequently abandoned, prescribed in Eugen Sandow's **Physical Strength and How to Obtain It** which, designed particularly for commercial men engaged in sedentary occupations, were to be made with mental concentration in front of a mirror so as to bring into play the various families of muscles and produce successively a pleasant rigidity, a more pleasant relaxation and the most pleasant repristination of juvenile agility.

Had any special agility been his in earlier youth?

Though ringweight lifting had been beyond his strength and the full circle gyration beyond his courage yet as a High school scholar he had excelled in his stable and protracted execution of the half lever movement on the parallel bars in consequence of his abnormally developed abdominal muscles.

Did either openly allude to their racial difference?

Neither.

What, reduced to their simplest reciprocal form, were Bloom's thoughts about Stephen's thoughts about Bloom and about Stephen's thoughts about Bloom's thoughts about Stephen?

He thought that he thought that he was a jew whereas he knew that he knew that he knew that he was not.

What, the enclosures of reticence removed, were their respective parentages?

Bloom, only born male transubstantial heir of Rudolf Virag (subsequently Rudolph Bloom) of Szombathely, Vienna, Budapest, Milan, London and Dublin and of Ellen Higgins, second daughter of Julius Higgins (born Karoly) and Fanny Higgins (born Hegarty). Stephen, eldest surviving male consubstantial heir of Simon Dedalus of Cork and Dublin and of Mary, daughter of Richard and Christina Goulding (born Grier).

Had Bloom and Stephen been baptised, and where and by whom, cleric or layman?

Bloom (three times), by the reverend Mr Gilmer Johnston M. A., alone, in the protestant church of Saint Nicholas Without, Coombe, by James O'Connor, Philip Gilligan and James Fitzpatrick, together, under a pump in the village of Swords, and by the reverend Charles Malone C. C., in the church of the Three Patrons, Rathgar. Stephen (once) by the reverend Charles Malone C. C., alone, in the church of the Three Patrons, Rathgar.

Did they find their educational careers similar?

Substituting Stephen for Bloom Stoom would have passed successively through a dame's school and the high school. Substituting Bloom for Stephen Blephen would have passed successively through the preparatory, junior, middle and senior grades of the intermediate and through the matriculation, first arts, second arts and arts degree courses of the royal university.

Why did Bloom refrain from stating that he had frequented the university of life?

Because of his fluctuating incertitude as to whether this observation had or had not been already made by him to Stephen or by Stephen to him.

What two temperaments did they individually represent?

The scientific. The artistic.

What proofs did Bloom adduce to prove that his tendency was towards applied, rather than towards pure, science?

Certain possible inventions of which he had cogitated when reclining in a state of supine repletion to aid digestion, stimulated by his appreciation of the importance of inventions now common but once revolutionary, for example, the aeronautic parachute, the reflecting telescope, the spiral corkscrew, the safety pin, the mineral water siphon, the canal lock with winch and sluice, the suction pump.

Were these inventions principally intended for an improved scheme of kindergarten?

Yes, rendering obsolete popguns, elastic airbladders, games of hazard, catapults. They comprised astronomical kaleidoscopes exhibiting the twelve constellations of the zodiac from Aries to Pisces, miniature mechanical orreries, arithmetical gelatine lozenges, geometrical to correspond with zoological biscuits, globemap playing balls, historically costumed dolls.

What also stimulated him in his cogitations?

The financial success achieved by Ephraim Marks and Charles A. James, the former by his 1d bazaar at 42 George's street, south, the latter at his 6 1/2d shop and world's fancy fair and waxwork exhibition at 30 Henry street, admission 2d, children 1d: and the infinite possibilities hitherto unexploited of the modern art of advertisement if condensed in triliteral monoideal symbols, vertically of maximum visibility (divined), horizontally of maximum legibility (deciphered) and of magnetising efficacy to arrest involuntary attention, to interest, to convince, to decide.

Such as?

K. II. Kino's 11/- Trousers. House of Keys. Alexander J. Keyes.

Such as not?

Look at this long candle. Calculate when it burns out and you receive gratis 1 pair of our special non-compo boots, guaranteed 1 candle power. Address: Barclay and Cook, 18 Talbot street.

Bacilikil (Insect Powder). Veribest (Boot Blacking). Uwantit (Combined pocket twoblade penknife with corkscrew, nailfile and pipecleaner).

Such as never?

What is home without Plumtree's Potted Meat?

Incomplete.

With it an abode of bliss.

Manufactured by George Plumtree, 23 Merchants' quay, Dublin, put up in 4 oz pots, and inserted by Councillor Joseph P. Nannetti, M. P., Rotunda Ward, 19 Hardwicke street, under the obituary notices and anniversaries of deceases. The name on the label is Plumtree. A plumtree in a meatpot, registered trade mark. Beware of imitations. Peatmot. Trumplee. Moutpat. Plamtroo.

Which example did he adduce to induce Stephen to deduce that originality, though producing its own reward, does not invariably conduce to success?

His own ideated and rejected project of an illuminated showcart, drawn by a beast of burden, in which two smartly dressed girls were to be seated engaged in writing.

What suggested scene was then constructed by Stephen?

Solitary hotel in mountain pass. Autumn. Twilight. Fire lit. In dark corner young man seated. Young woman enters. Restless. Solitary. She sits. She goes to window. She stands. She sits. Twilight. She thinks. On solitary hotel paper she writes. She thinks. She writes. She sighs. Wheels and hoofs. She hurries out. He comes from his dark corner. He seizes solitary paper. He holds it towards fire. Twilight. He reads. Solitary.

What?

In sloping, upright and backhands: Queen's Hotel, Queen's Hotel, Queen's Hotel. Queen's Ho...

What suggested scene was then reconstructed by Bloom?

The Queen's Hotel, Ennis, county Clare, where Rudolph Bloom (Rudolf Virag) died on the evening of the 27 June 1886, at some hour unstated, in consequence of an overdose of monkshood (aconite) selfadministered in the form of a neuralgic liniment composed of 2 parts of aconite liniment to I of chloroform liniment (purchased by him at 10.20 a.m. on the morning of 27 June 1886 at the medical hall of Francis Dennehy, 17 Church street, Ennis) after having, though not in consequence of having, purchased at 3.15 p.m. on the afternoon of 27 June 1886 a new boater straw hat, extra smart (after having, though not in consequence of having, purchased at the hour and in the place aforesaid, the toxin aforesaid), at the general drapery store of James Cullen, 4 Main street, Ennis.

Did he attribute this homonymity to information or coincidence or intuition?

Coincidence.

Did he depict the scene verbally for his guest to see?

He preferred himself to see another's face and listen to another's words by which potential narration was realised and kinetic temperament relieved.

Did he see only a second coincidence in the second scene narrated to him, described by the narrator as **A Pisgah Sight of Palestine or The Parable of the Plums**?

It, with the preceding scene and with others

unnarrated but existent by implication, to which add essays on various subjects or moral apothegms (e.g. **My Favourite Hero or Procrastination is the Thief of Time**) composed during schoolyears, seemed to him to contain in itself and in conjunction with the personal equation certain possibilities of financial, social, personal and sexual success, whether specially collected and selected as model pedagogic themes (of cent per cent merit) for the use of preparatory and junior grade students or contributed in printed form, following the precedent of Philip Beaufoy or Doctor Dick or Heblon's **Studies in Blue**, to a publication of certified circulation and solvency or employed verbally as intellectual stimulation for sympathetic auditors, tacitly appreciative of successful narrative and confidently augurative of successful achievement, during the increasingly longer nights gradually following the summer solstice on the day but three following, videlicet,

Tuesday, 21 June (S. Aloysius Gonzaga), sunrise 3.33 a.m., sunset 8.29 p.m.

Which domestic problem as much as, if not more than, any other frequently engaged his mind?

What to do with our wives.

What had been his hypothetical singular solutions?

Parlour games (dominos, halma, tiddledywinks, spilikins, cup and ball, nap, spoil five, bezique, twentyfive, beggar my neighbour, draughts, chess or backgammon): embroidery, darning or knitting for the policeaided clothing society: musical duets, mandoline and guitar, piano and flute, guitar and piano: legal scrivenery or envelope addressing: biweekly visits to variety entertainments: commercial activity as pleasantly commanding and pleasingly obeyed mistress proprietress in a cool dairy shop or warm cigar divan: the clandestine satisfaction of erotic irritation in masculine brothels, state inspected and medically controlled: social visits, at regular infrequent prevented intervals and with regular frequent preventive superintendence, to and from female acquaintances of recognised respectability in the vicinity: courses of evening instruction specially designed to render liberal instruction agreeable.

What instances of deficient mental development in his wife inclined him in favour of the lastmentioned (ninth) solution?

In disoccupied moments she had more than once covered a sheet of paper with signs and hieroglyphics which she stated were Greek and Irish and Hebrew characters. She had interrogated constantly at varying intervals as to the correct method of writing the capital initial of the name of a city in Canada, Quebec. She understood little of political complications, internal, or balance of power, external. In calculating the addenda of bills she frequently had recourse to digital aid. After completion of laconic epistolary compositions she abandoned the implement of calligraphy in the encaustic pigment, exposed to the corrosive action of copperas, green vitriol and nutgall. Unusual polysyllables of foreign origin she interpreted phonetically or by false analogy or by both: metempsychosis (met him pike hoses), **alias** (a mendacious person mentioned in sacred scripture).

What compensated in the false balance of her intelligence for these and such deficiencies of judgment regarding persons, places and things?

The false apparent parallelism of all perpendicular arms of all balances, proved true by construction. The counterbalance of her proficiency of judgment regarding one person, proved true by experiment.

How had he attempted to remedy this state of comparative ignorance?

Variously. By leaving in a conspicuous place a certain book open at a certain page: by assuming in her, when alluding explanatorily, latent knowledge: by open ridicule in her presence of some absent other's ignorant lapse.

With what success had he attempted direct instruction?

She followed not all, a part of the whole, gave attention with interest comprehended with surprise, with care repeated, with greater difficulty remembered, forgot with ease, with misgiving reremembered, rerepeated with error.

What system had proved more effective?

Indirect suggestion implicating selfinterest.

Example?

She disliked umbrella with rain, he liked woman with umbrella, she disliked new hat with rain, he liked woman with new hat, he bought new hat with rain, she carried umbrella with new hat.

Accepting the analogy implied in his guest's parable which examples of postexilic eminence did he adduce?

Three seekers of the pure truth, Moses of Egypt, Moses Maimonides, author of

More Nebukim (Guide of the Perplexed) and Moses Mendelssohn of such eminence that from Moses (of Egypt) to Moses (Mendelssohn) there arose none like Moses (Maimonides).

What statement was made, under correction, by Bloom concerning a fourth seeker of pure truth, by name Aristotle, mentioned, with permission, by Stephen?

That the seeker mentioned had been a pupil of a rabbinical philosopher, name uncertain.

Were other anapocryphal illustrious sons of the law and children of a selected or rejected race mentioned?

Felix Bartholdy Mendelssohn (composer), Baruch Spinoza (philosopher), Mendoza (pugilist), Ferdinand Lassalle (reformer, duellist).

What fragments of verse from the ancient Hebrew and ancient Irish languages were cited with modulations of voice and translation of texts by guest to host and by host to guest?

By Stephen: **suil, suil, suil arun, suil go siocair agus suil go cuin** (walk, walk, walk your way, walk in safety, walk with care).

By Bloom: **Kkifeloch, harimon rakatejch m'baad l'zamatejch** (thy temple amid thy hair is as a slice of pomegranate).

How was a glyphic comparison of the phonic symbols of both languages made in substantiation of the oral comparison?

By juxtaposition. On the penultimate blank page of a book of inferior literary style, entituled **Sweets of Sin** (produced by Bloom and so manipulated that its front cover came in contact with the surface of the table) with a pencil (supplied by Stephen) Stephen wrote the Irish characters for gee, eh, dee, em, simple and modified, and Bloom in turn wrote the Hebrew characters ghimel, aleph, daleth and (in the absence of mem) a substituted qoph, explaining their arithmetical values as ordinal and cardinal numbers, videlicet 3, 1, 4, and 100.

Was the knowledge possessed by both of each of these languages, the extinct and the revived, theoretical or practical?

Theoretical, being confined to certain grammatical rules of accidence and syntax and practically excluding vocabulary.

What points of contact existed between these languages and between the peoples who spoke them?

The presence of guttural sounds, diacritic aspirations, epenthetic and servile letters in both languages: their antiquity, both having been taught on the plain of Shinar 242 years after the deluge in the seminary instituted by Fenius Farsaigh, descendant of Noah, progenitor of Israel, and ascendant of Heber and Heremon, progenitors of Ireland: their archaeological, genealogical, hagiographical, exegetical, homiletic, toponomastic, historical and religious literatures comprising the works of rabbis and culdees, Torah, Talmud (Mischna and Ghemara), Massor, Pentateuch, Book of the Dun Cow, Book of Ballymote, Garland of Howth, Book of Kells: their dispersal, persecution, survival and revival: the isolation of their synagogical and ecclesiastical rites in ghetto (S. Mary's Abbey) and masshouse (Adam and Eve's tavern): the proscription of their national costumes in penal laws and jewish dress acts: the restoration in Chanah David of Zion and the possibility of Irish political autonomy or devolution.

What anthem did Bloom chant partially in anticipation of that multiple, ethnically irreducible consummation?

Kolod balejwaw pnimah
Nefesch, jehudi, homijah.

Why was the chant arrested at the conclusion of this first distich?

In consequence of defective mnemotechnic.

How did the chanter compensate for this deficiency?

By a periphrastic version of the general text.

In what common study did their mutual reflections merge?

The increasing simplification traceable from the Egyptian epigraphic hieroglyphs to the Greek and Roman alphabets and the anticipation of modern stenography and telegraphic code in the cuneiform inscriptions (Semitic) and the virgular quinquecostate ogham writing (Celtic). Did the guest comply with his host's request?

Doubly, by appending his signature in Irish and Roman characters.

What was Stephen's auditive sensation?

He heard in a profound ancient male unfamiliar melody the accumulation of the past.

What was Bloom's visual sensation?

He saw in a quick young male familiar form the predestination of a future.

What were Stephen's and Bloom's quasisimultaneous volitional quasisensations of concealed identities?

Visually, Stephen's: The traditional figure of hypostasis, depicted by Johannes Damascenus, Lentulus Romanus and Epiphanius Monachus as leucodermic, sesquipedalian with winedark hair. Auditively, Bloom's: The traditional accent of the ecstasy of catastrophe.

What future careers had been possible for Bloom in the past and with what exemplars?

In the church, Roman, Anglican or Nonconformist: exemplars, the very reverend John Conmee S. J., the reverend T. Salmon, D. D., provost of Trinity college, Dr Alexander J. Dowie. At the bar, English or Irish: exemplars, Seymour Bushe, K. C., Rufus Isaacs, K. C. On the stage modern or Shakespearean: exemplars, Charles Wyndham, high comedian Osmond Tearle (died 1901), exponent of Shakespeare.

Did the host encourage his guest to chant in a modulated voice a strange legend on an allied theme?

Reassuringly, their place, where none could hear them talk, being secluded, reassured, the decocted beverages, allowing for subsolid residual sediment of a mechanical mixture, water plus sugar plus cream plus cocoa, having been consumed.

Recite the first (major) part of this chanted legend.

Little Harry Hughes and his schoolfellows all
Went out for to play ball.
And the very first ball little Harry Hughes played
He drove it o'er the jew's garden wall.
And the very second ball little Harry Hughes played
He broke the jew's windows all.

How did the son of Rudolph receive this first part?

With unmixed feeling. Smiling, a jew he

heard with pleasure and saw the unbroken kitchen window.

Recite the second part (minor) of the legend.

**Then out there came the jew's
daughter
And she all dressed in green.
"Come back, come back, you pretty
little boy,
And play your ball again."**

**"I can't come back and I won't come
back
Without my schoolfellows all.
For if my master he did hear
He'd make it a sorry ball."
She took him by the lilywhite hand
And led him along the hall
Until she led him to a room
Where none could hear him call.**

She took a penknife out of her pocket

And cut off his little head.
And now he'll play his ball no more
For he lies among the dead.

How did the father of Millicent receive this second part?

With mixed feelings. Unsmiling, he heard and saw with wonder a jew's daughter, all dressed in green.

Condense Stephen's commentary.

One of all, the least of all, is the victim predestined. Once by inadvertence twice by design he challenges his destiny. It comes when he is abandoned and challenges him reluctant and, as an apparition of hope and youth, holds him unresisting. It leads him to a strange habitation, to a secret infidel apartment, and there, implacable, immolates him, consenting.

Why was the host (victim predestined) sad?

He wished that a tale of a deed should be told of a deed not by him should by him not be told.

Why was the host (reluctant, unresisting) still?

In accordance with the law of the conservation of energy.

Why was the host (secret infidel) silent?

He weighed the possible evidences for and against ritual murder: the incitations of the hierarchy, the superstition of the populace, the propagation of rumour in continued fraction of veridicity, the envy of opulence, the influence of retaliation, the sporadic reappearance of atavistic delinquency, the mitigating circumstances of fanaticism, hypnotic suggestion and somnambulism.

From which (if any) of these mental or physical disorders was he not totally immune?

From hypnotic suggestion: once, waking, he had not recognised his sleeping apartment: more than once, waking, he had been for an indefinite time incapable of moving or uttering sounds. From somnambulism:

once, sleeping, his body had risen, crouched and crawled in the direction of a heatless fire and, having attained its destination, there, curled, unheated, in night attire had lain, sleeping.

Had this latter or any cognate phenomenon declared itself in any member of his family?

Twice, in Holles street and in Ontario terrace, his daughter Millicent (Milly) at the ages of 6 and 8 years had uttered in sleep an exclamation of terror and had replied to the interrogations of two figures in night attire with a vacant mute expression.

What other infantile memories had he of her?

15 June 1889. A querulous newborn female infant crying to cause and lessen congestion. A child renamed Padney Socks she shook with shocks her moneybox: counted his three free moneypenny buttons, one, tloo, tlee: a doll, a boy, a sailor she cast away: blond, born of two dark, she had blond ancestry, remote, a violation,

Herr Hauptmann Hainau, Austrian army, proximate, a hallucination, lieutenant Mulvey, British navy.

What endemic characteristics were present?

Conversely the nasal and frontal formation was derived in a direct line of lineage which, though interrupted, would continue at distant intervals to more distant intervals to its most distant intervals.

What memories had he of her adolescence?

She relegated her hoop and skippingrope to a recess. On the duke's lawn, entreated by an English visitor, she declined to permit him to make and take away her photographic image (objection not stated). On the South Circular road in the company of Elsa Potter, followed by an individual of sinister aspect, she went half way down Stamer street and turned abruptly back (reason of change not stated). On the vigil of the 15th anniversary of her birth she wrote a letter from Mullingar, county Westmeath, making a brief allusion to a local student (faculty and year not stated).

Did that first division, portending a second division, afflict him?

Less than he had imagined, more than he had hoped.

What second departure was contemporaneously perceived by him similarly, if differently?

A temporary departure of his cat.

Why similarly, why differently?

Similarly, because actuated by a secret purpose the quest of a new male

(Mullingar student) or of a healing herb (valerian). Differently, because of different possible returns to the inhabitants or to the habitation.

In other respects were their differences similar?

In passivity, in economy, in the instinct of tradition, in unexpectedness.

As?

Inasmuch as leaning she sustained her

blond hair for him to ribbon it for her (cf neckarching cat). Moreover, on the free surface of the lake in Stephen's green amid inverted reflections of trees her uncommented spit, describing concentric circles of waterrings, indicated by the constancy of its permanence the locus of a somnolent prostrate fish (cf mousewatching cat).

Again, in order to remember the date, combatants, issue and consequences of a famous military engagement she pulled a plait of her hair (cf earwashing cat). Furthermore, silly Milly, she dreamed of having had an unspoken unremembered conversation with a horse whose name had been Joseph to whom (which) she had offered a tumblerful of lemonade which it (he) had appeared to have accepted (cf hearthdreaming cat). Hence, in passivity, in economy, in the instinct of tradition, in unexpectedness, their differences were similar.

In what way had he utilised gifts (1) an owl, (2) a clock, given as matrimonial auguries, to interest and to instruct her?

As object lessons to explain: 1) the nature and habits of oviparous animals, the possibility of aerial flight, certain abnormalities of vision, the secular process of imbalsamation: 2) the principle of the pendulum, exemplified in bob, wheelgear and regulator, the translation in terms of human or social regulation of the various positions of clockwise moveable indicators on an unmoving dial, the exactitude of the recurrence per hour of an instant in each hour when the longer and the shorter indicator were at the same angle of inclination, **videlicet**, 5 5/11 minutes past each hour per hour in arithmetical progression.

In what manners did she reciprocate?

She remembered: on the 27th anniversary of his birth she presented to him a breakfast moustachecup of imitation Crown Derby porcelain ware. She provided: at quarter day or thereabouts if or when purchases had been made by him not for her she showed herself attentive to his necessities, anticipating his desires. She admired: a natural phenomenon having been explained by him to her she expressed the immediate desire to possess without gradual acquisition a fraction of his science, the moiety, the quarter, a thousandth part.

What proposal did Bloom, diambulist, father of Milly, somnambulist, make to Stephen, noctambulist?

To pass in repose the hours intervening between Thursday (proper) and Friday (normal) on an extemporised cubicle in the apartment immediately above the kitchen and immediately adjacent to the sleeping apartment of his host and hostess.

What various advantages would or might have resulted from a prolongation of such an extemporisation?

For the guest: security of domicile and seclusion of study. For the host: rejuvenation of intelligence, vicarious satisfaction. For the hostess: disintegration of obsession, acquisition of correct Italian pronunciation.

Why might these several provisional contingencies between a guest and a hostess not necessarily preclude or be precluded by a permanent eventuality of reconciliatory union between a schoolfellow and a jew's daughter?

Because the way to daughter led through mother, the way to mother through daughter.

To what inconsequent polysyllabic question of his host did the guest return a monosyllabic negative answer?

If he had known the late Mrs Emily Sinico, accidentally killed at Sydney Parade railway station, 14 October 1903.

What inchoate corollary statement was consequently suppressed by the host?

A statement explanatory of his absence on the occasion of the interment of Mrs Mary Dedalus (born Goulding), 26 June 1903, vigil of the anniversary of the decease of

Rudolph Bloom (born Virag).

Was the proposal of asylum accepted?

Promptly, inexplicably, with amicability, gratefully it was declined. What exchange of money took place between host and guest?

The former returned to the latter, without interest, a sum of money (1-7-0), one pound seven shillings sterling, advanced by the latter to the former.

What counterproposals were alternately advanced, accepted, modified, declined, restated in other terms, reaccepted, ratified, reconfirmed?

To inaugurate a prearranged course of Italian instruction, place the residence of the instructed. To inaugurate a course of vocal instruction, place the residence of the instructress. To inaugurate a series of static semistatic and peripatetic intellectual dialogues, places the residence of both speakers (if both speakers were resident in the same place), the Ship hotel and tavern, 6 Lower Abbey street (W. and E. Connery, proprietors), the National Library of Ireland, 10 Kildare street, the National Maternity Hospital, 29, 30 and 31 Holles street, a public garden, the vicinity of a place of worship, a conjunction of two or more public thoroughfares, the point of bisection of a right line drawn between their residences (if both speakers were resident in different places).

What rendered problematic for Bloom the realisation of these mutually selfexcluding propositions?

The irreparability of the past: once at a performance of Albert Hengler's circus in the Rotunda, Rutland square, Dublin, an intuitive particoloured clown in quest of paternity had penetrated from the ring to a place in the auditorium where Bloom, solitary, was seated and had publicly declared to an exhilarated audience that he (Bloom) was his (the clown's) papa. The imprevidibility of the future: once in the summer of 1898 he (Bloom) had marked a florin (2/-) with three notches on the milled edge and tendered it m payment of an account due to and received by J. and T. Davy, family grocers, 1 Charlemont Mall, Grand Canal, for circulation on the waters of civic finance, for possible, circuitous or direct, return.

Was the clown Bloom's son?

No.

Had Bloom's coin returned?

Never.

Why would a recurrent frustration the more depress him?

Because at the critical turningpoint of human existence he desired to amend many social conditions, the product of inequality and avarice and international animosity. He believed then that human life was infinitely perfectible, eliminating these conditions?

There remained the generic conditions imposed by natural, as distinct from human law, as integral parts of the human whole: the necessity of destruction to procure alimentary sustenance: the painful character of the ultimate functions of separate existence, the agonies of birth and death: the monotonous menstruation of simian and (particularly) human females extending from the age of puberty to the menopause: inevitable accidents at sea, in mines and factories: certain very painful maladies and their resultant surgical operations, innate lunacy and congenital criminality, decimating epidemics: catastrophic cataclysms which make terror the basis of human mentality: seismic upheavals the epicentres of which are located in densely populated regions: the fact of vital growth, through convulsions of metamorphosis, from infancy through maturity to decay.

Why did he desist from speculation?

Because it was a task for a superior intelligence to substitute other more acceptable phenomena in the place of the less acceptable phenomena to be removed.

Did Stephen participate in his dejection?

He affirmed his significance as a conscious

rational animal proceeding syllogistically from the known to the unknown and a conscious rational reagent between a micro and a macrocosm ineluctably constructed upon the incertitude of the void.

Was this affirmation apprehended by Bloom?

Not verbally. Substantially.

What comforted his misapprehension?

That as a competent keyless citizen he had proceeded energetically from the unknown to the known through the incertitude of the void.

In what order of precedence, with what attendant ceremony was the exodus from the house of bondage to the wilderness of inhabitation effected?

Lighted Candle in Stick borne by

BLOOM

Diaconal Hat on Ashplant borne by

STEPHEN:

With what intonation secreto of what commemorative psalm?

The 113th, **modus peregrinus: In exitu Israel de Egypto: domus Jacob de populo barbaro**.

What did each do at the door of egress?

Bloom set the candlestick on the floor. Stephen put the hat on his head.

For what creature was the door of egress a door of ingress?

For a cat.

What spectacle confronted them when they, first the host, then the guest, emerged silently, doubly dark, from obscurity by a passage from the rere of the house into the penumbra of the garden?

The heaventree of stars hung with humid nightblue fruit.

With what meditations did Bloom accompany his demonstration to his companion of various constellations?

Meditations of evolution increasingly vaster: of the moon invisible in incipient lunation, approaching perigee: of the infinite lattiginous scintillating uncondensed milky way, discernible by daylight by an observer placed at the lower end of a cylindrical vertical shaft 5000 ft deep sunk from the surface towards the centre of the earth: of Sirius (alpha in Canis Maior) 10 lightyears (57,000,000,000,000 miles) distant and in volume 900 times the dimension of our planet: of Arcturus: of the precession of equinoxes: of Orion with belt and sextuple sun theta and nebula in which 100 of our solar systems could be contained: of moribund and of nascent new stars such as Nova in 1901: of our system plunging towards the constellation of Hercules: of the parallax or parallactic drift of socalled fixed stars, in reality evermoving wanderers from immeasurably remote eons to infinitely remote futures in comparison with which the years, threescore and ten, of allotted human life formed a parenthesis of infinitesimal brevity.

Were there obverse meditations of involution increasingly less vast?

Of the eons of geological periods recorded

in the stratifications of the earth: of the myriad minute entomological organic existences concealed in cavities of the earth, beneath removable stones, in hives and mounds, of microbes, germs, bacteria, bacilli, spermatozoa: of the incalculable trillions of billions of millions of imperceptible molecules contained by cohesion of molecular affinity in a single pinhead: of the universe of human serum constellated with red and white bodies, themselves universes of void space constellated with other bodies, each, in continuity, its universe of divisible component bodies of which each was again divisible in divisions of redivisible component bodies, dividends and divisors ever diminishing without actual division till, if the progress were carried far enough, nought nowhere was never reached.

Why did he not elaborate these calculations to a more precise result?

Because some years previously in 1886 when occupied with the problem of the quadrature of the circle he had learned of the existence of a number computed to a relative degree of accuracy to be of such magnitude and of so many places, e.g., the 9th power of the 9th power of 9, that, the result having been obtained, 33 closely printed volumes of 1000 pages each of innumerable quires and reams of India paper would have to be requisitioned in order to contain the complete tale of its printed integers of units, tens, hundreds, thousands, tens of thousands, hundreds of thousands, millions, tens of millions, hundreds of millions, billions, the nucleus of the nebula of every digit of every series containing succinctly the potentiality of being raised to the utmost kinetic elaboration of any power of any of its powers.

Did he find the problems of the inhabitability of the planets and their satellites by a race, given in species, and of the possible social and moral redemption of said race by a redeemer, easier of solution?

Of a different order of difficulty. Conscious that the human organism, normally capable of sustaining an atmospheric pressure of 19 tons, when elevated to a considerable altitude in the terrestrial atmosphere suffered with arithmetical progression of intensity, according as the line of demarcation between troposphere and stratosphere was approximated from nasal hemorrhage, impeded respiration and vertigo, when proposing this problem for solution, he had conjectured as a working hypothesis which could not be proved impossible that a more adaptable and differently anatomically constructed race of beings might subsist otherwise under Martian, Mercurial, Veneral, Jovian, Saturnian, Neptunian or Uranian sufficient and equivalent conditions, though an apogean humanity of beings created in varying forms with finite differences resulting similar to the whole and to one another would probably there as here remain inalterably and inalienably attached to vanities, to vanities of vanities and to all that is vanity.

And the problem of possible redemption?
The minor was proved by the major.

Which various features of the constellations were in turn considered?

The various colours significant of various degrees of vitality (white, yellow, crimson, vermilion, cinnabar): their degrees of brilliancy: their magnitudes revealed up to and including the 7th: their positions: the waggoner's star: Walsingham way: the chariot of David: the annular cinctures of Saturn: the condensation of spiral nebulae into suns: the interdependent gyrations of double suns: the independent synchronous discoveries of Galileo, Simon Marius, Piazzi, Le Verrier, Herschel, Galle: the systematisations attempted by Bode and Kepler of cubes of distances and squares of times of revolution: the almost infinite compressibility of hirsute comets and their vast elliptical egressive and reentrant orbits from perihelion to aphelion: the sidereal origin of meteoric stones: the Libyan floods on Mars about the period of the birth of the younger astroscopist: the annual recurrence of meteoric showers about the period of the feast of S. Lawrence (martyr, lo August): the monthly recurrence known as the new moon with the old moon in her arms: the posited influence of celestial on human bodies: the appearance of a star (1st magnitude) of exceeding brilliancy dominating by night and day (a new luminous sun generated by the collision and amalgamation in incandescence of two nonluminous exsuns) about the period of the birth of William Shakespeare over delta in the recumbent neversetting constellation of Cassiopeia and of a star (2nd magnitude) of similar origin but of lesser brilliancy which had appeared in and disappeared from the constellation of the Corona Septentrionalis about the period of the birth of Leopold Bloom and of other stars of (presumably) similar origin which had (effectively or presumably) appeared in and disappeared from the constellation of Andromeda about the period of the birth of Stephen Dedalus, and in and from the constellation of Auriga some years after the birth and death of Rudolph Bloom, junior, and in and from other constellations some years before or after the birth or death of other persons: the attendant phenomena of eclipses, solar and lunar, from immersion to emersion, abatement of wind, transit of shadow, taciturnity of winged creatures, emergence of nocturnal or crepuscular animals, persistence of infernal light, obscurity of terrestrial waters, pallor of human beings.

His (Bloom's) logical conclusion, having weighed the matter and allowing for possible error?

That it was not a heaventree, not a

heavengrot, not a heavenbeast, not a heavenman. That it was a Utopia, there being no known method from the known to the unknown: an infinity renderable equally finite by the suppositious apposition of one or more bodies equally of the same and of different magnitudes: a mobility of illusory forms immobilised in space, remobilised in air: a past which possibly had ceased to exist as a present before its probable spectators had entered actual present existence.

Was he more convinced of the esthetic value of the spectacle?

Indubitably in consequence of the reiterated examples of poets in the delirium of the frenzy of attachment or in the abasement of rejection invoking ardent sympathetic constellations or the frigidity of the satellite of their planet.

Did he then accept as an article of belief the theory of astrological influences upon sublunary disasters?

It seemed to him as possible of proof as of confutation and the nomenclature employed in its selenographical charts as attributable to verifiable intuition as to fallacious analogy: the lake of dreams, the sea of rains, the gulf of dews, the ocean of fecundity.

What special affinities appeared to him to exist between the moon and woman?

Her antiquity in preceding and surviving successive tellurian generations: her nocturnal predominance: her satellitic dependence: her luminary reflection: her constancy under all her phases, rising and setting by her appointed times, waxing and waning: the forced invariability of her aspect: her indeterminate response to inaffirmative interrogation: her potency over effluent and refluent waters: her power to enamour, to mortify, to invest with beauty, to render insane, to incite to and aid delinquency: the tranquil inscrutability of her visage: the terribility of her isolated dominant implacable resplendent propinquity: her omens of tempest and of calm: the stimulation of her light, her motion and her presence: the admonition of her craters, her arid seas, her silence: her splendour, when visible: her attraction, when invisible.

What visible luminous sign attracted Bloom's, who attracted Stephen's, gaze?

In the second storey (rere) of his (Bloom's) house the light of a paraffin oil lamp with oblique shade projected on a screen of roller blind supplied by Frank O'Hara, window blind, curtain pole and revolving shutter manufacturer, 16 Aungier street.

How did he elucidate the mystery of an invisible attractive person, his wife Marion (Molly) Bloom, denoted by a visible splendid sign, a lamp?

With indirect and direct verbal allusions or affirmations: with subdued affection and admiration: with description: with impediment: with suggestion.

Both then were silent?

Silent, each contemplating the other

in both mirrors of the reciprocal flesh of theirhisnothis fellowfaces.

Were they indefinitely inactive?

At Stephen's suggestion, at Bloom's instigation both, first Stephen, then Bloom, in penumbra urinated, their sides contiguous, their organs of micturition reciprocally rendered invisible by manual circumposition, their gazes, first Bloom's, then Stephen's, elevated to the projected luminous and semiluminous shadow.

Similarly?

The trajectories of their, first sequent, then simultaneous, urinations were dissimilar: Bloom's longer, less irruent, in the incomplete form of the bifurcated penultimate alphabetical letter, who in his ultimate year at High School (1880) had been capable of attaining the point of greatest altitude against the whole concurrent strength of the institution, 210 scholars: Stephen's higher, more sibilant, who in the ultimate hours of the previous day had augmented by diuretic consumption an insistent vesical pressure.

What different problems presented themselves to each concerning the invisible audible collateral organ of the other?

To Bloom: the problems of irritability, tumescence, rigidity, reactivity, dimension, sanitariness, pilosity.

To Stephen: the problem of the sacerdotal integrity of Jesus circumcised (I January, holiday of obligation to hear mass and abstain from unnecessary servile work) and the problem as to whether the divine prepuce, the carnal bridal ring of the holy Roman catholic apostolic church, conserved in Calcata, were deserving of simple hyperduly or of the fourth degree of latria accorded to the abscission of such divine excrescences as hair and toenails.

What celestial sign was by both simultaneously observed?

A star precipitated with great apparent velocity across the firmament from Vega in the Lyre above the zenith beyond the stargroup of the Tress of Berenice towards the zodiacal sign of Leo.

How did the centripetal remainer afford egress to the centrifugal departer?

By inserting the barrel of an arruginated male key in the hole of an unstable female lock, obtaining a purchase on the bow of the key and turning its wards from right to left, withdrawing a bolt from its staple, pulling inward spasmodically an obsolescent unhinged door and revealing an aperture for free egress and free ingress.

How did they take leave, one of the other, in separation?

Standing perpendicular at the same door and on different sides of its base, the lines of their valedictory arms, meeting at any point and forming any angle less than the sum of two right angles.

What sound accompanied the union of their tangent, the disunion of their (respectively) centrifugal and centripetal hands?

The sound of the peal of the hour of the

night by the chime of the bells in the church of Saint George.

What echoes of that sound were by both and each heard?

By Stephen:

Liliata rutilantium. Turma circumdet. Iubilantium te virginum. Chorus excipiat.

By Bloom:

Heigho, heigho,
Heigho, heigho.

Where were the several members of the company which with Bloom that day at the bidding of that peal had travelled from Sandymount in the south to Glasnevin in the north?

Martin Cunningham (in bed), Jack Power (in bed), Simon Dedalus (in bed), Ned Lambert (in bed), Tom Kernan (in bed), Joe Hynes (in bed), John Henry Menton (in bed), Bernard Corrigan (in bed), Patsy Dignam (in bed), Paddy Dignam (in the grave).

Alone, what did Bloom hear?

The double reverberation of retreating feet on the heavenborn earth, the double vibration of a jew's harp in the resonant lane.

Alone, what did Bloom feel?

The cold of interstellar space, thousands of degrees below freezing point or the absolute zero of Fahrenheit, Centigrade or Réaumur: the incipient intimations of proximate dawn.

Of what did bellchime and handtouch and footstep and lonechill remind him?

Of companions now in various manners in different places defunct: Percy Apjohn (killed in action, Modder River), Philip Gilligan (phthisis, Jervis Street hospital), Matthew F. Kane (accidental drowning, Dublin Bay), Philip Moisel (pyemia, Heytesbury street), Michael Hart (phthisis, Mater Misericordiae hospital), Patrick Dignam (apoplexy, Sandymount).

What prospect of what phenomena

inclined him to remain?

The disparition of three final stars, the diffusion of daybreak, the apparition of a new solar disk.

Had he ever been a spectator of those phenomena?

Once, in 1887, after a protracted performance of charades in the house of Luke Doyle, Kimmage, he had awaited with patience the apparition of the diurnal phenomenon, seated on a wall, his gaze turned in the direction of Mizrach, the east.

He remembered the initial paraphenomena?

More active air, a matutinal distant cock, ecclesiastical clocks at various points, avine music, the isolated tread of an early wayfarer, the visible diffusion of the light of an invisible luminous body, the first golden limb of the resurgent sun perceptible low on the horizon.

Did he remain?

With deep inspiration he returned,

retraversing the garden, reentering the passage, reclosing the door. With brief suspiration he reassumed the candle, reascended the stairs, reapproached the door of the front room, hallfloor, and reentered.

What suddenly arrested his ingress?

The right temporal lobe of the hollow sphere of his cranium came into contact with a solid timber angle where, an infinitesimal but sensible fraction of a second later, a painful sensation was located in consequence of antecedent sensations transmitted and registered.

Describe the alterations effected in the disposition of the articles of furniture.

A sofa upholstered in prune plush had been translocated from opposite the door to the ingleside near the compactly furled Union Jack (an alteration which he had frequently intended to execute): the blue and white checker inlaid majolicatopped table had been placed opposite the door in the place vacated by the prune plush sofa: the walnut sideboard (a projecting angle of which had momentarily arrested his ingress) had been moved from its position beside the door to a more advantageous but more perilous position in front of the door: two chairs had been moved from right and left of the ingleside to the position originally occupied by the blue and white checker inlaid majolicatopped table.

Describe them.

One: a squat stuffed easychair, with stout arms extended and back slanted to the rere, which, repelled in recoil, had then upturned an irregular fringe of a rectangular rug and now displayed on its amply upholstered seat a centralised diffusing and diminishing discolouration. The other: a slender splayfoot chair of glossy cane curves, placed directly opposite the former, its frame from top to seat and from seat to base being varnished dark brown, its seat being a bright circle of white plaited rush.

What significances attached to these two chairs?

Significances of similitude, of posture, of symbolism, of circumstantial evidence, of testimonial supermanence.

What occupied the position originally occupied by the sideboard?

A vertical piano (Cadby) with exposed keyboard, its closed coffin supporting a pair of long yellow ladies' gloves and an emerald ashtray containing four consumed matches, a partly consumed cigarette and two discoloured ends of cigarettes, its musicrest supporting the music in the key of G natural for voice and piano of **Love's Old Sweet Song** (words by G. Clifton Bingham, composed by J. L. Molloy, sung by Madam Antoinette Sterling) open at the last page with the final indications **ad libitum, forte**, pedal, **animato**, sustained pedal, **ritirando**, close.

With what sensations did Bloom contemplate in rotation these objects?

With strain, elevating a candlestick: with pain, feeling on his right temple a contused tumescence: with attention, focussing his gaze on a large dull passive and a slender bright active: with solicitation, bending and downturning the upturned rugfringe: with amusement, remembering Dr Malachi Mulligan's scheme of colour containing the gradation of green: with pleasure, repeating the words and antecedent act and perceiving through various channels of internal sensibility the consequent and concomitant tepid pleasant diffusion of gradual discolouration.

His next proceeding?

From an open box on the majolicatopped table he extracted a black diminutive cone, one inch in height, placed it on its circular base on a small tin plate, placed his candlestick on the right corner of the mantelpiece, produced from his waistcoat a folded page of prospectus (illustrated) entitled Agendath Netaim, unfolded the same, examined it superficially, rolled it into a thin cylinder, ignited it in the candleflame, applied it when ignited to the apex of the cone till the latter reached the stage of rutilance, placed the cylinder in the basin of the candlestick disposing its unconsumed part in such a manner as to facilitate total combustion.

What followed this operation?

The truncated conical crater summit of the diminutive volcano emitted a vertical and serpentine fume redolent of aromatic oriental incense.

What homothetic objects, other than the candlestick, stood on the mantelpiece?

A timepiece of striated Connemara marble, stopped at the hour of 4.46 a.m. on the 21 March 1896, matrimonial gift of Matthew Dillon: a dwarf tree of glacial arborescence under a transparent bellshade, matrimonial gift of Luke and Caroline Doyle: an embalmed owl, matrimonial gift of Alderman John Hooper.

What interchanges of looks took place between these three objects and Bloom?

In the mirror of the giltbordered pierglass the undecorated back of the dwarf tree regarded the upright back of the embalmed owl. Before the mirror the matrimonial gift of Alderman John Hooper with a clear melancholy wise bright motionless compassionate gaze regarded Bloom while Bloom with obscure tranquil profound motionless compassionated gaze regarded the matrimonial gift of Luke and Caroline Doyle.

What composite asymmetrical image in the mirror then attracted his attention?

The image of a solitary (ipsorelative) mutable (aliorelative) man.

Why solitary (ipsorelative)?

Brothers and sisters had he none. Yet that man's father was his grandfather's son.

Why mutable (aliorelative)?

From infancy to maturity he had resembled his maternal procreatrix. From maturity to senility he would increasingly resemble his paternal procreator.

What final visual impression was communicated to him by the mirror?

The optical reflection of several inverted volumes improperly arranged and not in the order of their common letters with scintillating titles on the two bookshelves opposite.

Catalogue these books.

Thom's Dublin Post Office Directory, 1886. Denis Florence M'Carthy's **Poetical Works** (copper beechleaf bookmark at p. 5). Shakespeare's **Works** (dark crimson morocco, goldtooled).

The Useful Ready Reckoner (brown cloth).

The Secret History of the Court of Charles II (red cloth, tooled binding). **The Child's Guide** (blue cloth).

The Beauties of Killarney (wrappers).

When We Were Boys by William O'Brien M. P. (green cloth, slightly faded, envelope bookmark at p. 217).

Thoughts from Spinoza (maroon leather).

The Story of the Heavens by Sir Robert Ball (blue cloth). Ellis's **Three Trips to Madagascar** (brown cloth, title obliterated).

The Stark-Munro Letters by A. Conan Doyle, property of the City of Dublin Public Library, 106 Capel street, lent 21 May (Whitsun Eve) 1904, due 4 June 1904, 13 days overdue (black cloth binding, bearing white letternumber ticket).

Voyages in China by "Viator" (recovered with brown paper, red ink title).

Philosophy of the Talmud (sewn pamphlet). Lockhart's **Life of Napoleon** (cover wanting, marginal annotations, minimising victories, aggrandising defeats of the protagonist).

Soll und Haben by Gustav Freytag (black boards, Gothic characters, cigarette coupon bookmark at p. 24). Hozier's **History of the Russo-Turkish War** (brown cloth, a volumes, with gummed label, Garrison

Library, Governor's Parade, Gibraltar, on verso of cover).

Laurence Bloomfield in Ireland by William Allingham (second edition, green cloth, gilt trefoil design, previous owner's name on recto of flyleaf erased).

A Handbook of Astronomy (cover, brown leather, detached, S plates, antique letterpress long primer, author's footnotes nonpareil, marginal clues brevier, captions small pica).

The Hidden Life of Christ (black boards).

In the Track of the Sun (yellow cloth, titlepage missing, recurrent title intestation).

Physical Strength and How to Obtain It by Eugen Sandow (red cloth).

Short but yet Plain Elements of Geometry written in French by F. Ignat. Pardies and rendered into English by John Harris D. D. London, printed for R. Knaplock at the Bifhop's Head, MDCCXI, with dedicatory epiftle to his worthy friend Charles Cox, efquire, Member of Parliament for the burgh of Southwark and having ink calligraphed statement on the flyleaf certifying that the book was the property of Michael Gallagher, dated this 10th day of May 1822 and requefting the perfon who should find it, if the book should be loft or go aftray, to reftore it to Michael Gallagher, carpenter, Dufery Gate, Ennifcorthy, county Wicklow, the fineft place in the world.

What reflections occupied his mind during the process of reversion of the inverted volumes?

The necessity of order, a place for everything and everything in its place: the deficient appreciation of literature possessed by females: the incongruity of an apple incuneated in a tumbler and of an umbrella inclined in a closestool: the insecurity of hiding any secret document behind, beneath or between the pages of a book.

Which volume was the largest in bulk?

Hozier's **History of the Russo-Turkish**

war.

What among other data did the second volume of the work in question contain?

The name of a decisive battle (forgotten), frequently remembered by a decisive officer, major Brian Cooper Tweedy (remembered).

Why, firstly and secondly, did he not consult the work in question?

Firstly, in order to exercise mnemotechnic: secondly, because after an interval of amnesia, when, seated at the central table, about to consult the work in question, he remembered by mnemotechnic the name of the military engagement, Plevna.

What caused him consolation in his sitting posture?

The candour, nudity, pose, tranquility, youth, grace, sex, counsel of a statue erect in the centre of the table, an image of Narcissus purchased by auction from P. A. Wren, 9 Bachelor's Walk.

What caused him irritation in his sitting posture? Inhibitory pressure of collar (size

17) and waistcoat (5 buttons), two articles of clothing superfluous in the costume of mature males and inelastic to alterations of mass by expansion.

How was the irritation allayed?

He removed his collar, with contained black necktie and collapsible stud, from his neck to a position on the left of the table. He unbuttoned successively in reversed direction waistcoat, trousers, shirt and vest along the medial line of irregular incrispated black hairs extending in triangular convergence from the pelvic basin over the circumference of the abdomen and umbilicular fossicle along the medial line of nodes to the intersection of the sixth pectoral vertebrae, thence produced both ways at right angles and terminating in circles described about two equidistant points, right and left, on the summits of the mammary prominences. He unbraced successively each of six minus one braced trouser buttons, arranged in pairs, of which one incomplete.

What involuntary actions followed?

He compressed between 2 fingers the flesh circumjacent to a cicatrice in the left infracostal region below the diaphragm resulting from a sting inflicted 2 weeks and 3 days previously (23 May 1904) by a bee. He scratched imprecisely with his right hand, though insensible of prurition, various points and surfaces of his partly exposed, wholly abluted skin. He inserted his left hand into the left lower pocket of his waistcoat and extracted and replaced a silver coin (I shilling), placed there (presumably) on the occasion (17 October 1903) of the interment of Mrs Emily Sinico, Sydney Parade.

Compile the budget for 16 June 1904.

Did the process of divestiture continue?

Sensible of a benignant persistent ache in his footsoles he extended his foot to one side and observed the creases, protuberances and salient points caused by foot pressure in the course of walking repeatedly in several different directions, then, inclined, he disnoded the laceknots, unhooked and loosened the laces, took off each of his two boots for the second time, detached the partially moistened right sock through the fore part of which the nail of his great toe had again effracted, raised his right foot and, having unhooked a purple elastic sock suspender, took off his right sock, placed his unclothed right foot on the margin of the seat of his chair, picked at and gently lacerated the protruding part of the great toenail, raised the part lacerated to his nostrils and inhaled the odour of the quick, then, with satisfaction, threw away the lacerated ungual fragment.

Why with satisfaction?

Because the odour inhaled corresponded to other odours inhaled of other ungual fragments, picked and lacerated by Master Bloom, pupil of Mrs Ellis's juvenile school, patiently each night in the act of brief genuflection and nocturnal prayer and ambitious meditation.

In what ultimate ambition had all concurrent and consecutive ambitions now coalesced?

Not to inherit by right of primogeniture, gavelkind or borough English, or possess in perpetuity an extensive demesne of a sufficient number of acres, roods and perches, statute land measure (valuation £ 42), of grazing turbary surrounding a baronial hall with gatelodge and carriage drive nor, on the other hand, a terracehouse or semidetached villa, described as **Rus in Urbe** or **Qui si sana**, but to purchase by private treaty in fee simple a thatched bungalowshaped 2 storey dwellinghouse of southerly aspect, surmounted by vane and lightning conductor, connected with the earth, with porch covered by parasitic plants (ivy or Virginia creeper), halldoor, olive green, with smart carriage finish and neat doorbrasses, stucco front with gilt tracery at eaves and gable, rising, if possible, upon a gentle eminence with agreeable prospect from balcony with stone pillar parapet over unoccupied and unoccupyable interjacent pastures and standing in 5 or 6 acres of its own ground, at such a distance from the nearest public thoroughfare as to render its houselights visible at night above and through a quickset hornbeam hedge of topiary cutting, situate at a given point not less than 1 statute mile from the periphery of the metropolis, within a time limit of not more than 15 minutes from tram or train line (e.g., Dundrum, south, or Sutton, north, both localities equally reported by trial to resemble the terrestrial poles in being favourable climates for phthisical subjects), the premises to be held under feefarm grant, lease 999 years, the messuage to consist of 1 drawingroom with baywindow (2 lancets), thermometer affixed, 1 sittingroom, 4 bedrooms, 2 servants' rooms, tiled kitchen with close range and scullery, lounge hall fitted with linen wallpresses, fumed oak sectional bookcase containing the Encyclopaedia Britannica and New Century Dictionary, transverse obsolete medieval and oriental weapons, dinner gong, alabaster lamp, bowl pendant, vulcanite automatic telephone receiver with adjacent directory, handtufted Axminster carpet with cream ground and trellis border, loo table with pillar and claw legs, hearth with massive firebrasses and ormolu mantel chronometer clock, guaranteed timekeeper with cathedral chime, barometer with hygrographic chart, comfortable lounge settees and corner fitments, upholstered in ruby plush with good springing and sunk centre, three banner Japanese screen and cuspidors (club style, rich winecoloured leather, gloss renewable with a minimum of labour by use of linseed oil and vinegar) and pyramidically prismatic central chandelier lustre, bentwood perch with fingertame parrot (expurgated language), embossed mural paper at 10/- per dozen with transverse swags of carmine floral design and top crown frieze, staircase, three continuous flights at successive right angles, of varnished cleargrained oak, treads and risers, newel, balusters and handrail, with steppedup panel dado, dressed with camphorated wax: bathroom, hot and cold supply, reclining and shower: water closet on mezzanine provided with opaque singlepane oblong window, tipup seat, bracket lamp, brass tierod and brace, armrests, footstool and artistic oleograph on inner face of door: ditto, plain: servants' apartments with separate sanitary and hygienic necessaries for cook, general and betweenmaid (salary, rising by biennial unearned increments of £ 2, with comprehensive fidelity insurance, annual bonus (£ 1) and retiring allowance (based on the 65 system) after 30 years' service), pantry, buttery, larder, refrigerator, outoffices, coal and wood cellarage with winebin (still and sparkling vintages) for distinguished guests, if entertained to dinner (evening dress), carbon monoxide gas supply throughout.

What additional attractions might the grounds contain?

As addenda, a tennis and fives court, a shrubbery, a glass summerhouse with tropical palms, equipped in the best botanical manner, a rockery with waterspray, a beehive arranged on humane principles, oval flowerbeds in rectangular grassplots set with eccentric ellipses of scarlet and chrome tulips, blue scillas, crocuses, polyanthus, sweet William, sweet pea, lily of the valley (bulbs obtainable from sir James W. Mackey (Limited) wholesale and retail seed and bulb merchants and nurserymen, agents for chemical manures, 23 Sackville street, upper), an orchard, kitchen garden and vinery protected against illegal trespassers by glasstopped mural enclosures, a lumbershed with padlock for various inventoried implements.

As?

Eeltraps, lobsterpots, fishingrods, hatchet, steelyard, grindstone, clodcrusher, swatheturner, carriagesack, telescope ladder, 10 tooth rake, washing clogs, haytedder, tumbling rake, billhook, paintpot, brush, hoe and so on.

What improvements might be subsequently introduced?

A rabbitry and fowlrun, a dovecote, a botanical conservatory, 2 hammocks (lady's and gentleman's), a sundial shaded and sheltered by laburnum or lilac trees, an exotically harmonically accorded Japanese tinkle gatebell affixed to left lateral gatepost, a capacious waterbutt, a lawnmower with side delivery and grassbox, a lawnsprinkler with hydraulic hose.

What facilities of transit were desirable?

When citybound frequent connection by train or tram from their respective intermediate station or terminal. When countrybound velocipedes, a chainless freewheel roadster cycle with side basketcar attached, or draught conveyance, a donkey with wicker trap or smart phaeton with good working solidungular cob (roan gelding, 14 h).

What might be the name of this erigible or erected residence?

Bloom Cottage. Saint Leopold's. Flowerville.

Could Bloom of 7 Eccles street foresee Bloom of Flowerville?

In loose allwool garments with Harris tweed cap, price 8/6, and useful garden boots with elastic gussets and wateringcan, planting aligned young firtrees, syringing, pruning, staking, sowing hayseed, trundling a weedladen wheelbarrow without excessive fatigue at sunset amid the scent of newmown hay, ameliorating the soil, multiplying wisdom, achieving longevity.

What syllabus of intellectual pursuits was simultaneously possible?

Snapshot photography, comparative study of religions, folklore relative to various amatory and superstitious practices, contemplation of the celestial constellations.

What lighter recreations?

Outdoor: garden and fieldwork, cycling on level macadamised causeways ascents of moderately high hills, natation in secluded fresh water and unmolested river boating in secure wherry or light curricle with kedge anchor on reaches free from weirs and rapids (period of estivation), vespertinal perambulation or equestrian circumprocession with inspection of sterile landscape and contrastingly agreeable cottagers' fires of smoking peat turves (period of hibernation). Indoor: discussion in tepid security of unsolved historical and criminal problems: lecture of unexpurgated exotic erotic masterpieces: house carpentry with toolbox containing hammer, awl nails, screws, tintacks, gimlet, tweezers, bullnose plane and turnscrew. Might he become a gentleman farmer of field produce and live stock?

Not impossibly, with 1 or 2 stripper cows, 1 pike of upland hay and requisite farming implements, e.g., an end-to-end churn, a turnip pulper etc.

What would be his civic functions and social status among the county families and landed gentry?

Arranged successively in ascending powers of hierarchical order, that of gardener, groundsman, cultivator, breeder, and at the zenith of his career, resident magistrate or justice of the peace with a family crest and coat of arms and appropriate classical motto (**Semper paratus**), duly recorded in the court directory (Bloom, Leopold P., M. P., P. C., K. P., L. L. D. (**honoris causa**), Bloomville, Dundrum) and mentioned in court and fashionable intelligence (Mr and Mrs Leopold Bloom have left Kingstown for England).

What course of action did he outline for himself in such capacity?

A course that lay between undue clemency and excessive rigour: the dispensation in a heterogeneous society of arbitrary classes, incessantly rearranged in terms of greater and lesser social inequality, of unbiassed homogeneous indisputable justice, tempered with mitigants of the widest possible latitude but exactable to the uttermost farthing with confiscation of estate, real and personal, to the crown. Loyal to the highest constituted power in the land, actuated by an innate love of rectitude his aims would be the strict maintenance of public order, the repression of many abuses though not of all simultaneously (every measure of reform or retrenchment being a preliminary solution to be contained by fluxion in the final solution), the upholding of the letter of the law (common, statute and law merchant) against all traversers in covin and trespassers acting in contravention of bylaws and regulations, all resuscitators (by trespass and petty larceny of kindlings) of venville rights, obsolete by desuetude, all orotund instigators of international persecution, all perpetuators of international animosities, all menial molestors of domestic conviviality, all recalcitrant violators of domestic connubiality.

Prove that he had loved rectitude from his earliest youth.

To Master Percy Apjohn at High School in 1880 he had divulged his disbelief in the tenets of the Irish (protestant) church (to which his father Rudolf Virag (later Rudolph Bloom) had been converted from the Israelitic faith and communion in 1865 by the Society for promoting Christianity among the jews) subsequently abjured by him in favour of Roman catholicism at the epoch of and with a view to his matrimony in 1888. To Daniel Magrane and Francis Wade in 1882 during a juvenile friendship (terminated by the premature emigration of the former) he had advocated during nocturnal perambulations the political theory of colonial (e.g. Canadian) expansion and the evolutionary theories of Charles Darwin, expounded in **The Descent of Man** and **The Origin of Species**. In 1885 he had publicly expressed his adherence to the collective and national economic programme advocated by James Fintan Lalor, John Fisher Murray, John Mitchel, J. F. X. O'Brien and others, the agrarian policy of Michael Davitt, the constitutional agitation of Charles Stewart Parnell (M. P. for Cork City), the programme of peace, retrenchment and reform of William Ewart Gladstone (M. P. for Midlothian, N. B.) and, in support of his political convictions, had climbed up into a secure position amid the ramifications of a tree on Northumberland road to see the entrance (2 February 1888) into the capital of a demonstrative torchlight procession of 20,000 torchbearers, divided into 120 trade corporations, bearing 2000 torches in escort of the marquess of Ripon and (honest) John Morley.

How much and how did he propose to pay for this country residence?

As per prospectus of the Industrious Foreign Acclimatised Nationalised Friendly Stateaided Building Society (incorporated

1874), a maximum of £ 60 per annum, being 1/6 of an assured income, derived from giltedged securities, representing at 5 % simple interest on capital of £ 1200 (estimate of price at 20 years' purchase), of which to be paid on acquisition and the balance in the form of annual rent, viz. £ 800 plus 2 1/2 % interest on the same, repayable quarterly in equal annual instalments until extinction by amortisation of loan advanced for purchase within a period of 20 years, amounting to an annual rental of £ 64, headrent included, the titledeeds to remain in possession of the lender or lenders with a saving clause envisaging forced sale, foreclosure and mutual compensation in the event of protracted failure to pay the terms assigned, otherwise the messuage to become the absolute property of the tenant occupier upon expiry of the period of years stipulated.

What rapid but insecure means to opulence might facilitate immediate purchase?

A private wireless telegraph which would transmit by dot and dash system the result of a national equine handicap (flat or steeplechase) of I or more miles and furlongs won by an outsider at odds of 50 to 1 at 3 hr 8 m p.m. at Ascot (Greenwich time), the message being received and available for betting purposes in Dublin at 2.59 p.m. (Dunsink time). The unexpected discovery of an object of great monetary value (precious stone, valuable adhesive or impressed postage stamps (7 schilling, mauve, imperforate, Hamburg, 1866: 4 pence, rose, blue paper, perforate, Great Britain, 1855: 1 franc, stone, official, rouletted, diagonal surcharge, Luxemburg, 1878), antique dynastical ring, unique relic) in unusual repositories or by unusual means: from the air (dropped by an eagle in flight), by fire (amid the carbonised remains of an incendiated edifice), in the sea (amid flotsam, jetsam, lagan and derelict), on earth (in the gizzard of a comestible fowl). A Spanish prisoner's donation of a distant treasure of valuables or specie or bullion lodged with a solvent banking corporation loo years previously at 5% compound interest of the collective worth of £ 5,000,000 stg (five million pounds sterling). A contract with an inconsiderate contractee for the delivery of 32 consignments of some given commodity in consideration of cash payment on delivery per delivery at the initial rate of 1/4d to be increased constantly in the geometrical progression of 2 (1/4d, 1/2d, 1d, 2d, 4d, 8d, 1s 4d, 2s 8d to 32 terms). A prepared scheme based on a study of the laws of probability to break the bank at Monte Carlo. A solution of the secular problem of the quadrature of the circle, government premium £ 1,000,000 sterling.

Was vast wealth acquirable through industrial channels?

The reclamation of dunams of waste arenary soil, proposed in the prospectus of Agendath Netaim, Bleibtreustrasse, Berlin, W. 15, by the cultivation of orange plantations and melonfields and reafforestation. The utilisation of waste paper, fells of sewer rodents, human excrement possessing chemical properties, in view of the vast production of the first, vast number of the second and immense quantity of the third, every normal human being of average vitality and appetite producing annually, cancelling byproducts of water, a sum total of 80 lbs. (mixed animal and vegetable diet), to be multiplied by 4,386,035, the total population of Ireland according to census returns of 1901.

Were there schemes of wider scope?

A scheme to be formulated and submitted for approval to the harbour commissioners for the exploitation of white coal (hydraulic power), obtained by hydroelectric plant at peak of tide at Dublin bar or at head of water at Poulaphouca or Powerscourt or catchment basins of main streams for the economic production of 500,000 W. H. P. of electricity. A scheme to enclose the peninsular delta of the North Bull at Dollymount and erect on the space of the foreland, used for golf links and rifle ranges, an asphalted esplanade with casinos, booths, shooting galleries, hotels, boardinghouses, readingrooms, establishments for mixed bathing. A scheme for the use of dogvans and goatvans for the delivery of early morning milk. A scheme for the development of Irish tourist traffic in and around Dublin by means of petrolpropelled riverboats, plying in the fluvial fairway between Island bridge and Ringsend, charabancs, narrow gauge local railways, and pleasure steamers for coastwise navigation (10/- per person per day, guide (trilingual) included). A scheme for the repristination of passenger and goods traffics over Irish waterways, when freed from weedbeds. A scheme to connect by tramline the Cattle Market (North Circular road and Prussia street) with the quays (Sheriff street, lower, and East Wall), parallel with the Link line railway laid (in conjunction with the Great Southern and Western railway line) between the cattle park, Liffey junction, and terminus of Midland Great Western Railway 43 to 45 North

Wall, in proximity to the terminal stations or Dublin branches of Great Central Railway, Midland Railway of England, City of Dublin Steam Packet Company, Lancashire and Yorkshire Railway Company, Dublin and Glasgow Steam Packet Company, Glasgow, Dublin and Londonderry Steam Packet Company (Laird line), British and Irish Steam Packet Company, Dublin and Morecambe Steamers, London and North Western Railway Company, Dublin Port and Docks Board Landing Sheds and transit sheds of Palgrave, Murphy and Company, steamship owners, agents for steamers from Mediterranean, Spain, Portugal, France, Belgium and Holland and for Liverpool Underwriters' Association, the cost of acquired rolling stock for animal transport and of additional mileage operated by the Dublin United Tramways Company, limited, to be covered by graziers' fees.

Positing what protasis would the contraction for such several schemes become a natural and necessary apodosis?

Given a guarantee equal to the sum sought, the support, by deed of gift and transfer vouchers during donor's lifetime or by bequest after donor's painless extinction, of eminent financiers (Blum Pasha, Rothschild Guggenheim, Hirsch, Montefiore, Morgan, Rockefeller) possessing fortunes in 6 figures, amassed during a successful life, and joining capital with opportunity the thing required was done.

What eventuality would render him independent of such wealth?

The independent discovery of a goldseam of inexhaustible ore.

For what reason did he meditate on schemes so difficult of realisation?

It was one of his axioms that similar meditations or the automatic relation to himself of a narrative concerning himself or tranquil recollection of the past when practised habitually before retiring for the night alleviated fatigue and produced as a result sound repose and renovated vitality.

His justifications?

As a physicist he had learned that of the 70 years of complete human life at least 2/7, viz. 20 years are passed in sleep. As a philosopher he knew that at the termination of any allotted life only an infinitesimal part of any person's desires has been realised. As a physiologist he believed in the artificial placation of malignant agencies chiefly operative during somnolence.

What did he fear?

The committal of homicide or suicide during sleep by an aberration of the light of reason, the incommensurable categorical intelligence situated in the cerebral convolutions.

What were habitually his final meditations?

Of some one sole unique advertisement to cause passers to stop in wonder, a poster novelty, with all extraneous accretions excluded, reduced to its simplest and most efficient terms not exceeding the span of casual vision and congruous with the velocity of modern life.

What did the first drawer unlocked contain?

A Vere Foster's handwriting copybook, property of Milly (Millicent) Bloom, certain pages of which bore diagram drawings, marked **Papli**, which showed a large globular head with 5 hairs erect, 2 eyes in profile, the trunk full front with 3 large buttons, 1 triangular foot: 2 fading photographs of queen Alexandra of England and of Maud Branscombe, actress and professional beauty: a Yuletide card, bearing on it a pictorial representation of a parasitic plant, the legend **Mizpah**, the date Xmas 1892, the name of the senders: from Mr + Mrs M. Comerford, the versicle: **May this Yuletide bring to thee, Joy and peace and welcome glee**: a butt of red partly liquefied sealing wax, obtained from the stores department of

Messrs Hely's, Ltd., 89, 90, and 91 Dame street: a box containing the remainder of a gross of gilt "J" pennibs, obtained from same department of same firm: an old sandglass which rolled containing sand which rolled: a sealed prophecy (never unsealed) written by Leopold Bloom in 1886 concerning the consequences of the passing into law of William Ewart Gladstone's Home Rule bill of 1886 (never passed into law): a bazaar ticket, no 2004, of S. Kevin's Charity Fair, price 6d, 100 prizes: an infantile epistle, dated, small em monday, reading: capital pee Papli comma capital aitch How are you note of interrogation capital eye I am very well full stop new paragraph signature with flourishes capital em Milly no stop: a cameo brooch, property of Ellen Bloom (born Higgins), deceased: a cameo scarfpin, property of Rudolph Bloom (born Virag), deceased: 3 typewritten letters, addressee, Henry Flower, c/o. P. O. Westland Row, addresser, Martha Clifford, c/o. P. O. Dolphin's Barn: the transliterated name and address of the addresser of the 3 letters in reversed alphabetic boustrophedonic punctated quadrilinear cryptogram (vowels suppressed) N. IGS./WI. UU. OX/W. OKS. MH/Y. IM: a press cutting from an English weekly periodical **Modern Society**, subject corporal chastisement in girls' schools: a pink ribbon which had festooned an Easter egg in the year 1899: two partly uncoiled rubber preservatives with reserve pockets, purchased by post from Box 32, P. O., Charing Cross, London, W. C.: 1 pack of 1 dozen creamlaid envelopes and feintruled notepaper, watermarked, now reduced by 3: some assorted Austrian-Hungarian coins: 2 coupons of the Royal and Privileged Hungarian Lottery: a lowpower magnifying glass: 2 erotic photocards showing a) buccal coition between nude senorita (rere presentation, superior position) and nude torero (fore presentation, inferior position) b) anal violation by male religious (fully clothed, eyes abject) of female religious (partly clothed, eyes direct), purchased by post from Box 32, P. O., Charing Cross, London, W. C.: a press cutting of recipe for renovation of old tan boots: a Id adhesive stamp, lavender, of the reign of Queen Victoria: a chart of the measurements of Leopold Bloom compiled before, during and after 2 months' consecutive use of Sandow-Whiteley's pulley exerciser (men's 15/-, athlete's 20/-) viz. chest 28 in and 29 1/2 in, biceps 9 in and 10 in, forearm 8 1/2 in and 9 in, thigh 10 in and 12 in, calf 11 in and 12 in: 1 prospectus of The Wonderworker, the world's greatest remedy for rectal complaints, direct from Wonderworker, Coventry House, South Place, London E C, addressed (erroneously) to Mrs L. Bloom with brief accompanying note commencing (erroneously): Dear Madam.

Quote the textual terms in which the prospectus claimed advantages for this thaumaturgic remedy.

It heals and soothes while you sleep, in case of trouble in breaking wind, assists nature in the most formidable way, insuring instant relief in discharge of gases, keeping parts clean and free natural action, an initial outlay of 7/6 making a new man of you and life worth living. Ladies find Wonderworker especially useful, a pleasant surprise when they note delightful result like a cool drink of fresh spring water on a sultry summer's day. Recommend it to your lady and gentlemen friends, lasts a lifetime. Insert long round end. Wonderworker.

Were there testimonials?

Numerous. From clergyman, British naval officer, wellknown author, city man, hospital nurse, lady, mother of five, absentminded beggar.

How did absentminded beggar's concluding testimonial conclude?

What a pity the government did not supply our men with wonderworkers during the South African campaign! What a relief it would have been!

What object did Bloom add to this collection

of objects?

A 4th typewritten letter received by Henry Flower (let H. F. be L. B.) from Martha Clifford (find M. C.).

What pleasant reflection accompanied this action?

The reflection that, apart from the letter in question, his magnetic face, form and address had been favourably received during the course of the preceding day by a wife (Mrs Josephine Breen, born Josie Powell), a nurse, Miss Callan (Christian name unknown), a maid, Gertrude (Gerty, family name unknown).

What possibility suggested itself?

The possibility of exercising virile power of fascination in the not immediate future after an expensive repast in a private apartment in the company of an elegant courtesan, of corporal beauty, moderately mercenary, variously instructed, a lady by origin.

What did the 2nd drawer contain?

Documents: the birth certificate of Leopold

Paula Bloom: an endowment assurance policy of £ 500 in the Scottish Widows' Assurance Society, intestated Millicent (Milly) Bloom, coming into force at 25 years as with profit policy of £ 430, £ 462-10-0 and £ 500 at 60 years or death, 65 years or death and death, respectively, or with profit policy (paidup) of £ 299-10-0 together with cash payment of £ 133-10-0, at option: a bank passbook issued by the Ulster Bank, College Green branch showing statement of a/c for halfyear ending 31 December 1903, balance in depositor's favour: £ 18-14-6 (eighteen pounds, fourteen shillings and sixpence, sterling), net personalty: certificate of possession of £ 900, Canadian 4 percent (inscribed) government stock (free of stamp duty): dockets of the Catholic Cemeteries' (Glasnevin) Committee, relative to a graveplot purchased: a local press cutting concerning change of name by deedpoll.

Quote the textual terms of this notice.

I, Rudolph Virag, now resident at no 52

Clanbrassil street, Dublin, formerly of Szombathely in the kingdom of Hungary, hereby give notice that I have assumed and intend henceforth upon all occasions and at all times to be known by the name of Rudolph Bloom.

What other objects relative to Rudolph Bloom (born Virag) were in the 2nd drawer?

An indistinct daguerreotype of Rudolf Virag and his father Leopold Virag executed in the year 1852 in the portrait atelier of their (respectively) 1st and 2nd cousin, Stefan Virag of Szesfehervar, Hungary. An ancient haggadah book in which a pair of hornrimmed convex spectacles inserted marked the passage of thanksgiving in the ritual prayers for Pessach (Passover): a photocard of the Queen's Hotel, Ennis, proprietor, Rudolph Bloom: an envelope addressed: **To My Dear Son Leopold**.

What fractions of phrases did the lecture of those five whole words evoke?

Tomorrow will be a week that I received...

it is no use Leopold to be ... with your dear mother... that is not more to stand... to her... all for me is out... be kind to Athos, Leopold... my dear son... always... of me... **das Herz... Gott... dein**...

What reminiscences of a human subject suffering from progressive melancholia did these objects evoke in Bloom?

An old man, widower, unkempt of hair, in bed, with head covered, sighing: an infirm dog, Athos: aconite, resorted to by increasing doses of grains and scruples as a palliative of recrudescent neuralgia: the face in death of a septuagenarian, suicide by poison.

Why did Bloom experience a sentiment of remorse?

Because in immature impatience he had treated with disrespect certain beliefs and practices.

As?

The prohibition of the use of fleshmeat and milk at one meal: the hebdomadary symposium of incoordinately abstract, perfervidly concrete mercantile coexreligionist excompatriots: the circumcision of male infants: the supernatural character of Judaic scripture: the ineffability of the tetragrammaton: the sanctity of the sabbath.

How did these beliefs and practices now appear to him?

Not more rational than they had then appeared, not less rational than other beliefs and practices now appeared.

What first reminiscence had he of Rudolph Bloom (deceased)?

Rudolph Bloom (deceased) narrated to his son Leopold Bloom (aged 6) a retrospective arrangement of migrations and settlements in and between Dublin, London, Florence, Milan, Vienna, Budapest, Szombathely with statements of satisfaction (his grandfather having seen Maria Theresia, empress of Austria, queen of Hungary), with commercial advice (having taken care of pence, the pounds having taken care of themselves). Leopold Bloom (aged 6) had accompanied these narrations by constant consultation of a geographical map of Europe (political) and by suggestions for the establishment of affiliated business premises in the various centres mentioned.

Had time equally but differently obliterated the memory of these migrations in narrator and listener?

In narrator by the access of years and in consequence of the use of narcotic toxin: in listener by the access of years and in consequence of the action of distraction upon vicarious experiences.

What idiosyncracies of the narrator were concomitant products of amnesia?

Occasionally he ate without having previously removed his hat. Occasionally he drank voraciously the juice of gooseberry fool from an inclined plate. Occasionally he removed from his lips the traces of food by means of a lacerated envelope or other accessible fragment of paper.

What two phenomena of senescence were more frequent?

The myopic digital calculation of coins, eructation consequent upon repletion.

What object offered partial consolation for these reminiscences?

The endowment policy, the bank passbook, the certificate of the possession of scrip.

Reduce Bloom by cross multiplication of reverses of fortune, from which these supports protected him, and by elimination of all positive values to a negligible negative irrational unreal quantity.

Successively, in descending helotic order: Poverty: that of the outdoor hawker of imitation jewellery, the dun for the recovery of bad and doubtful debts, the poor rate and deputy cess collector. Mendicancy: that of the fraudulent bankrupt with negligible assets paying 1s. 4d. in the £, sandwichman, distributor of throwaways, nocturnal vagrant, insinuating sycophant, maimed sailor, blind stripling, superannuated bailiffs man, marfeast, lickplate, spoilsport, pickthank, eccentric public laughingstock seated on bench of public park under discarded perforated umbrella. Destitution: the inmate of Old Man's House (Royal Hospital) Kilmainham, the inmate of Simpson's Hospital for reduced but respectable men permanently disabled by gout or want of sight. Nadir of misery: the aged impotent disfranchised ratesupported moribund lunatic pauper.

With which attendant indignities?

The unsympathetic indifference of previously amiable females, the contempt of muscular males, the acceptance of fragments of bread, the simulated ignorance of casual acquaintances, the latration of illegitimate unlicensed vagabond dogs, the infantile discharge of decomposed vegetable missiles, worth little or nothing, nothing or less than nothing.

By what could such a situation be

precluded?

By decease (change of state): by departure (change of place).

Which preferably?

The latter, by the line of least resistance.

What considerations rendered departure not entirely undesirable?

Constant cohabitation impeding mutual toleration of personal defects. The habit of independent purchase increasingly cultivated. The necessity to counteract by impermanent sojourn the permanence of arrest.

What considerations rendered departure not irrational?

The parties concerned, uniting, had increased and multiplied, which being done, offspring produced and educed to maturity, the parties, if not disunited were obliged to reunite for increase and multiplication, which was absurd, to form by reunion the original couple of uniting parties, which was impossible.

What considerations rendered departure desirable?

The attractive character of certain localities in Ireland and abroad, as represented in general geographical maps of polychrome design or in special ordnance survey charts by employment of scale numerals and hachures.

In Ireland?

The cliffs of Moher, the windy wilds of Connemara, lough Neagh with submerged petrified city, the Giant's Causeway, Fort Camden and Fort Carlisle, the Golden Vale of Tipperary, the islands of Aran, the pastures of royal Meath, Brigid's elm in Kildare, the Queen's Island shipyard in Belfast, the Salmon Leap, the lakes of Killarney.

Abroad?

Ceylon (with spicegardens supplying tea to Thomas Kernan, agent for Pulbrook, Robertson and Co, 2 Mincing Lane, London, E. C., 5 Dame street, Dublin), Jerusalem, the holy city (with mosque of Omar and gate of Damascus, goal of aspiration), the straits of Gibraltar (the unique birthplace of Marion Tweedy), the Parthenon (containing statues of nude Grecian divinities), the Wall street money market (which controlled international finance), the Plaza de Toros at La Linea, Spain (where O'Hara of the Camerons had slain the bull), Niagara (over which no human being had passed with impunity), the land of the Eskimos (eaters of soap), the forbidden country of Thibet (from which no traveller returns), the bay of Naples (to see which was to die), the Dead Sea.

Under what guidance, following what signs?

At sea, septentrional, by night the polestar, located at the point of intersection of the right line from beta to alpha in Ursa Maior produced and divided externally at omega and the hypotenuse of the rightangled triangle formed by the line alpha omega so produced and the line alpha delta of Ursa Maior. On land, meridional, a bispherical moon, revealed in imperfect varying phases of lunation through the posterior interstice of the imperfectly occluded skirt of a carnose negligent perambulating female, a pillar of the cloud by day.

What public advertisement would divulge the occultation of the departed?

£ 5 reward, lost, stolen or strayed from his residence 7 Eccles street, missing gent about 40, answering to the name of Bloom, Leopold (Poldy), height 5 ft 9 1/2 inches, full build, olive complexion, may have since grown a beard, when last seen was wearing a black suit. Above sum will be paid for information leading to his discovery.

What universal binomial denominations would be his as entity and nonentity?

Assumed by any or known to none. Everyman or Noman.

What tributes his?

Honour and gifts of strangers, the friends of Everyman. A nymph immortal, beauty, the bride of Noman.

Would the departed never nowhere nohow reappear?

Ever he would wander, selfcompelled, to the extreme limit of his cometary orbit, beyond the fixed stars and variable suns and telescopic planets, astronomical waifs and strays, to the extreme boundary of space, passing from land to land, among peoples, amid events. Somewhere imperceptibly he would hear and somehow reluctantly, suncompelled, obey the summons of recall. Whence, disappearing from the constellation of the Northern Crown he would somehow reappear reborn above delta in the constellation of Cassiopeia and after incalculable eons of peregrination return an estranged avenger, a wreaker of justice on malefactors, a dark crusader, a sleeper awakened, with financial resources (by supposition) surpassing those of Rothschild or the silver king.

What would render such return irrational?

An unsatisfactory equation between an

exodus and return in time through reversible space and an exodus and return in space through irreversible time.

What play of forces, inducing inertia, rendered departure undesirable?

The lateness of the hour, rendering procrastinatory: the obscurity of the night, rendering invisible: the uncertainty of thoroughfares, rendering perilous: the necessity for repose, obviating movement: the proximity of an occupied bed, obviating research: the anticipation of warmth (human) tempered with coolness (linen), obviating desire and rendering desirable: the statue of Narcissus, sound without echo, desired desire.

What advantages were possessed by an occupied, as distinct from an unoccupied bed?

The removal of nocturnal solitude, the superior quality of human (mature female) to inhuman (hotwaterjar) calefaction, the stimulation of matutinal contact, the economy of mangling done on the premises in the case of trousers accurately folded and placed lengthwise between the spring mattress (striped) and the woollen mattress (biscuit section).

What past consecutive causes, before rising preapprehended, of accumulated fatigue did Bloom, before rising, silently recapitulate?

Thepreparationofbreakfast(burntoffering): intestinal congestion and premeditative defecation (holy of holies): the bath (rite of John): the funeral (rite of Samuel): the advertisement of Alexander Keyes (Urim and Thummim): the unsubstantial lunch (rite of Melchisedek): the visit to museum and national library (holy place): the bookhunt along Bedford row, Merchants› Arch, Wellington Quay (Simchath Torah): the music in the Ormond Hotel (Shira Shirim): the altercation with a truculent troglodyte in Bernard Kiernan›s premises (holocaust): a blank period of time including a cardrive, a visit to a house of mourning, a leavetaking (wilderness): the eroticism produced by feminine exhibitionism (rite of Onan): the prolonged delivery of Mrs Mina Purefoy (heave offering): the visit to the disorderly house of Mrs Bella Cohen, 82 Tyrone street, lower and subsequent brawl and chance medley in Beaver street (Armageddon) – nocturnal perambulation to and from the cabman›s shelter, Butt Bridge (atonement).

What selfimposed enigma did Bloom about to rise in order to go so as to conclude lest he should not conclude involuntarily apprehend?

The cause of a brief sharp unforeseen heard loud lone crack emitted by the insentient material of a strainveined timber table.

What selfinvolved enigma did Bloom risen, going, gathering multicoloured multiform multitudinous garments, voluntarily apprehending, not comprehend?

Who was M›Intosh?

What selfevident enigma pondered with desultory constancy during 30 years did Bloom now, having effected natural obscurity by the extinction of artificial light, silently suddenly comprehend?

Where was Moses when the candle went out?

What imperfections in a perfect day did Bloom, walking, charged with collected articles of recently disvested male wearing apparel, silently, successively, enumerate?

A provisional failure to obtain renewal of an advertisement: to obtain a certain quantity of tea from Thomas Kernan (agent for Pulbrook, Robertson and Co, 5 Dame Street, Dublin, and 2 Mincing Lane, London E. C.): to certify the presence or absence of posterior rectal orifice in the case of Hellenic female divinities: to obtain admission (gratuitous or paid) to the performance of Leah by Mrs Bandmann Palmer at the Gaiety Theatre, 46, 47, 48, 49 South King street.

What impression of an absent face did Bloom, arrested, silently recall?

The face of her father, the late Major Brian Cooper Tweedy, Royal Dublin Fusiliers, of Gibraltar and Rehoboth, Dolphin›s Barn.

What recurrent impressions of the same were possible by hypothesis?

Retreating, at the terminus of the Great Northern Railway, Amiens street, with constant uniform acceleration, along parallel lines meeting at infinity, if produced: along parallel lines, reproduced from infinity, with constant uniform retardation, at the terminus of the Great Northern Railway, Amiens street, returning.

What miscellaneous effects of female personal wearing apparel were perceived by him?

A pair of new inodorous halfsilk black ladies› hose, a pair of new violet garters, a pair of outsize ladies› drawers of India mull, cut on generous lines, redolent of opoponax, jessamine and Muratti›s Turkish cigarettes and containing a long bright steel safety pin, folded curvilinear, a camisole of batiste with thin lace border, an accordion underskirt of blue silk moirette, all these objects being disposed irregularly on the top of a rectangular trunk, quadruple battened, having capped corners, with multicoloured labels, initialled on its fore side in white lettering B. C. T. (Brian Cooper Tweedy).

What impersonal objects were perceived?

A commode, one leg fractured, totally covered by square cretonne cutting, apple design, on which rested a lady›s black straw hat. Orangekeyed ware, bought of Henry Price, basket, fancy goods, chinaware and ironmongery manufacturer, 21, 22, 23 Moore street, disposed irregularly on the washstand and floor and consisting of basin, soapdish and brushtray (on the washstand, together), pitcher and night article (on the floor, separate).

Bloom›s acts?

He deposited the articles of clothing on

a chair, removed his remaining articles of clothing, took from beneath the bolster at the head of the bed a folded long white nightshirt, inserted his head and arms into the proper apertures of the nightshirt, removed a pillow from the head to the foot of the bed, prepared the bedlinen accordingly and entered the bed.

How?

With circumspection, as invariably when entering an abode (his own or not his own): with solicitude, the snakespiral springs of the mattress being old, the brass quoits and pendent viper radii loose and tremulous under stress and strain: prudently, as entering a lair or ambush of lust or adders: lightly, the less to disturb: reverently, the bed of conception and of birth, of consummation of marriage and of breach of marriage, of sleep and of death.

What did his limbs, when gradually extended, encounter?

New clean bedlinen, additional odours, the

presence of a human form, female, hers, the imprint of a human form, male, not his, some crumbs, some flakes of potted meat, recooked, which he removed.

If he had smiled why would he have smiled?

To reflect that each one who enters imagines himself to be the first to enter whereas he is always the last term of a preceding series even if the first term of a succeeding one, each imagining himself to be first, last, only and alone whereas he is neither first nor last nor only nor alone in a series originating in and repeated to infinity.

What preceding series?

Assuming Mulvey to be the first term of his series, Penrose, Bartell d›Arcy, professor Goodwin, Julius Mastiansky, John Henry Menton, Father Bernard Corrigan, a farmer at the Royal Dublin Society›s Horse Show, Maggot O›Reilly, Matthew Dillon, Valentine Blake Dillon (Lord Mayor of Dublin), Christopher Callinan, Lenehan, an Italian organgrinder, an unknown gentleman in the Gaiety Theatre, Benjamin Dollard, Simon Dedalus, Andrew (Pisser) Burke, Joseph Cuffe, Wisdom Hely, Alderman John Hooper, Dr Francis Brady, Father Sebastian of Mount Argus, a bootblack at the General Post Office, Hugh E. (Blazes) Boylan and so each and so on to no last term.

What were his reflections concerning the last member of this series and late occupant of the bed?

Reflections on his vigour (a bounder), corporal proportion (a billsticker), commercial ability (a bester), impressionability (a boaster).

Why for the observer impressionability in addition to vigour, corporal proportion and commercial ability?

Because he had observed with augmenting frequency in the preceding members of the same series the same concupiscence, inflammably transmitted, first with alarm, then with understanding, then with desire, finally with fatigue, with alternating symptoms of epicene comprehension and apprehension.

With what antagonistic sentiments were his subsequent reflections affected?

Envy, jealousy, abnegation, equanimity.

Envy?

Of a bodily and mental male organism specially adapted for the superincumbent posture of energetic human copulation and energetic piston and cylinder movement necessary for the complete satisfaction of a constant but not acute concupiscence resident in a bodily and mental female organism, passive but not obtuse.

Jealousy?

Because a nature full and volatile in its free state, was alternately the agent and reagent of attraction. Because attraction between agent(s) and reagent(s) at all instants varied, with inverse proportion of increase and decrease, with incessant circular extension and radial reentrance.

Because the controlled contemplation of the fluctuation of attraction produced, if desired, a fluctuation of pleasure.

Abnegation?

In virtue of a) acquaintance initiated in September 1903 in the establishment of George Mesias, merchant tailor and outfitter, 5 Eden Quay, b) hospitality extended and received in kind, reciprocated and reappropriated in person, c) comparative youth subject to impulses of ambition and magnanimity, colleagual altruism and amorous egoism, d) extraracial attraction, intraracial inhibition, supraracial prerogative, e) an imminent provincial musical tour, common current expenses, net proceeds divided.

Equanimity?

As as natural as any and every natural act of a nature expressed or understood executed in natured nature by natural creatures in accordance with his, her and their natured natures, of dissimilar similarity.

As not so calamitous as a cataclysmic annihilation of the planet in consequence of a collision with a dark sun. As less reprehensible than theft, highway robbery, cruelty to children and animals, obtaining money under false pretences, forgery, embezzlement, misappropriation of public money, betrayal of public trust, malingering, mayhem, corruption of minors, criminal libel, blackmail, contempt of court, arson, treason, felony, mutiny on the high seas, trespass, burglary, jailbreaking, practice of unnatural vice, desertion from armed forces in the field, perjury, poaching, usury, intelligence with the king›s enemies, impersonation, criminal assault, manslaughter, wilful and premeditated murder. As not more abnormal than all other parallel processes of adaptation to altered conditions of existence, resulting in a reciprocal equilibrium between the bodily organism and its attendant circumstances, foods, beverages, acquired habits, indulged inclinations, significant disease. As more than inevitable, irreparable.

Why more abnegation than jealousy, less envy than equanimity?

From outrage (matrimony) to outrage (adultery) there arose nought but outrage (copulation) yet the matrimonial violator of the matrimonially violated had not been outraged by the adulterous violator of the adulterously violated.

What retribution, if any?

Assassination, never, as two wrongs did not make one right. Duel by combat, no. Divorce, not now. Exposure by mechanical artifice (automatic bed) or individual testimony (concealed ocular witnesses), not yet. Suit for damages by legal influence or simulation of assault with evidence of injuries sustained (selfinflicted), not impossibly. Hushmoney by moral influence possibly. If any, positively, connivance, introduction of emulation (material, a prosperous rival agency of publicity: moral, a successful rival agent of intimacy), depreciation, alienation, humiliation, separation protecting the one separated from the other, protecting the separator from both.

By what reflections did he, a conscious reactor against the void of incertitude, justify to himself his sentiments?

The preordained frangibility of the hymen: the presupposed intangibility of the thing in itself: the incongruity and disproportion between the selfprolonging tension of the thing proposed to be done and the selfabbreviating relaxation of the thing done; the fallaciously inferred debility of the female: the muscularity of the male: the variations of ethical codes: the natural grammatical transition by inversion involving no alteration of sense of an aorist preterite proposition (parsed as masculine subject, monosyllabic onomatopoeic transitive verb with direct feminine object) from the active voice into its correlative aorist preterite proposition (parsed as feminine subject, auxiliary verb and quasimonosyllabic onomatopoeic past participle with complementary masculine agent) in the passive voice: the continued product of seminators by generation: the continual production of semen by distillation: the futility of triumph or protest or vindication: the inanity of extolled virtue: the lethargy of nescient matter: the apathy of the stars.

In what final satisfaction did these antagonistic sentiments and reflections, reduced to their simplest forms, converge?

Satisfaction at the ubiquity in eastern and western terrestrial hemispheres, in all habitable lands and islands explored or unexplored (the land of the midnight sun, the islands of the blessed, the isles of Greece, the land of promise), of adipose anterior and posterior female hemispheres, redolent of milk and honey and of excretory sanguine and seminal warmth, reminiscent of secular families of curves of amplitude, insusceptible of moods of impression or of contrarieties of expression, expressive of mute immutable mature animality.

The visible signs of antesatisfaction?

An approximate erection: a solicitous adversion: a gradual elevation: a tentative revelation: a silent contemplation.

Then?

He kissed the plump mellow yellow smellow melons of her rump, on each plump melonous hemisphere, in their mellow yellow furrow, with obscure prolonged provocative melonsmellonous osculation.

The visible signs of postsatisfaction?

A silent contemplation: a tentative velation: a gradual abasement: a solicitous aversion: a proximate erection.

What followed this silent action?

Somnolent invocation, less somnolent recognition, incipient excitation, catechetical interrogation.

With what modifications did the narrator reply to this interrogation?

Negative: he omitted to mention the clandestine correspondence between Martha Clifford and Henry Flower, the public altercation at, in and in the vicinity of the licensed premises of Bernard Kiernan and Co, Limited, 8, 9 and 10 Little Britain street, the erotic provocation and response thereto caused by the exhibitionism of Gertrude (Gerty), surname unknown. Positive: he included mention of a performance by Mrs Bandmann Palmer of LEAH at the Gaiety Theatre, 46, 47, 48, 49 South King street, an invitation to supper at Wynn›s (Murphy›s) Hotel, 35, 36 and 37 Lower Abbey street, a volume of peccaminous pornographical tendency entituled SWEETS OF SIN, anonymous author a gentleman of fashion, a temporary concussion caused by a falsely calculated movement in the course of a postcenal gymnastic display, the victim (since completely recovered) being Stephen Dedalus, professor and author, eldest surviving son of Simon Dedalus, of no fixed occupation, an aeronautical feat executed by him (narrator) in the presence of a witness, the professor and author aforesaid, with promptitude of decision and gymnastic flexibility.

Was the narration otherwise unaltered by modifications?

Absolutely.

Which event or person emerged as the salient point of his narration?

Stephen Dedalus, professor and author.

What limitations of activity and inhibitions of conjugal rights were perceived by listener and narrator concerning themselves during the course of this intermittent and increasingly more laconic narration?

By the listener a limitation of fertility inasmuch as marriage had been celebrated 1 calendar month after the 18th anniversary of her birth (8 September 1870), viz. 8 October, and consummated on the same date with female issue born 15 June 1889, having been anticipatorily consummated on the lo September of the same year and complete carnal intercourse, with ejaculation of semen within the natural female organ, having last taken place 5 weeks previous, viz. 27 November 1893, to the birth on 29 December 1893 of second (and only male) issue, deceased 9 January 1894, aged 11 days, there remained a period of 10 years, 5 months and 18 days during which carnal intercourse had been incomplete, without ejaculation of semen within the natural female organ. By the narrator a limitation of activity, mental and corporal, inasmuch as complete mental intercourse between himself and the listener had not taken place since the consummation of puberty, indicated by catamenic hemorrhage, of the female issue of narrator and listener, 15 September 1903, there remained a period of 9 months and 1 day during which, in consequence of a preestablished natural comprehension in incomprehension between the consummated females (listener and issue), complete corporal liberty of action had been circumscribed.

How?

Chapter Seventeen

By various reiterated feminine interrogation concerning the masculine destination whither, the place where, the time at which, the duration for which, the object with which in the case of temporary absences, projected or effected.

What moved visibly above the listener›s and the narrator›s invisible thoughts?

The upcast reflection of a lamp and shade, an inconstant series of concentric circles of varying gradations of light and shadow.

In what directions did listener and narrator lie?

Listener, S. E. by E.: Narrator, N. W. by W.: on the 53rd parallel of latitude, N., and 6th meridian of longitude, W.: at an angle of 45 degrees to the terrestrial equator.

In what state of rest or motion?

At rest relatively to themselves and to each other. In motion being each and both carried westward, forward and rereward respectively, by the proper perpetual motion of the earth through everchanging tracks of neverchanging space.

In what posture?

Listener: reclined semilaterally, left, left hand under head, right leg extended in a straight line and resting on left leg, flexed, in the attitude of Gea-Tellus, fulfilled, recumbent, big with seed. Narrator: reclined laterally, left, with right and left legs flexed, the index finger and thumb of the right hand resting on the bridge of the nose, in the attitude depicted in a snapshot photograph made by Percy Apjohn, the childman weary, the manchild in the womb.

Womb? Weary?

He rests. He has travelled.

With?

Sinbad the Sailor and Tinbad the Tailor and Jinbad the Jailer and Whinbad the Whaler and Ninbad the Nailer and Finbad the Failer and Binbad the Bailer and Pinbad the Pailer and Minbad the Mailer and Hinbad the Hailer and Rinbad the Railer and Dinbad the Kailer and Vinbad the Quailer and Linbad the Yailer and Xinbad the Phthailer.

When?

Going to dark bed there was a square round Sinbad the Sailor roc›s auk›s egg in the night of the bed of all the auks of the rocs of Darkinbad the Brightdayler.

Where?

CHAPTER EIGHTEEN

YES BECAUSE he never did a thing like that before as ask to get his breakfast in bed with a couple of eggs since the **City Arms** hotel when he used to be pretending to be laid up with a sick voice doing his highness to make himself interesting for that old faggot Mrs Riordan that he thought he had a great leg of and she never left us a farthing all for masses for herself and her soul greatest miser ever was actually afraid to lay out 4d for her methylated spirit telling me all her ailments she had too much old chat in her about politics and earthquakes and the end of the world let us have a bit of fun first God help the world if all the women were her sort down on bathingsuits and lownecks of course nobody wanted her to wear them I suppose she was pious because no man would look at her twice I hope Ill never be like her a wonder she didnt want us to cover our faces but she was a welleducated woman certainly and her gabby talk about Mr Riordan here and Mr Riordan there I suppose he was glad to get shut of her and her dog smelling my fur and always edging to get up under my petticoats especially then still I like that in him polite to old women like that and waiters and beggars too hes not proud out of nothing but not always if ever he got anything really serious the matter with him its much better for them to go into a hospital where everything is clean but I suppose Id have to dring it into him for a month yes and then wed have a hospital nurse next thing on the carpet have him staying there till they throw him out or a nun maybe like the smutty photo he has shes as much a nun as Im not yes because theyre so weak and puling when theyre sick they want a woman to get well if his nose bleeds youd think it was O tragic and that dyinglooking one off the south circular when he sprained his foot at the choir party at the sugarloaf Mountain the day I wore that dress Miss Stack bringing him flowers the worst old ones she could find at the bottom of the basket anything at all to get into a mans bedroom with her old maids voice trying to imagine he was dying on account of her to never see thy face again though he looked more like a man with his beard a bit grown in the bed father was the same besides I hate bandaging and dosing when he cut his toe with the razor paring his corns afraid hed get bloodpoisoning but if it was a thing I was sick then wed see what attention only of course the woman hides it not to give all the trouble they do yes he came somewhere Im sure by his appetite anyway love its not or hed be off his feed thinking of her so either it was one of those night women if it was down there he was really and the hotel story he made up a pack of lies to hide it planning it Hynes kept me who did I meet ah yes I met do you remember Menton and who else who let me see that big babbyface I saw him and he not long married flirting with a young girl at Pooles Myriorama and turned my back on him when he slinked out looking quite conscious what harm but he had the impudence to make up to me one time well done to him mouth almighty and his boiled eyes of all the big stupoes I ever met and thats called a solicitor only for I hate having a long wrangle in bed or else if its not that its some little bitch or other he got in with somewhere or picked up on the sly if they only knew him as well as I do yes because the day before yesterday he was scribbling something a letter when I came into the front room to show him Dignams death in the paper as if something told me and he covered it up with the blottingpaper pretending to be thinking about business so very probably that was it to somebody who thinks she has a softy in him because all men get a bit like that at his age especially getting on to forty he is now so as to wheedle any money she can out of him no fool like an old fool and then the usual kissing my bottom was to hide it not that I care two straws now who he does it with or knew before that way though Id like to find out so long as I dont have the two of them under my nose all the time like that slut that Mary we had in Ontario terrace padding out her false bottom to excite him bad enough to get the smell of those painted women off him once or twice I had a suspicion by getting him to come near me when I found the long hair on his coat without that one when I went into the kitchen pretending he was drinking water 1 woman is not enough for them it was all his fault of course ruining servants then proposing that she could eat at our table on Christmas day if you please O no thank you not in my house stealing my potatoes and the oysters 2/6 per doz going out to see her aunt if you please common robbery so it was but I was sure he had something on with that one it takes me to find out a thing like that he said you have no proof it was her proof O yes her aunt was very fond of oysters but I told her what I thought of her suggesting me to go out to be alone with her I wouldnt lower myself to spy on them the garters I found in her room the Friday she was out that was enough for me a little bit too much her face swelled up on her with temper when I gave her her weeks notice I saw to that better do without them altogether do out the rooms myself quicker only for the damn cooking and throwing out the dirt I gave it to him anyhow either she or me leaves the house I couldnt even touch him if I thought he was with a dirty barefaced liar and sloven like that one denying it up to my face and singing about the place in the W C too because she knew she was too well off yes because he couldnt possibly do without it that long so he must do it somewhere and the last time he came on my bottom when was it the night Boylan gave my hand a great squeeze going along by the Tolka in my hand there steals another I just pressed the back of his like that with my thumb to squeeze back singing the young May moon shes beaming love because he has an idea about him and me hes not such a fool he said Im dining out and going to the Gaiety though Im not going to give him the satisfaction in any case God knows hes a change in a way not to be always and ever wearing the same old hat unless I paid some nicelooking boy to do it since I cant do it myself a young boy would like me Id confuse him a little alone with him if we were Id let him see my garters the new ones and make him turn red looking at him seduce him I know what boys feel with that down on their cheek doing that frigging drawing out the thing by the hour question and answer would you do this that and the other with the coalman yes with a bishop yes I would because I told him about some dean or bishop was sitting beside me in the jews temples gardens when I was knitting that woollen thing a stranger to Dublin what place was it and so on about the monuments and he tired me out with statues encouraging him making him worse than he is who is in your mind now tell me who are you thinking of who is it tell me his name who tell me who the german Emperor is it yes imagine Im him think of him can you feel him trying to make a whore of me what he never will he ought to give it up now at this age of his life simply ruination for any woman and no satisfaction in it pretending to like it till he comes and then finish it off myself anyway and it makes your lips pale anyhow its done now once and for all with all the talk of the world about it people make its only the first time after that its just the ordinary do it and think no more about it why cant you kiss a man without going and marrying him first you sometimes love to wildly when you feel that way so nice all over you you cant help yourself I wish some man or other would take me sometime when hes there and kiss me in his arms theres nothing like a kiss long and hot down to your soul almost paralyses you then I hate that confession when I used to go to Father Corrigan he touched me father and what harm if he did where and I said on the canal bank like a fool but whereabouts on your person my child on the leg behind high up was it yes rather high up was it where you sit down yes O Lord couldnt he say bottom right out and have done with it what has that got to do with it and did you whatever way he put it I forget no father and I always think of the real father what did he want to know for when I already confessed it to God he had a nice fat hand the palm moist always I wouldnt mind feeling it neither would he Id say by the bullneck in his horsecollar I wonder did he know me in the box I could see his face he couldnt see mine of course hed never turn or let on still his eyes were red when his father died theyre lost for a woman of course must be terrible when a man cries let alone them Id like to be embraced by one in his vestments and the smell of incense off him like the pope besides theres no danger with a priest if youre married hes too careful about himself then give something to H H the pope for a penance I wonder was he satisfied with me one thing I didnt like his slapping me behind going away so familiarly in the hall though I laughed Im not a horse or an ass am I I suppose he was thinking of his fathers I wonder is he awake thinking of me or dreaming am I in it who gave him that flower he said he bought he smelt of some kind of drink not whisky or stout or perhaps the sweety kind of paste they stick their bills up with some liqueur Id like to sip those richlooking green and yellow expensive drinks those stagedoor johnnies drink with the opera hats I tasted once with my finger dipped out of that American that had the squirrel talking stamps with father he had all he could do to keep himself from falling asleep after the last time after we took the port and potted meat it had a fine salty taste yes because I felt lovely and tired myself and fell asleep as sound as a top the moment I popped straight into bed till that thunder woke me up God be merciful to us I thought the heavens were coming down about us to punish us when I blessed myself and said a Hail Mary like those awful thunderbolts in Gibraltar as if the world was coming to an end and then they come and tell you theres no God what could you do if it was running and rushing about nothing only make an act of contrition the candle I lit that evening in Whitefriars street chapel for the month of

May see it brought its luck though hed scoff if he heard because he never goes to church mass or meeting he says your soul you have no soul inside only grey matter because he doesnt know what it is to have one yes when I lit the lamp because he must have come 3 or 4 times with that tremendous big red brute of a thing he has I thought the vein or whatever the dickens they call it was going to burst though his nose is not so big after I took off all my things with the blinds down after my hours dressing and perfuming and combing it like iron or some kind of a thick crowbar standing all the time he must have eaten oysters I think a few dozen he was in great singing voice no I never in all my life felt anyone had one the size of that to make you feel full up he must have eaten a whole sheep after whats the idea making us like that with a big hole in the middle of us or like a Stallion driving it up into you because thats all they want out of you with that determined vicious look in his eye I had to halfshut my eyes still he hasnt such a tremendous amount of spunk in him when I made him pull out and do it on me considering how big it is so much the better in case any of it wasnt washed out properly the last time I let him finish it in me nice invention they made for women for him to get all the pleasure but if someone gave them a touch of it themselves theyd know what I went through with Milly nobody would believe cutting her teeth too and Mina Purefoys husband give us a swing out of your whiskers filling her up with a child or twins once a year as regular as the clock always with a smell of children off her the one they called budgers or something like a nigger with a shock of hair on it Jesusjack the child is a black the last time I was there a squad of them falling over one another and bawling you couldnt hear your ears supposed to be healthy not satisfied till they have us swollen out like elephants or I dont know what supposing I risked having another not off him though still if he was married Im sure hed have a fine strong child but I dont know Poldy has more spunk in him yes thatd be awfully jolly I suppose it was meeting Josie Powell and the funeral and thinking about me and Boylan set him off well he can think what he likes now if thatll do him any good I know they were spooning a bit when I came on the scene he was dancing and sitting out with her the night of Georgina Simpsons housewarming and then he wanted to ram it down my neck it was on account of not liking to see her a wallflower that was why we had the standup row over politics he began it not me when he said about Our Lord being a carpenter at last he made me cry of course a woman is so sensitive about everything I was fuming with myself after for giving in only for I knew he was gone on me and the first socialist he said He was he annoyed me so much I couldnt put him into a temper still he knows a lot of mixedup things especially about the body and the inside I often wanted to study up that myself what we have inside us in that family physician I could always hear his voice talking when the room was crowded and watch him after that I pretended I had a coolness on with her over him because he used to be a bit on the jealous side whenever he asked who are you going to and I said over to Floey and he made me the present of Byron's poems and the three pairs of gloves so that finished that I could quite easily get him to make it up any time I know how Id even supposing he got in with her again and was going out to see her somewhere Id know if he refused to eat the onions I know plenty of ways ask him to tuck down the collar of my blouse or touch him with my veil and gloves on going out I kiss then would send them all spinning however alright well see then let him go to her she of course would only be too delighted to pretend shes mad in love with him that I wouldnt so much mind Id just go to her and ask her do you love him and look her square in the eyes she couldnt fool me but he might imagine he was and make a declaration to her with his plabbery kind of a manner like he did to me though I had the devils own job to get it out of him though I liked him for that it showed he could hold in and wasnt to be got for the asking he was on the pop of asking me too the night in the kitchen I was rolling the potato cake theres something I want to say to you only for I put him off letting on I was in a temper with my hands and arms full of pasty flour in any case I let out too much the night before talking of dreams so I didnt want to let him know more than was good for him she used to be always embracing me Josie whenever he was there meaning him of course glauming me over and when I said I washed up and down as far as possible asking me and did you wash possible the women are always egging on to that putting it on thick when hes there they know by his sly eye blinking a bit putting on the indifferent when they come out with something the kind he is what spoils him I dont wonder in the least because he was very handsome at that time trying to look like Lord Byron I said I liked though he was too beautiful for a man and he was a little before we got engaged afterwards though she didnt like it so much the day I was in fits of laughing with the giggles I couldnt stop about all my hairpins falling out one after another with the mass of hair I had youre always in great humour she said yes because it grigged her because she knew what it meant because I used to tell her a good bit of what went on between us not all but just enough to make her mouth water but that wasnt my fault she didnt darken the door much after we were married I wonder what shes got like now after living with that dotty husband of hers she had her face beginning to look drawn and run down the last time I saw her she must have been just after a row with him because I saw on the moment she was edging to draw down a conversation about husbands and talk about him to run him down what was it she told me O yes that sometimes he used to go to bed with his muddy boots on when the maggot takes him just imagine having to get into bed with a thing like that that might murder you any moment what a man well its not the one way everyone goes mad Poldy anyhow whatever he does always wipes his feet on the mat when he comes in wet or shine and always blacks his own boots too and he always takes off his hat when he comes up in the street like then and now hes going about in his slippers to look for £ 10000 for a postcard U p up O sweetheart May wouldnt a thing like that simply bore you stiff to extinction actually too stupid even to take his boots off now what could you make of a man like that Id rather die 20 times over than marry another of their sex of course hed never find another woman like me to put up with him the way I do know me come sleep with me yes and he knows that too at the bottom of his heart take that Mrs Maybrick that poisoned her husband for what I wonder in love with some other man yes it was found out on her wasnt she the downright villain to go and do a thing like that of course some men can be dreadfully aggravating drive you mad and always the worst word in the world what do they ask us to marry them for if were so bad as all that comes to yes because they cant get on without us white Arsenic she put in his tea off flypaper wasnt it I wonder why they call it that if I asked him hed say its from the Greek leave us as wise as we were before she must have been madly in love with the other fellow to run the chance of being hanged O she didnt care if that was her nature what could she do besides theyre not brutes enough to go and hang a woman surely are they

theyre all so different Boylan talking about the shape of my foot he noticed at once even before he was introduced when I was in the D B C with Poldy laughing and trying to listen I was waggling my foot we both ordered 2 teas and plain bread and butter I saw him looking with his two old maids of sisters when I stood up and asked the girl where it was what do I care with it dropping out of me and that black closed breeches he made me buy takes you half an hour to let them down wetting all myself always with some brandnew fad every other week such a long one I did I forgot my suede gloves on the seat behind that I never got after some robber of a woman and he wanted me to put it in the Irish times lost in the ladies lavatory D B C Dame street finder return to Mrs Marion Bloom and I saw his eyes on my feet going out through the turning door he was looking when I looked back and I went there for tea 2 days after in the hope but he wasnt now how did that excite him because I was crossing them when we were in the other room first he meant the shoes that are too tight to walk in my hand is nice like that if I only had a ring with the stone for my month a nice aquamarine Ill stick him for one and a gold bracelet I dont like my foot so much still I made him spend once with my foot the night after Goodwins botchup of a concert so cold and windy it was well we had that rum in the house to mull and the fire wasnt black out when he asked to take off my stockings lying on the hearthrug in Lombard street west and another time it was my muddy boots hed like me to walk in all the horses dung I could find but of course hes not natural like the rest of the world that I what did he say I could give 9 points in 10 to Katty Lanner and beat her what does that mean I asked him I forget what he said because the stoppress edition just passed and the man with the curly hair in the Lucan dairy thats so polite I think I saw his face before somewhere I noticed him when I was tasting the butter so I took my time Bartell dArcy too that he used to make fun of when he commenced kissing me on the choir stairs after I sang Gounods **Ave Maria** what are we waiting for O my heart kiss me straight on the brow and part which is my brown part he was pretty hot for all his tinny voice too my low notes he was always raving about if you can believe him I liked the way he used his mouth singing then he said wasnt it terrible to do that there in a place like that I dont see anything so terrible about it Ill tell him about that some day not now and surprise him ay and Ill take him there and show him the very place too we did it so now there you are like it or lump it he thinks nothing can happen without him knowing he hadnt an idea about my mother till we were engaged otherwise hed never have got me so cheap as he did he was lo times worse himself anyhow begging me to give him a tiny bit cut off my drawers that was the evening coming along Kenilworth square he kissed me in the eye of my glove and I had to take it off asking me questions is it permitted to enquire the shape of my bedroom so I let him keep it as if I forgot it to think of me when I saw him slip it into his pocket of course hes mad on the subject of drawers thats plain to be seen always skeezing at those brazenfaced things on the bicycles with their skirts blowing up to their navels even when Milly and I were out with him at the open air fete that one in the cream muslin standing right against the sun so he could see every atom she had on when he saw me from behind following in the rain I saw him before he saw me however standing at the corner of the Harolds cross road with a new raincoat on him with the muffler in the Zingari colours to show off his complexion and the brown hat looking slyboots as usual what was he doing there where hed no business they can go and get whatever they like from anything at all with a skirt on it and were not to ask any questions but they want to know where were you where are you going I could feel him coming along skulking after me his eyes on my neck he had been keeping away from the house he felt it was getting too warm for him so I halfturned and stopped then he pestered me to say yes till I took off my glove slowly watching him he said my openwork sleeves were too cold for the rain anything for an excuse to put his hand anear me drawers drawers the whole blessed time till I promised to give him the pair off my doll to carry about in his waistcoat pocket **O Maria Santisima** he did look a big fool dreeping in the rain splendid set of teeth he had made me hungry to look at them and beseeched of me to lift the orange petticoat I had on with the sunray pleats that there was nobody he said hed kneel down in the wet if I didnt so persevering he would too and ruin his new raincoat you never know what freak theyd take alone with you theyre so savage for it if anyone was passing so I lifted them a bit and touched his trousers outside the way I used to Gardner after with my ring hand to keep him from doing worse where it was too public I was dying to find out was he circumcised he was shaking like a jelly all over they want to do everything too quick take all the pleasure out of it and father waiting all the time for his dinner he told me to say I left my purse in the butchers and had to go back for it what a Deceiver then he wrote me that letter with all those words in it how could he have the face to any woman after his company manners making it so awkward after when we met asking me have I offended you with my eyelids down of course he saw I wasnt he had a few brains not like that other fool Henny Doyle he was always breaking or tearing something in the charades I hate an unlucky man and if I knew what it meant of course I had to say no for form sake dont understand you I said and wasnt it natural so it is of course it used to be written up with a picture of a womans on that wall in Gibraltar with that word I couldnt find anywhere only for children seeing it too young then writing every morning a letter sometimes twice a day I liked the way he made love then he knew the way to take a woman when he sent me the 8 big poppies because mine was the 8th then I wrote the night he kissed my heart at Dolphins barn I couldnt describe it simply it makes you feel like nothing on earth but he never knew how to embrace well like Gardner I hope hell come on Monday as he said at the same time four I hate people who come at all hours answer the door you think its the vegetables then its somebody and you all undressed or the door of the filthy sloppy kitchen blows open the day old frostyface Goodwin called about the concert in Lombard street and I just after dinner all flushed and tossed with boiling old stew dont look at me professor I had to say Im a fright yes but he was a real old gent in his way it was impossible to be more respectful nobody to say youre out you have to peep out through the blind like the messengerboy today I thought it was a putoff first him sending the port and the peaches first and I was just beginning to yawn with nerves thinking he was trying to make a fool of me when I knew his tattarrattat at the door he must have been a bit late because it was l/4 after 3 when I saw the 2 Dedalus girls coming from school I never know the time even that watch he gave me never seems to go properly Id want to get it looked after when I threw the penny to that lame sailor for England home and beauty when I was whistling there is a charming girl I love and I hadnt even put on my clean shift or powdered myself or a thing then this day week were to go to Belfast just as well he has to go to Ennis his fathers anniversary the 27th it wouldnt be pleasant if he did suppose our rooms at the hotel were beside each other and any fooling went on in the new bed I couldnt tell him to stop and not bother me with him in the next room or perhaps some protestant clergyman with a cough knocking on the wall then hed never believe the next day we didnt do something its all very well a husband but you cant fool a lover after me telling him we never did anything of course he didnt believe me no its better hes going where he is besides something always happens with him the time going to the Mallow concert at Maryborough ordering boiling soup for the two of us then the bell rang out he walks down the platform with the soup splashing about taking spoonfuls of it hadnt he the nerve and the waiter after him making a holy show of us screeching and confusion for the engine to start but he wouldnt pay till he finished it the two gentlemen in the 3rd class carriage said he was quite right so he was too hes so pigheaded sometimes when he gets a thing into his head a good job he was able to open the carriage door with his knife or theyd have taken us on to Cork I suppose that was done out of revenge on him O I love jaunting in a train or a car with lovely soft cushions I wonder will he take a 1st class for me he might want to do it in the train by tipping the guard well O I suppose therell be the usual idiots of men gaping at us with their eyes as stupid as ever they can possibly be that was an exceptional man that common workman that left us alone in the carriage that day going to Howth Id like to find out something about him I or 2 tunnels perhaps then you have to look out of the window all the nicer then coming back suppose I never came back what would they say eloped with him that gets you on on the stage the last concert I sang at where its over a year ago when was it St Teresas hall Clarendon St little chits of missies they have now singing Kathleen Kearney and her like on account of father being in the army and my singing the absentminded beggar and wearing a brooch for Lord Roberts when I had the map of it all and Poldy not Irish enough was it him managed it this time I wouldnt put it past him like he got me on to sing in the **Stabat Mater** by going around saying he was putting Lead Kindly Light to music I put him up to that till the jesuits found out he was a freemason thumping the piano lead Thou me on copied from some old opera yes and he was going about with some of them Sinner Fein lately or whatever they call themselves talking his usual trash and nonsense he says that little man he showed me without the neck is very intelligent the coming man Griffiths is he well he doesnt look it thats all I can say still it must have been him he knew there was a boycott I hate the mention of their politics after the war that Pretoria and Ladysmith and Bloemfontein where Gardner lieut Stanley G 8th Bn 2nd East Lancs Rgt of enteric fever he was a lovely fellow in khaki and just the right height over me Im sure he was brave too he said I was lovely the evening we kissed goodbye at the canal lock my Irish beauty he was pale with excitement about going away or wed be seen from the road he couldnt stand properly and I so hot as I never felt they could have made their peace in the beginning or old oom Paul and the rest of the other old Krugers go and fight it out between them instead of dragging on for years killing any finelooking men there were with their fever if he was even decently shot it wouldnt have been so bad I love to see a regiment pass in review the first time I saw the Spanish cavalry at La Roque it was lovely after looking across the bay from Algeciras all the lights of the rock like fireflies or those sham battles on the 15 acres the Black Watch with their kilts in time at the march past the 10th hussars the prince of Wales own or the lancers O the lancers theyre grand or the Dublins that won Tugela his father made his money over selling the horses for the cavalry well he could buy me a nice present up in Belfast after what I gave him theyve lovely linen up there or one of those nice kimono things I must buy a mothball like I had before to keep in the drawer with them it would be exciting going round with him shopping buying those things in a new city better leave this ring behind want to keep turning and turning to get it over the knuckle there or they might bell it round the town in their papers or tell the police on me but theyd think were married O let them all go and smother themselves for the fat lot I care he has plenty of money and hes not a marrying man so somebody better get it out of him if I could find out whether he likes me I looked a bit washy of course when I looked close in the handglass powdering a mirror never gives you the expression besides scrooching down on me like that all the time with his big hipbones hes heavy too with his hairy chest for this heat always having to lie down for them better for him put it into me from behind the way Mrs Mastiansky told me her husband made her like the dogs do it and stick out her tongue as far as ever she could and he so quiet and mild with his tingating cither can you ever be up to men the way it takes them lovely stuff in that blue suit he had on and stylish tie and socks with the skyblue silk things on them hes certainly well off I know by the cut his clothes have and his heavy watch but he was like a perfect devil for a few minutes after he came back with the stoppress tearing up the tickets and swearing blazes because he lost 20 quid he said he lost over that outsider that won and half he put on for me on account of Lenehans tip cursing him to the lowest pits that sponger he was making free with me after the Glencree dinner coming back that long joult over the featherbed mountain after the lord Mayor looking at me with his dirty eyes Val Dillon that big heathen I first noticed him at dessert when I was cracking the nuts with my teeth I wished I could have picked every morsel of that chicken out of my fingers it was so tasty and browned and as tender as anything only for I didnt want to eat everything on my plate those forks and fishslicers were hallmarked silver too I wish I had some I could easily have slipped a couple into my muff when I was playing with them then always hanging out of them for money in a restaurant for the bit you put down your throat we have to be thankful for our mangy cup of tea itself as a great compliment to be noticed the way the world is divided in any case if its going to go on I want at least two other good chemises for one thing and but I dont know what kind of drawers he likes none at all I think didnt he say yes and half the girls in Gibraltar never wore them either naked as God made them that Andalusian singing her Manola she didnt make much secret of what she hadnt yes and the second pair of silkette stockings is laddered after one days wear I could have brought them back to Lewers this morning and kicked up a row and made that one change them only not to upset myself and run the risk of walking into him and ruining the whole thing and one of those kidfitting corsets Id want advertised cheap in the Gentlewoman with elastic gores on the hips he saved the one I have but thats no good what did they say they give a delightful figure line 11/6 obviating that unsightly broad appearance across the lower back to reduce flesh my belly is a bit too big Ill have to knock off the stout at dinner or am I getting too fond of it the last they sent from ORourkes was as flat as a pancake he makes his money easy Larry they call him the old mangy parcel he sent at Xmas a cottage cake and a bottle of hogwash he tried to palm off as claret that he couldnt get anyone to drink God spare his spit for fear hed die of the drouth or I must do a few breathing exercises I wonder is that antifat any good might overdo it the thin ones are not so much the fashion now garters that much I have the violet pair I wore today thats all he bought me out of the cheque he got on the first O no there was the face lotion I finished the last of yesterday that made my skin like new I told him over and over again get that made up in the same place and dont forget it God only knows whether he did after all I said to him 111 know by the bottle anyway if not I suppose 111 only have to wash in my piss like beeftea or chickensoup with some of that opoponax and violet I thought it was beginning to look coarse or old a bit the skin underneath is much finer where it peeled off there on my finger after the burn its a pity it isnt all like that and the four paltry handkerchiefs about 6/- in all sure you cant get on in this world without style all going in food and rent when I get it Ill lash it around I tell you in fine style I always want to throw a handful of tea into the pot measuring and mincing if I buy a pair of old brogues itself do you like those new shoes yes were they Ive no clothes at all the brown costume and the skirt and jacket and the one at the cleaners 3 whats that for any woman cutting up this old hat and patching up the other the men wont look at you and women try to walk on you because they know youve no man then with all the things getting dearer every day for the 4 years more I have of life up to 35 no Im what am I at all 111 be 33 in September will I what O well look at that Mrs Galbraith shes much older than me I saw her when I was out last week her beautys on the wane she was a lovely woman magnificent head of hair on her down to her waist tossing it back like that like Kitty OShea in Grantham street 1st thing I did every morning to look across see her combing it as if she loved it and was full of it pity I only got to know her the day before we left and that Mrs Langtry the jersey lily the prince of Wales was in love with I suppose hes like the first man going the roads only for the name of a king theyre all made the one way only a black mans Id like to try a beauty up to what was she 45 there was some funny story about the jealous old husband what was it at all and an oyster knife he went no he made her wear a kind of a tin thing round her and the prince of Wales yes he had the oyster knife cant be true a thing like that like some of those books he brings me the works of Master Francois Somebody supposed to be a priest about a child born out of her ear because her bumgut fell out a nice word for any priest to write and her a – e as if any fool wouldnt know what that meant I hate that pretending of all things with that old blackguards face on him anybody can see its not true and that Ruby and Fair Tyrants he brought me that twice I remember when I came to page 5 o the part about where she hangs him up out of a hook with a cord flagellate sure theres nothing for a woman in that all invention made up about he drinking the champagne out of her slipper after the ball was over like the infant Jesus in the crib at Inchicore in the Blessed Virgins arms sure no woman could have a child that big taken out of her and I thought first it came out of her side because how could she go to the chamber when she wanted to and she a rich lady of course she felt honoured H R H he was in Gibraltar the year I was born I bet he found lilies there too where he planted the tree he planted more than that in his time he might have planted me too if hed come a bit sooner then I wouldnt be here as I am he ought to chuck that Freeman with the paltry few shillings he knocks out of it and go into an office or something where hed get regular pay or a bank where they could put him up on a throne to count the money all the day of course he prefers plottering about the house so you cant stir with him any side whats your programme today I wish hed even smoke a pipe like father to get the smell of a man or pretending to be mooching about for advertisements when he could have been in Mr Cuffes still only for what he did then sending me to try and patch it up I could have got him promoted there to be the manager he gave me a great mirada once or twice first he was as stiff as the mischief really and truly Mrs Bloom only I felt rotten simply with the old rubbishy dress that I lost the leads out of the tails with no cut in it but theyre coming into fashion again I bought it simply to please him I knew it was no good by the finish pity I changed my mind of going to Todd and Bums as I said and not Lees it was just like the shop itself rummage sale a lot of trash I hate those rich shops get on your nerves nothing kills me altogether only he thinks he knows a great lot about a womans dress and cooking mathering everything he can scour off the shelves into it if I went by his advices every blessed hat I put on does that suit me yes take that thats alright the one like a weddingcake standing up miles off my head he said suited me or the dishcover one coming down on my backside on pins and needles about the shopgirl in that place in Grafton street I had the misfortune to bring him into and she as insolent as ever she could be with her smirk saying Im afraid were giving you too much trouble what shes there for but I stared it out of her yes he was awfully stiff and no wonder but he changed the second time he looked Poldy pigheaded as usual like the soup but I could see him looking very hard at my chest when he stood up to open the door for me it was nice of him to show me out in any case Im extremely sorry Mrs Bloom believe me without making it too marked the first time after him being insulted and me being supposed to be his wife I just half smiled I know my chest was out that way at the door when he said Im extremely sorry and Im sure you were

yes I think he made them a bit firmer sucking them like that so long he made me thirsty titties he calls them I had to laugh yes this one anyhow stiff the nipple gets for the least thing Ill get him to keep that up and Ill take those eggs beaten up with marsala fatten them out for him what are all those veins and things curious the way its made 2 the same in case of twins theyre supposed to represent beauty placed up there like those statues in the museum one of them pretending to hide it with her hand are they so beautiful of course compared with what a man looks like with his two bags full and his other thing hanging down out of him or sticking up at you like a hatrack no wonder they hide it with a cabbageleaf that disgusting Cameron highlander behind the meat market or that other wretch with the red head behind the tree where the statue of the fish used to be when I was passing pretending he was pissing standing out for me to see it with his babyclothes up to one side the Queens own they were a nice lot its well the Surreys relieved them theyre always trying to show it to you every time nearly I passed outside the mens greenhouse near the Harcourt street station just to try some fellow or other trying to catch my eye as if it was I of the 7 wonders of the world O and the stink of those rotten places the night coming home with Poldy after the Comerfords party oranges and lemonade to make you feel nice and watery I went into r of them it was so biting cold I couldnt keep it when was that 93 the canal was frozen yes it was a few months after a pity a couple of the Camerons werent there to see me squatting in the mens place meadero I tried to draw a picture of it before I tore it up like a sausage or something I wonder theyre not afraid going about of getting a kick or a bang of something there the woman is beauty of course thats admitted when he said I could pose for a picture naked to some rich fellow in Holles street when he lost the job in Helys and I was selling the clothes and strumming in the coffee palace would I be like that bath of the nymph with my hair down yes only shes younger or Im a little like that dirty bitch in that Spanish photo he has nymphs used they go about like that I asked him about her and that word met something with hoses in it and he came out with some jawbreakers about the incarnation he never can explain a thing simply the way a body can understand then he goes and burns the bottom out of the pan all for his Kidney this one not so much theres the mark of his teeth still where he tried to bite the nipple I had to scream out arent they fearful trying to hurt you I had a great breast of milk with Milly enough for two what was the reason of that he said I could have got a pound a week as a wet nurse all swelled out the morning that delicate looking student that stopped in no 28 with the Citrons Penrose nearly caught me washing through the window only for I snapped up the towel to my face that was his studenting hurt me they used to weaning her till he got doctor Brady to give me the belladonna prescription I had to get him to suck them they were so hard he said it was sweeter and thicker than cows then he wanted to milk me into the tea well hes beyond everything I declare somebody ought to put him in the budget if I only could remember the I half of the things and write a book out of it the works of Master Poldy yes and its so much smoother the skin much an hour he was at them Im sure by the clock like some kind of a big infant I had at me they want everything in their mouth all the pleasure those men get out of a woman I can feel his mouth O Lord I must stretch myself I wished he was here or somebody to let myself go with and come again like that I feel all fire inside me or if I could dream it when he made me spend the 2nd time tickling me behind with his finger I was coming for about 5 minutes with my legs round him I had to hug him after O Lord I wanted to shout out all sorts of things fuck or shit or anything at all only not to look ugly or those lines from the strain who knows the way hed take it you want to feel your way with a man theyre not all like him thank God some of them want you to be so nice about it

I noticed the contrast he does it and doesnt talk I gave my eyes that look with my hair a bit loose from the tumbling and my tongue between my lips up to him the savage brute Thursday Friday one Saturday two Sunday three O Lord I cant wait till Monday

frseeeeeeeefronnnng train somewhere whistling the strength those engines have in them like big giants and the water rolling all over and out of them all sides like the end of Loves old sweeeetsonnnng the poor men that have to be out all the night from their wives and families in those roasting engines stifling it was today Im glad I burned the half of those old Freemans and Photo Bits leaving things like that lying about hes getting very careless and threw the rest of them up in the W C 111 get him to cut them tomorrow for me instead of having them there for the next year to get a few pence for them have him asking wheres last Januarys paper and all those old overcoats I bundled out of the hall making the place hotter than it is that rain was lovely and refreshing just after my beauty sleep I thought it was going to get like Gibraltar my goodness the heat there before the levanter came on black as night and the glare of the rock standing up in it like a big giant compared with their 3 Rock mountain they think is so great with the red sentries here and there the poplars and they all whitehot and the smell of the rainwater in those tanks watching the sun all the time weltering down on you faded all that lovely frock fathers friend Mrs Stanhope sent me from the B Marche paris what a shame my dearest Doggerina she wrote on it she was very nice whats this her other name was just a p c to tell you I sent the little present have just had a jolly warm bath and feel a very clean dog now enjoyed it wogger she called him wogger wd give anything to be back in Gib and hear you sing Waiting and in old Madrid Concone is the name of those exercises he bought me one of those new some word I couldnt make out shawls amusing things but tear for the least thing still there lovely I think dont you will always think of the lovely teas we had together scrumptious currant scones and raspberry wafers I adore well now dearest Doggerina be sure and write soon kind she left out regards to your father also captain Grove with love yrs affly Hester x x x x x she didnt look a bit married just like a girl he was years older than her wogger he was awfully fond of me when he held down the wire with his foot for me to step over at the bullfight at La Linea when that matador Gomez was given the bulls ear these clothes we have to wear whoever invented them expecting you to walk up Killiney hill then for example at that picnic all staysed up you cant do a blessed thing in them in a crowd run or jump out of the way thats why I was afraid when that other ferocious old Bull began to charge the banderilleros with the sashes and the 2 things in their hats and the brutes of men shouting bravo toro sure the women were as bad in their nice white mantillas ripping all the whole insides out of those poor horses I never heard of such a thing in all my life yes he used to break his heart at me taking off the dog barking in bell lane poor brute and it sick what became of them ever I suppose theyre dead long ago the 2 of them its like all through a mist makes you feel so old I made the scones of course I had everything all to myself then a girl Hester we used to compare our hair mine was thicker than hers she showed me how to settle it at the back when I put it up and whats this else how to make a knot on a thread with the one hand we were like cousins what age was I then the night of the storm I slept in her bed she had her arms round me then we were fighting in the morning with the pillow what fun he was watching me whenever he got an opportunity at the band on the Alameda esplanade when I was with father and captain Grove I looked up at the church first and then at the windows then down and our eyes met I felt something go through me like all needles my eyes were dancing I remember after when I looked at myself in the glass hardly recognised myself the change he was attractive to a girl in spite of his being a little bald intelligent looking disappointed and gay at the same time he was like Thomas in the shadow of Ashlydyat I had a splendid skin from the sun and the excitement like a rose I didnt get a wink of sleep it wouldnt have been nice on account of her but I could have stopped it in time she gave me the Moonstone to read that was the first I read of Wilkie Collins East Lynne I read and the shadow of Ashlydyat Mrs Henry Wood Henry Dunbar by that other woman I lent him afterwards with Mulveys photo in it so as he see I wasnt without and Lord Lytton Eugene Aram Molly bawn she gave me by Mrs Hungerford on account of the name I dont like books with a Molly in them like that one he brought me about the one from Flanders a whore always shoplifting anything she could cloth and stuff and yards of it O this blanket is too heavy on me thats better I havent even one decent nightdress this thing gets all rolled under me besides him and his fooling thats better I used to be weltering then in the heat my shift drenched with the sweat stuck in the cheeks of my bottom on the chair when I stood up they were so fattish and firm when I got up on the sofa cushions to see with my clothes up and the bugs tons of them at night and the mosquito nets I couldnt read a line Lord how long ago it seems centuries of course they never came back and she didnt put her address right on it either she may have noticed her wogger people were always going away and we never I remember that day with the waves and the boats with their high heads rocking and the smell of ship those Officers uniforms on shore leave made me seasick he didnt say anything he was very serious I had the high buttoned boots on and my skirt was blowing she kissed me six or seven times didnt I cry yes I believe I did or near it my lips were taittering when I said goodbye she had a Gorgeous wrap of some special kind of blue colour on her for the voyage made very peculiarly to one side like and it was extremely pretty it got as dull as the devil after they went I was almost planning to run away mad out of it somewhere were never easy where we are father or aunt or marriage waiting always waiting to guiiiide him toooo me waiting nor speeeed his flying feet their damn guns bursting and booming all over the shop especially the Queens birthday and throwing everything down in all directions if you didnt open the windows when general Ulysses Grant whoever he was or did supposed to be some great fellow landed off the ship and old Sprague the consul that was there from before the flood dressed up poor man and he in mourning for the son then the same old bugles for reveille in the morning and drums rolling and the unfortunate poor devils of soldiers walking about with messtins smelling the place more than the old longbearded jews in their jellibees and levites assembly and sound clear and gunfire for the men to cross the lines and the warden marching with his keys to lock the gates and the bagpipes and only captain Groves and father talking about Rorkes drift and Plevna and sir Garnet Wolseley and Gordon at Khartoum lighting their pipes for them everytime they went out drunken old devil with his grog on the windowsill catch him leaving any of it picking his nose trying to think of some other dirty story to tell up in a corner but he never forgot himself when I was there sending me out of the room on some blind excuse paying his compliments the Bushmills whisky talking of course but hed do the same to the next woman that came along I suppose he died of galloping drink ages ago the days like years not a letter from a living soul except the odd few I posted to myself with bits of paper in them so bored sometimes I could fight with my nails listening to that old Arab with the one eye and his heass of an instrument singing his heah heah aheah all my compriments on your hotchapotch of your heass as bad as now with the hands hanging off me looking out of the window if there was a nice fellow even in the opposite house that medical in Holles street the nurse was after when I put on my gloves and hat at the window to show I was going out not a notion what I meant arent they thick never understand what you say even youd want to print it up on a big poster for them not even if you shake hands twice with the left he didnt recognise me either when I half frowned at him outside Westland row chapel where does their great intelligence come in Id like to know grey matter they have it all in their tail if you ask me those country gougers up in the City Arms intelligence they had a damn sight less than the bulls and cows they were selling the meat and the coalmans bell that noisy bugger trying to swindle me with the wrong bill he took out of his hat what a pair of paws and pots and pans and kettles to mend any broken bottles for a poor man today and no visitors or post ever except his cheques or some advertisement like that wonderworker they sent him addressed dear Madam only his letter and the card from Milly this morning see she wrote a letter to him who did I get the last letter from O Mrs Dwenn now what possessed her to write from Canada after so many years to know the recipe I had for pisto madrileno Floey Dillon since she wrote to say she was married to a very rich architect if Im to believe all I hear with a villa and eight rooms her father was an awfully nice man he was near seventy always goodhumoured well now Miss Tweedy or Miss Gillespie theres the piannyer that was a solid silver coffee service he had too on the mahogany sideboard then dying so far away I hate people that have always their poor story to tell everybody has their own troubles that poor Nancy Blake died a month ago of acute neumonia well I didnt know her so well as all that she was Floeys friend more than mine poor Nancy its a bother having to answer he always tells me the wrong things and no stops to say like making a speech your sad bereavement symphathy I always make that mistake and newphew with 2 double yous in I hope hell write me a longer letter the next time if its a thing he really likes me O thanks be to the great God I got somebody to give me what I badly wanted to put some heart up into me youve no chances at all in this place like you used long ago I wish somebody would write me a loveletter his wasnt much and I told him he could write what he liked yours ever Hugh Boylan in old Madrid stuff silly women believe love is sighing I am dying still if he wrote it I suppose thered be some truth in it true or no it fills up your whole day and life always something to think about every moment and see it all round you like a new world I could write the answer in bed to let him imagine me short just a few words not those long crossed letters Atty Dillon used to write to the fellow that was something in the four courts that jilted her after out of the ladies letterwriter when I told her to say a few simple words he could twist how he liked not acting with precipat precip itancy with equal candour the greatest earthly happiness answer to a gentlemans proposal affirmatively my goodness theres nothing else its all very fine for them but as for being a woman as soon as youre old they might as well throw you out in the bottom of the ashpit.

Mulveys was the first when I was in bed that morning and Mrs Rubio brought it in with the coffee she stood there standing when I asked her to hand me and I pointing at them I couldnt think of the word a hairpin to open it with ah horquilla disobliging old thing and it staring her in the face with her switch of false hair on her and vain about her appearance ugly as she was near 80 or a loo her face a mass of wrinkles with all her religion domineering because she never could get over the Atlantic fleet coming in half the ships of the world and the Union Jack flying with all her carabineros because 4 drunken English sailors took all the rock from them and because I didnt run into mass often enough in Santa Maria to please her with her shawl up on her except when there was a marriage on with all her miracles of the saints and her black blessed virgin with the silver dress and the sun dancing 3 times on Easter Sunday morning and when the priest was going by with the bell bringing the vatican to the dying blessing herself for his Majestad an admirer he signed it I near jumped out of my skin I wanted to pick him up when I saw him following me along the Calle Real in the shop window then he tipped me just in passing but I never thought hed write making an appointment I had it inside my petticoat bodice all day reading it up in every hole and corner while father was up at the drill instructing to find out by the handwriting or the language of stamps singing I remember shall I wear a white rose and I wanted to put on the old stupid clock to near the time he was the first man kissed me under the Moorish wall my sweetheart when a boy it never entered my head what kissing meant till he put his tongue in my mouth his mouth was sweetlike young I put my knee up to him a few times to learn the way what did I tell him I was engaged for for fun to the son of a Spanish nobleman named Don Miguel de la Flora and he believed me that I was to be married to him in 3 years time theres many a true word spoken in jest there is a flower that bloometh a few things I told him true about myself just for him to be imagining the Spanish girls he didnt like I suppose one of them wouldnt have him I got him excited he crushed all the flowers on my bosom he brought me he couldnt count the pesetas and the perragordas till I taught him Cappoquin he came from he said on the black water but it was too short then the day before he left May yes it was May when the infant king of Spain was born Im always like that in the spring Id like a new fellow every year up on the tiptop under the rockgun near OHaras tower I told him it was struck by lightning and all about the old Barbary apes they sent to Clapham without a tail careering all over the show on each others back Mrs Rubio said she was a regular old rock scorpion robbing the chickens out of Inces farm and throw stones at you if you went anear he was looking at me I had that white blouse on open in the front to encourage him as much as I could without too openly they were just beginning to be plump I said I was tired we lay over the firtree cove a wild place I suppose it must be the highest rock in existence the galleries and casemates and those frightful rocks and Saint Michaels cave with the icicles or whatever they call them hanging down and ladders all the mud plotching my boots Im sure thats the way down the monkeys go under the sea to Africa when they die the ships out far like chips that was the Malta boat passing yes the sea and the sky you could do what you liked lie there for ever he caressed them outside they love doing that its the roundness there I was leaning over him with my white ricestraw hat to take the newness out of it the left side of my face the best my blouse open for his last day transparent kind of shirt he had I could see his chest pink he wanted to touch mine with his for a moment but I wouldnt lee him he was awfully put out first for fear you never know consumption or leave me with a child embarazada that old servant Ines told me that one drop even if it got into you at all after I tried with the Banana but I was afraid it might break and get lost up in me somewhere because they once took something down out of a woman that was up there for years covered with limesalts theyre all mad to get in there where they come out of youd think they could never go far enough up and then theyre done with you in a way till the next time yes because theres a wonderful feeling there so tender all the time how did we finish it off yes O yes I pulled him off into my handkerchief pretending not to be excited but I opened my legs I wouldnt let him touch me inside my petticoat because I had a skirt opening up the side I tormented the life out of him first tickling him I loved rousing that dog in the hotel rrrsssstt awokwokawok his eyes shut and a bird flying below us he was shy all the same I liked him like that moaning I made him blush a little when I got over him that way when I unbuttoned him and took his out and drew back the skin it had a kind of eye in it theyre all Buttons men down the middle on the wrong side of them Molly darling he called me what was his name Jack Joe Harry Mulvey was it yes I think a lieutenant he was rather fair he had a laughing kind of a voice so I went round to the whatyoucallit everything was whatyoucallit moustache had he he said hed come back Lord its just like yesterday to me and if I was married hed do it to me and I promised him yes faithfully Id let him block me now flying perhaps hes dead or killed or a captain or admiral its nearly 20 years if I said firtree cove he would if he came up behind me and put his hands over my eyes to guess who I might recognise him hes young still about 40 perhaps hes married some girl on the black water and is quite changed they all do they havent half the character a woman has she little knows what I did with her beloved husband before he ever dreamt of her in broad daylight too in the sight of the whole world you might say they could have put an article about it in the Chronicle I was a bit wild after when I blew out the old bag the biscuits were in from Benady Bros and exploded it Lord what a bang all the woodcocks and pigeons screaming coming back the same way that we went over middle hill round by the old guardhouse and the jews burialplace pretending to read out the Hebrew on them I wanted to fire his pistol he said he hadnt one he didnt know what to make of me with his peak cap on that he always wore crooked as often as I settled it straight H M S Calypso swinging my hat that old Bishop that spoke off the altar his long preach about womans higher functions about girls now riding the bicycle and wearing peak caps and the new woman bloomers God send him sense and me more money I suppose theyre called after him I never thought that would be my name Bloom when I used to write it in print to see how it looked on a visiting card or practising for the butcher and oblige M Bloom youre looking blooming Josie used to say after I married him well its better than

Breen or Briggs does brig or those awful names with bottom in them Mrs Ramsbottom or some other kind of a bottom Mulvey I wouldnt go mad about either or suppose I divorced him Mrs Boylan my mother whoever she was might have given me a nicer name the Lord knows after the lovely one she had Lunita Laredo the fun we had running along Williss road to Europa point twisting in and out all round the other side of Jersey they were shaking and dancing about in my blouse like Millys little ones now when she runs up the stairs I loved looking down at them I was jumping up at the pepper trees and the white poplars pulling the leaves off and throwing them at him he went to India he was to write the voyages those men have to make to the ends of the world and back its the least they might get a squeeze or two at a woman while they can going out to be drowned or blown up somewhere I went up Windmill hill to the flats that Sunday morning with captain

Rubios that was dead spyglass like the sentry had he said hed have one or two from on board I wore that frock from the B Marche paris and the coral necklace the straits shining I could see over to Morocco almost the bay of Tangier white and the Atlas mountain with snow on it and the straits like a river so clear Harry Molly darling I was thinking of him on the sea all the time after at mass when my petticoat began to slip down at the elevation weeks and weeks I kept the handkerchief under my pillow for the smell of him there was no decent perfume to be got in that Gibraltar only that cheap peau dEspagne that faded and left a stink on you more than anything else I wanted to give him a memento he gave me that clumsy Claddagh ring for luck that I gave Gardner going to south Africa where those Boers killed him with their war and fever but they were well beaten all the same as if it brought its bad luck with it like an opal or pearl still it must have been pure 18 carrot gold because it was very heavy but what could you get in a place like that the sandfrog shower from Africa and that derelict ship that came up to the harbour Marie the Marie whatyoucallit no he hadnt a moustache that was Gardner yes I can see his face cleanshaven Frseeeeeeeeeeeeeeeeeeeefrong that train again weeping tone once in the dear deaead days beyondre call close my eyes breath my lips forward kiss sad look eyes open piano ere oer the world the mists began I hate that istsbeg comes loves sweet sooooooooooong Ill let that out full when I get in front of the footlights again Kathleen Kearney and her lot of squealers Miss This Miss That Miss Theother lot of sparrowfarts skitting around talking about politics they know as much about as my backside anything in the world to make themselves someway interesting Irish homemade beauties soldiers daughter am I ay and whose are you bootmakers and publicans I beg your pardon coach I thought you were a wheelbarrow theyd die down dead off their feet if ever they got a chance of walking down the Alameda on an officers arm like me on the bandnight my eyes flash my bust that they havent passion God help their poor head I knew more about men and life when I was I S than theyll all know at 50 they dont know how to sing a song like that Gardner said no man could look at my mouth and teeth smiling like that and not think of it I was afraid he mightnt like my accent first he so English all father left me in spite of his stamps Ive my mothers eyes and figure anyhow he always said theyre so snotty about themselves some of those cads he wasnt a bit like that he was dead gone on my lips let them get a husband first thats fit to be looked at and a daughter like mine or see if they can excite a swell with money that can pick and choose whoever he wants like Boylan to do it 4 or 5 times locked in each others arms or the voice either I could have been a prima donna only I married him comes looooves old deep down chin back not too much make it double My Ladys Bower is too long for an encore about the moated grange at twilight and vaunted rooms yes Ill sing Winds that blow from the south that he gave after the choirstairs performance Ill change that lace on my black dress to show off my bubs and Ill yes by God Ill get that big fan mended make them burst with envy my hole is itching me always when I think of him I feel I want to I feel some wind in me better go easy not wake him have him at it again slobbering after washing every bit of myself back belly and sides if we had even a bath itself or my own room anyway I wish hed sleep in some bed by himself with his cold feet on me give us room even to let a fart God or do the least thing better yes hold them like that a bit on my side piano quietly sweeeee theres that train far away pianissimo eeeee one more song that was a relief wherever you be let your wind go free who knows if that pork chop I took with my cup of tea after was quite good with the heat I couldnt smell anything off it Im sure that queerlooking man in the porkbutchers is a great rogue I hope that lamp is not smoking fill my nose up with smuts better than having him leaving the gas on all night I couldnt rest easy in my bed in Gibraltar even getting up to see why am I so damned nervous about that though I like it in the winter its more company O Lord it was rotten cold too that winter when I was only about ten was I yes I had the big doll with all the funny clothes dressing her up and undressing that icy wind skeeting across from those mountains the something Nevada sierra nevada standing at the fire with the little bit of a short shift I had up to heat myself I loved dancing about in it then make a race back into bed Im sure that fellow opposite used to be there the whole time watching with the lights out in the summer and I in my skin hopping around I used to love myself then stripped at the washstand dabbing and creaming only when it came to the chamber performance I put out the light too so then there were 2 of us goodbye to my sleep for this night anyhow I hope hes not going to get in with those medicals leading him astray to imagine hes young again coming in at 4 in the morning it must be if not more still he had the manners not to wake me what do they find to gabber about all night squandering money and getting drunker and drunker couldnt they drink water then he starts giving us his orders for eggs and tea and Findon haddy and hot buttered toast I suppose well have him sitting up like the king of the country pumping the wrong end of the spoon up and down in his egg wherever he learned that from and I love to hear him falling up the stairs of a morning with the cups rattling on the tray and then play with the cat she rubs up against you for her own sake I wonder has she fleas shes as bad as a woman always licking and lecking but I hate their claws I wonder do they see anything that we cant staring like that when she sits at the top of the stairs so long and listening as I wait always what a robber too that lovely fresh place I bought I think Ill get a bit of fish tomorrow or today is it Friday yes I will with some blancmange with black currant jam like long ago not those 2 lb pots of mixed plum and apple from the London and Newcastle Williams and Woods goes twice as far only for the bones I hate those eels cod yes Ill get a nice piece of cod Im always getting enough for 3 forgetting anyway Im sick of that everlasting butchers meat from Buckleys loin chops and leg beef and rib steak and scrag of mutton and calfs pluck the very name is enough or a picnic suppose we all gave 5/- each and or let him pay it and invite some other woman for him who Mrs Fleming and drove out to the furry glen or the strawberry beds wed have him examining all the horses toenails first like he does with the letters no not with Boylan there yes with some cold veal and ham mixed sandwiches there are little houses down at the bottom of the banks there on purpose but its as hot as blazes he says not a bank holiday anyhow I hate those ruck of Mary Ann coalboxes out for the day Whit Monday is a cursed day too no wonder that bee bit him better the seaside but Id never again in this life get into a boat with him after him at Bray telling the boatman he knew how to row if anyone asked could he ride the steeplechase for the gold cup hed say yes then it came on to get rough the old thing crookeding about and the weight all down my side telling me pull the right reins now pull the left and the tide all swamping in floods in through the bottom and his oar slipping out of the stirrup its a mercy we werent all drowned he can swim of course me no theres no danger whatsoever keep yourself calm in his flannel trousers Id like to have tattered them down off him before all the people and give him what that one calls flagellate till he was black and blue do him all the good in the world only for that longnosed chap I dont know who he is with that other beauty Burke out of the City Arms hotel was there spying around as usual on the slip always where he wasnt wanted if there was a row on youd vomit a better face there was no love lost between us thats 1 consolation I wonder what kind is that book he brought me Sweets of Sin by a gentleman of fashion some other Mr de Kock I suppose the people gave him that nickname going about with his tube from one woman to another I couldnt even change my new white shoes all ruined with the saltwater and the hat I had with that feather all blowy and tossed on me how annoying and provoking because the smell of the sea excited me of course the sardines and the bream in Catalan bay round the back of the rock they were fine all silver in the fishermens baskets old Luigi near a hundred they said came from

Genoa and the tall old chap with the earrings I dont like a man you have to climb up to to get at I suppose theyre all dead and rotten long ago besides I dont like being alone in this big barracks of a place at night I suppose Ill have to put up with it I never brought a bit of salt in even when we moved in the confusion musical academy he was going to make on the first floor drawingroom with a brassplate or Blooms private hotel he suggested go and ruin himself altogether the way his father did down in Ennis like all the things he told father he was going to do and me but I saw through him telling me all the lovely places we could go for the honeymoon Venice by moonlight with the gondolas and the lake of Como he had a picture cut out of some paper of and mandolines and lanterns O how nice I said whatever I liked he was going to do immediately if not sooner will you be my man will you carry my can he ought to get a leather medal with a putty rim for all the plans he invents then leaving us here all day youd never know what old beggar at the door for a crust with his long story might be a tramp and put his foot in the way to prevent me shutting it like that picture of that hardened criminal he was called in Lloyds Weekly news 20 years in jail then he comes out and murders an old woman for her money imagine his poor wife or mother or whoever she is such a face youd run miles away from I couldnt rest easy till I bolted all the doors and windows to make sure but its worse again being locked up like in a prison or a madhouse they ought to be all shot or the cat of nine tails a big brute like that that would attack a poor old woman to murder her in her bed Id cut them off him so I would not that hed be much use still better than nothing the night I was sure I heard burglars in the kitchen and he went down in his shirt with a candle and a poker as if he was looking for a mouse as white as a sheet frightened out of his wits making as much noise as he possibly could for the burglars benefit there isnt much to steal indeed the Lord knows still its the feeling especially now with Milly away such an idea for him to send the girl down there to learn to take photographs on account of his grandfather instead of sending her to Skerrys academy where shed have to learn not like me getting all IS at school only hed do a thing like that all the same on account of me and Boylan thats why he did it Im certain the way he plots and plans everything out I couldnt turn round with her in the place lately unless I bolted the door first gave me the fidgets coming in without knocking first when I put the chair against the door just as I was washing myself there below with the glove get on your nerves then doing the loglady all day put her in a glasscase with two at a time to look at her if he knew she broke off the hand off that little gimcrack statue with her roughness and carelessness before she left that I got that little Italian boy to mend so that you cant see the join for 2 shillings wouldnt even teem the potatoes for you of course shes right not to ruin her hands I noticed he was always talking to her lately at the table explaining things in the paper and she pretending to understand sly of course that comes from his side of the house he cant say I pretend things can he Im too honest as a matter of fact and helping her into her coat but if there was anything wrong with her its me shed tell not him I suppose he thinks Im finished out and laid on the shelf well Im not no nor anything like it well see well see now shes well on for flirting too with Tom Devans two sons imitating me whistling with those romps of Murray girls calling for her can Milly come out please shes in great demand to pick what they can out of her round in Nelson street riding Harry Devans bicycle at night its as well he sent her where she is she was just getting out of bounds wanting to go on the skatingrink and smoking their cigarettes through their nose I smelt it off her dress when I was biting off the thread of the button I sewed on to the bottom of her jacket she couldnt hide much from me I tell you only I oughtnt to have stitched it and it on her it brings a parting and the last plumpudding too split in 2 halves see it comes out no matter what they say her tongue is a bit too long for my taste your blouse is open too low she says to me the pan calling the kettle blackbottom and I had to tell her not to cock her legs up like that on show on the windowsill before all the people passing they all look at her like me when I was her age of course any old rag looks well on you then a great touchmenot too in her own way at the Only Way in the Theatre royal take your foot away out of that I hate people touching me afraid of her life Id crush her skirt with the pleats a lot of that touching must go on in theatres in the crush in the dark theyre always trying to wiggle up to you that fellow in the pit at the Gaiety for Beerbohm Tree in Trilby the last time Ill ever go there to be squashed like that for any Trilby or her barebum every two minutes tipping me there and looking away hes a bit daft I think I saw him after trying to get near two stylishdressed ladies outside Switzers window at the same little game I recognised him on the moment the face and everything but he didnt remember me yes and she didnt even want me to kiss her at the Broadstone going away well I hope shell get someone to dance attendance on her the way I did when she was down with the mumps and her glands swollen wheres this and wheres that of course she cant feel anything deep yet I never came properly till I was what 22 or so it went into the wrong place always only the usual girls nonsense and giggling that Conny Connolly writing to her in white ink on black paper sealed with sealingwax though she clapped when the curtain came down because he looked so handsome then we had Martin Harvey for breakfast dinner and supper I thought to myself afterwards it must be real love if a man gives up his life for her that way for nothing I suppose there are a few men like that left its hard to believe in it though unless it really happened to me the majority of them with not a particle of love in their natures to find two people like that nowadays full up of each other that would feel the same way as you do theyre usually a bit foolish in the head his father must have been a bit queer to go and poison himself after her still poor old man I suppose he felt lost shes always making love to my things too the few old rags I have wanting to put her hair up at I S my powder too only ruin her skin on her shes time enough for that all her life after of course shes restless knowing shes pretty with her lips so red a pity they wont stay that way I was too but theres no use going to the fair with the thing answering me like a fishwoman when I asked to go for a half a stone of potatoes the day we met Mrs Joe Gallaher at the trottingmatches and she pretended not to see us in her trap with Friery the solicitor we werent grand enough till I gave her 2 damn fine cracks across the ear for herself take that now for answering me like that and that for your impudence she had me that exasperated of course contradicting I was badtempered too because how was it there was a weed in the tea or I didnt sleep the night before cheese I ate was it and I told her over and over again not to leave knives crossed like that because she has nobody to command her as she said herself well if he doesnt correct her faith I will that was the last time she turned on the teartap I was just like that myself they darent order me about the place its his fault of course having the two of us slaving here instead of getting in a woman long ago am I ever going to have a proper servant again of course then shed see him coming Id have to let her know or shed revenge it arent they a nuisance that old Mrs Fleming you have to be walking round after her putting the things into her hands sneezing and farting into the pots well of course shes old she cant help it a good job I found that rotten old smelly dishcloth that got lost behind the dresser I knew there was something and opened the area window to let out the smell bringing in his friends to entertain them like the night he walked home with a dog if you please that might have been mad especially Simon Dedalus son his father such a criticiser with his glasses up with his tall hat on him at the cricket match and a great big hole in his sock one thing laughing at the other and his son that got all those prizes for whatever he won them in the intermediate imagine climbing over the railings if anybody saw him that knew us I wonder he didnt tear a big hole in his grand funeral trousers as if the one nature gave wasnt enough for anybody hawking him down into the dirty old kitchen now is he right in his head I ask pity it wasnt washing day my old pair of drawers might have been hanging up too on the line on exhibition for all hed ever care with the ironmould mark the stupid old bundle burned on them he might think was something else and she never even rendered down the fat I told her and now shes going such as she was on account of her paralysed husband getting worse theres always something wrong with them disease or they have to go under an operation or if its not that its drink and he beats her Ill have to hunt around again for someone every day I get up theres some new thing on sweet God sweet God well when Im stretched out dead in my grave I suppose 111 have some peace I want to get up a minute if Im let wait O Jesus wait yes that thing has come on me yes now wouldnt that afflict you of course all the poking and rooting and ploughing he had up in me now what am I to do Friday Saturday Sunday wouldnt that pester the soul out of a body unless he likes it some men do God knows theres always something wrong with us 5 days every 3 or 4 weeks usual monthly auction isnt it simply sickening that night it came on me like that the one and only time we were in a box that Michael Gunn gave him to see Mrs Kendal and her husband at the Gaiety something he did about insurance for him in Drimmies I was fit to be tied though I wouldnt give in with that gentleman of fashion staring down at me with his glasses and him the other side of me talking about Spinoza and his soul thats dead I suppose millions of years ago I smiled the best I could all in a swamp leaning forward as if I was interested having to sit it out then to the last tag I wont forget that wife of Scarli in a hurry supposed to be a fast play about adultery that idiot in the gallery hissing the woman adulteress he shouted I suppose he went and had a woman in the next lane running round all the back ways after to make up for it I wish he had what I had then hed boo I bet the cat itself is better off than us have we too much blood up in us or what O patience above its pouring out of me like the sea anyhow he didnt make me pregnant as big as he is I dont want to ruin the clean sheets I just put on I suppose the clean linen I wore brought it on too damn it damn it and they always want to see a stain on the bed to know youre a virgin for them all thats troubling them theyre such fools too you could be a widow or divorced 40 times over a daub of red ink would do or blackberry juice no thats too purply O Jamesy let me up out of this pooh sweets of sin whoever suggested that business for women what between clothes and cooking and children this damned old bed too jingling like the dickens I suppose they could hear us away over the other side of the park till I suggested to put the quilt on the floor with the pillow under my bottom I wonder is it nicer in the day I think it is easy I think Ill cut all this hair off me there scalding me I might look like a young girl wouldnt he get the great suckin the next time he turned up my clothes on me Id give anything to see his face wheres the chamber gone easy Ive a holy horror of its breaking under me after that old commode I wonder was I too heavy sitting on his knee I made him sit on the easychair purposely when I took off only my blouse and skirt first in the other room he was so busy where he oughtnt to be he never felt me I hope my breath was sweet after those kissing comfits easy God I remember one time I could scout it out straight whistling like a man almost easy O Lord how noisy I hope theyre bubbles on it for a wad of money from some fellow 111 have to perfume it in the morning dont forget I bet he never saw a better pair of thighs than that look how white they are the smoothest place is right there between this bit here how soft like a peach easy God I wouldnt mind being a man and get up on a lovely woman O Lord what a row youre making like the jersey lily easy easy O how the waters come down at Lahore who knows is there anything the matter with my insides or have I something growing in me getting that thing like that every week when was it last I Whit Monday yes its only about 3 weeks I ought to go to the doctor only it would be like before I married him when I had that white thing coming from me and Floey made me go to that dry old stick Dr Collins for womens diseases on Pembroke road your vagina he called it I suppose thats how he got all the gilt mirrors and carpets getting round those rich ones off Stephens green running up to him for every little fiddlefaddle her vagina and her cochinchina theyve money of course so theyre all right I wouldnt marry him not if he was the last man in the world besides theres something queer about their children always smelling around those filthy bitches all sides asking me if what I did had an offensive odour what did he want me to do but the one thing gold maybe what a question if I smathered it all over his wrinkly old face for him with all my compriments I suppose hed know then and could you pass it easily pass what I thought he was talking about the rock of Gibraltar the way he put it thats a very nice invention too by the way only I like letting myself down after in the hole as far as I can squeeze and pull the chain then to flush it nice cool pins and needles still theres something in it I suppose I always used to know by Millys when she was a child whether she had worms or not still all the same paying him for that how much is that doctor one guinea please and asking me had I frequent omissions where do those old fellows get all the words they have omissions with his shortsighted eyes on me cocked sideways I wouldnt trust him too far to give me chloroform or God knows what else still I liked him when he sat down to write the thing out frowning so severe his nose intelligent like that you be damned you lying strap O anything no matter who except an idiot he was clever enough to spot that of course that was all thinking of him and his mad crazy letters my Precious one everything connected with your glorious Body everything underlined that comes from it is a thing of beauty and of joy for ever something he got out of some nonsensical book that he had me always at myself 4 and 5 times a day sometimes and I said I hadnt are you sure O yes I said I am quite sure in a way that shut him up I knew what was coming next only natural weakness it was he excited me I dont know how the first night ever we met when I was living in Rehoboth terrace we stood staring at one another for about lo minutes as if we met somewhere I suppose on account of my being jewess looking after my mother he used to amuse me the things he said with the half sloothering smile on him and all the Doyles said he was going to stand for a member of Parliament O wasnt I the born fool to believe all his blather about home rule and the land league sending me that long strool of a song out of the Huguenots to sing in French to be more classy O beau pays de la Touraine that I never even sang once explaining and rigmaroling about religion and persecution he wont let you enjoy anything naturally then might he as a great favour the very 1st opportunity he got a chance in Brighton square running into my bedroom pretending the ink got on his hands to wash it off with the Albion milk and sulphur soap I used to use and the gelatine still round it O I laughed myself sick at him that day I better not make an alnight sitting on this affair they ought to make chambers a natural size so that a woman could sit on it properly he kneels down to do it I suppose there isnt in all creation another man with the habits he has look at the way hes sleeping at the foot of the bed how can he without a hard bolster its well he doesnt kick or he might knock out all my teeth breathing with his hand on his nose like that Indian god he took me to show one wet Sunday in the museum in Kildare street all yellow in a pinafore lying on his side on his hand with his ten toes sticking out that he said was a bigger religion than the jews and Our Lords both put together all over Asia imitating him as hes always imitating everybody I suppose he used to sleep at the foot of the bed too with his big square feet up in his wifes mouth damn this stinking thing anyway wheres this those napkins are ah yes I know I hope the old press doesnt creak ah I knew it would hes sleeping hard had a good time somewhere still she must have given him great value for his money of course he has to pay for it from her O this nuisance of a thing I hope theyll have something better for us in the other world tying ourselves up God help us thats all right for tonight now the lumpy old jingly bed always reminds me of old Cohen I suppose he scratched himself in it often enough and he thinks father bought it from Lord Napier that I used to admire when I was a little girl because I told him easy piano O I like my bed God here we are as bad as ever after 16 years how many houses were we in at all Raymond terrace and Ontario terrace and Lombard street and Holles street and he goes about whistling every time were on the run again his huguenots or the frogs march pretending to help the men with our 4 sticks of furniture and then the City Arms hotel worse and worse says Warden Daly that charming place on the landing always somebody inside praying then leaving all their stinks after them always know who was in there last every time were just getting on right something happens or he puts his big foot in it Thoms and Helys and Mr Cuffes and Drimmies either hes going to be run into prison over his old lottery tickets that was to be all our salvations or he goes and gives impudence well have him coming home with the sack soon out of the Freeman too like the rest on account of those Sinner Fein or the freemasons then well see if the little man he showed me dribbling along in the wet all by himself round by Coadys lane will give him much consolation that he says is so capable and sincerely Irish he is indeed judging by the sincerity of the trousers I saw on him wait theres Georges church bells wait 3 quarters the hour I wait 2 oclock well thats a nice hour of the night for him to be coming home at to anybody climbing down into the area if anybody saw him Ill knock him off that little habit tomorrow first Ill look at his shirt to see or Ill see if he has that French letter still in his pocketbook I suppose he thinks I dont know deceitful men all their 20 pockets arent enough for their lies then why should we tell them even if its the truth they dont believe you then tucked up in bed like those babies in the Aristocrats Masterpiece he brought me another time as if we hadnt enough of that in real life without some old Aristocrat or whatever his name is disgusting you more with those rotten pictures children with two heads and no legs thats the kind of villainy theyre always dreaming about with not another thing in their empty heads they ought to get slow poison the half of them then tea and toast for him buttered on both sides and newlaid eggs I suppose Im nothing any more when I wouldnt let him lick me in Holles street one night man man tyrant as ever for the one thing he slept on the floor half the night naked the way the jews used when somebody dies belonged to them and wouldnt eat any breakfast or speak a word wanting to be petted so I thought I stood out enough for one time and let him he does it all wrong too thinking only of his own pleasure his tongue is too flat or I dont know what he forgets that wethen I dont Ill make him do it again if he doesnt mind himself and lock him down to sleep in the coalcellar with the blackbeetles I wonder was it her Josie off her head with my castoffs hes such a born liar too no hed never have the courage with a married woman thats why he wants me and Boylan though as for her Denis as she calls him that forlornlooking spectacle you couldnt call him a husband yes its some little bitch hes got in with even when I was with him with Milly at the College races that Hornblower with the childs bonnet on the top of his nob let us into by the back way he was throwing his sheeps eyes at those two doing skirt duty up and down I tried to wink at him first no use of course and thats the way his money goes this is the fruits of Mr Paddy Dignam yes they were all in great style at the grand funeral in the paper Boylan brought in if they saw a real officers funeral thatd be something reversed arms muffled drums the poor horse walking behind in black L Boom and Tom Kernan that drunken little barrelly man that bit his tongue off falling down the mens W C drunk in some place or other and Martin Cunningham and the two Dedaluses and Fanny MCoys husband white head of cabbage skinny thing with a turn in her eye trying to sing my songs shed want to be born all over again and her old green dress with the lowneck as she cant attract them any other way like dabbling on a rainy day I see it all now plainly and they call that friendship killing and then burying one another and they all with their wives and families at home more especially Jack Power keeping that barmaid he does of course his wife is always sick or going to be sick or just getting better of it and hes a goodlooking man still though hes getting a bit grey over the ears theyre a nice lot all of them well theyre not going to get my husband again into their clutches if I can help it making fun of him then behind his back I know well when he goes on with his idiotics because he has sense enough not to squander every penny piece he earns down their gullets and looks after his wife and family goodfornothings poor Paddy Dignam all the same Im sorry in a way for him what are his wife and 5 children going to do unless he was insured comical little teetotum always stuck up in some pub corner and her or her son waiting Bill Bailey wont you please come home her widows weeds wont improve her appearance theyre awfully becoming though if youre goodlooking what men wasnt he yes he was at the

Glencree dinner and Ben Dollard base barreltone the night he borrowed the swallowtail to sing out of in Holles street squeezed and squashed into them and grinning all over his big Dolly face like a wellwhipped childs botty didnt he look a balmy ballocks sure enough that must have been a spectacle on the stage imagine paying 5/- in the preserved seats for that to see him trotting off in his trowlers and Simon Dedalus too he was always turning up half screwed singing the second verse first the old love is the new was one of his so sweetly sang the maiden on the hawthorn bough he was always on for flirtyfying too when I sang Maritana with him at Freddy Mayers private opera he had a delicious glorious voice Phoebe dearest goodbye **sweet**heart sweetheart he always sang it not like Bartell Darcy sweet tart goodbye of course he had the gift of the voice so there was no art in it all over you like a warm showerbath O Maritana wildwood flower we sang splendidly though it was a bit too high for my register even transposed and he was married at the time to May Goulding but then hed say or do something to knock the good out of it hes a widower now I wonder what sort is his son he says hes an author and going to be a university professor of Italian and Im to take lessons what is he driving at now showing him my photo its not good of me I ought to have got it taken in drapery that never looks out of fashion still I look young in it I wonder he didnt make him a present of it altogether and me too after all why not I saw him driving down to the Kingsbridge station with his father and mother I was in mourning thats 11 years ago now yes hed be 11 though what was the good in going into mourning for what was neither one thing nor the other the first cry was enough for me I heard the deathwatch too ticking in the wall of course he insisted hed go into mourning for the cat I suppose hes a man now by this time he was an innocent boy then and a darling little fellow in his lord Fauntleroy suit and curly hair like a prince on the stage when I saw him at Mat Dillons he liked me too I remember they all do wait by God yes wait yes hold on he was on the cards this morning when I laid out the deck union with a young stranger neither dark nor fair you met before I thought it meant him but hes no chicken nor a stranger either besides my face was turned the other way what was the 7th card after that the 10 of spades for a journey by land then there was a letter on its way and scandals too the 3 queens and the 8 of diamonds for a rise in society yes wait it all came out and 2 red 8s for new garments look at that and didnt I dream something too yes there was something about poetry in it I hope he hasnt long greasy hair hanging into his eyes or standing up like a red Indian what do they go about like that for only getting themselves and their poetry laughed at I always liked poetry when I was a girl first I thought he was a poet like lord Byron and not an ounce of it in his composition I thought he was quite different I wonder is he too young hes about wait 88 I was married 88 Milly is 15 yesterday 89 what age was he then at Dillons 5 or 6 about 88 I suppose hes 20 or more Im not too old for him if hes 23 or 24 I hope hes not that stuckup university student sort no otherwise he wouldnt go sitting down in the old kitchen with him taking Eppss cocoa and talking of course he pretended to understand it all probably he told him he was out of Trinity college hes very young to be a professor I hope hes not a professor like Goodwin was he was a potent professor of John Jameson they all write about some woman in their poetry well I suppose he wont find many like me where softly sighs of love the light guitar where poetry is in the air the blue sea and the moon shining so beautifully coming back on the nightboat from Tarifa the lighthouse at Europa point the guitar that fellow played was so expressive will I ever go back there again all new faces two glancing eyes a lattice hid Ill sing that for him theyre my eyes if hes anything of a poet two eyes as darkly bright as loves own star arent those beautiful words as loves young star itll be a change the Lord knows to have an intelligent person to talk to about yourself not always listening to him and Billy Prescotts ad and Keyess ad and Tom the Devils ad then if anything goes wrong in their business we have to suffer Im sure hes very distinguished Id like to meet a man like that God not those other ruck besides hes young those fine young men I could see down in Margate strand bathingplace from the side of the rock standing up in the sun naked like a God or something and then plunging into the sea with them why arent all men like that thered be some consolation for a woman like that lovely little statue he bought I could look at him all day long curly head and his shoulders his finger up for you to listen theres real beauty and poetry for you I often felt I wanted to kiss him all over also his lovely young cock there so simple I wouldnt mind taking him in my mouth if nobody was looking as if it was asking you to suck it so clean and white he looks with his boyish face I would too in 1/2 a minute even if some of it went down what its only like gruel or the dew theres no danger besides hed be so clean compared with those pigs of men I suppose never dream of washing it from I years end to the other the most of them only thats what gives the women the moustaches Im sure itll be grand if I can only get in with a handsome young poet at my age Ill throw them the 1st thing in the morning till I see if the wishcard comes out or Ill try pairing the lady herself and see if he comes out Ill read and study all I can find or learn a bit off by heart if I knew who he likes so he wont think me stupid if he thinks all women are the same and I can teach him the other part Ill make him feel all over him till he half faints under me then hell write about me lover and mistress publicly too with our 2 photographs in all the papers when he becomes famous O but then what am I going to do about him though no thats no way for him has he no manners nor no refinement nor no nothing in his nature slapping us behind like that on my bottom because I didnt call him Hugh the ignoramus that doesnt know poetry from a cabbage thats what you get for not keeping them in their proper place pulling off his shoes and trousers there on the chair before me so barefaced without even asking permission and standing out that vulgar way in the half of a shirt they wear to be admired like a priest or a butcher or those old hypocrites in the time of Julius Caesar of course hes right enough in his way to pass the time as a joke sure you might as well be in bed with what with a lion God Im sure hed have something better to say for himself an old Lion would O well I suppose its because they were so plump and tempting in my short petticoat he couldnt resist they excite myself sometimes its well for men all the amount of pleasure they get off a womans body were so round and white for them always I wished I was one myself for a change just to try with that thing they have swelling up on you so hard and at the same time so soft when you touch it my uncle John has a thing long I heard those cornerboys saying passing the comer of Marrowbone lane my aunt Mary has a thing hairy because it was dark and they knew a girl was passing it didnt make me blush why should it either its only nature and he puts his thing long into my aunt Marys hairy etcetera and turns out to be you put the handle in a sweepingbrush men again all over they can pick and choose what they please a married woman or a fast widow or a girl for their different tastes like those houses round behind Irish street no but were to be always chained up theyre not going to be chaining me up no damn fear once I start I tell you for their stupid husbands jealousy why cant we all remain friends over it instead of quarrelling her husband found it out what they did together well naturally and if he did can he undo it hes coronado anyway whatever he does and then he going to the other mad extreme about the wife in Fair Tyrants of course the man never even casts a 2nd thought on the husband or wife either its the woman he wants and he gets her what else were we given all those desires for Id like to know I cant help it if Im young still can I its a wonder Im not an old shrivelled hag before my time living with him so cold never embracing me except sometimes when hes asleep the wrong end of me not knowing I suppose who he has any man thatd kiss a womans bottom Id throw my hat at him after that hed kiss anything unnatural where we havent I atom of any kind of expression in us all of us the same 2 lumps of lard before ever Id do that to a man pfooh the dirty brutes the mere thought is enough I kiss the feet of you senorita theres some sense in that didnt he kiss our halldoor yes he did what a madman nobody understands his cracked ideas but me still of course a woman wants to be embraced 20 times a day almost to make her look young no matter by who so long as to be in love or loved by somebody if the fellow you want isnt there sometimes by the Lord God I was thinking would I go around by the quays there some dark evening where nobodyd know me and pick up a sailor off the sea thatd be hot on for it and not care a pin whose I was only do it off up in a gate somewhere or one of those wildlooking gipsies in Rathfarnham had their camp pitched near the Bloomfield laundry to try and steal our things if they could I only sent mine there a few times for the name model laundry sending me back over and over some old ones odd stockings that blackguardlooking fellow with the fine eyes peeling a switch attack me in the dark and ride me up against the wall without a word or a murderer anybody what they do themselves the fine gentlemen in their silk hats that K C lives up somewhere this way coming out of Hardwicke lane the night he gave us the fish supper on account of winning over the boxing match of course it was for me he gave it I knew him by his gaiters and the walk and when I turned round a minute after just to see there was a woman after coming out of it too some filthy prostitute then he goes home to his wife after that only I suppose the half of those sailors are rotten again with disease O move over your big carcass out of that for the love of Mike listen to him the winds that waft my sighs to thee so well he may sleep and sigh the great Suggester Don Poldo de la Flora if he knew how he came out on the cards this morning hed have something to sigh for a dark man in some perplexity between 2 7s too in prison for Lord knows what he does that I dont know and Im to be slooching around down in the kitchen to get his lordship his breakfast while hes rolled up like a mummy will I indeed did you ever see me running Id just like to see myself at it show them attention and they treat you like dirt I dont care what anybody says itd be much better for the world to be governed by the women in it you wouldnt see women going and killing one another and slaughtering when do you ever see women rolling around drunk like they do or gambling every penny they have and losing it on horses yes because a woman whatever she does she knows where to stop sure they wouldnt be in the world at all only for us they dont know what it is to be a woman and a mother how could they where would they all of them be if they hadnt all a mother to look after them what I never had thats why I suppose hes running wild now out at night away from his books and studies and not living at home on account of the usual rowy house I suppose well its a poor case that those that have a fine son like that theyre not satisfied and I none was he not able to make one it wasnt my fault we came together when I was watching the two dogs up in her behind in the middle of the naked street that disheartened me altogether I suppose I oughtnt to have buried him in that little woolly jacket I knitted crying as I was but give it to some poor child but I knew well Id never have another our 1st death too it was we were never the same since O Im not going to think myself into the glooms about that any more I wonder why he wouldnt stay the night I felt all the time it was somebody strange he brought in instead of roving around the city meeting God knows who nightwalkers and pickpockets his poor mother wouldnt like that if she was alive ruining himself for life perhaps still its a lovely hour so silent I used to love coming home after dances the air of the night they have friends they can talk to weve none either he wants what he wont get or its some woman ready to stick her knife in you I hate that in women no wonder they treat us the way they do we are a dreadful lot of bitches I suppose its all the troubles we have makes us so snappy Im not like that he could easy have slept in there on the sofa in the other room I suppose he was as shy as a boy he being so young hardly 20 of me in the next room hed have heard me on the chamber arrah what harm Dedalus I wonder its like those names in Gibraltar Delapaz Delagracia they had the devils queer names there father Vilaplana of Santa Maria that gave me the rosary Rosales y OReilly in the Calle las Siete Revueltas and Pisimbo and Mrs Opisso in Governor street O what a name Id go and drown myself in the first river if I had a name like her O my and all the bits of streets Paradise ramp and Bedlam ramp and Rodgers ramp and Crutchetts ramp and the devils gap steps well small blame to me if I am a harumscarum I know I am a bit I declare to God I dont feel a day older than then I wonder could I get my tongue round any of the Spanish como esta usted muy bien gracias y usted see I havent forgotten it all I thought I had only for the grammar a noun is the name of any person place or thing pity I never tried to read that novel cantankerous Mrs Rubio lent me by Valera with the questions in it all upside down the two ways I always knew wed go away in the end I can tell him the Spanish and he tell me the Italian then hell see Im not so ignorant what a pity he didnt stay Im sure the poor fellow was dead tired and wanted a good sleep badly I could have brought him in his breakfast in bed with a bit of toast so long as I didnt do it on the knife for bad luck or if the woman was going her rounds with the watercress and something nice and tasty there are a few olives in the kitchen he might like I never could bear the look of them in Abrines I could do the criada the room looks all right since I changed it the other way you see something was telling me all the time Id have to introduce myself not knowing me from Adam very funny wouldnt it Im his wife or pretend we were in Spain with him half awake without a Gods notion where he is dos huevos estrellados senor Lord the crackedthingscomeintomyheadsometimes itd be great fun supposing he stayed with us why not theres the room upstairs empty and Millys bed in the back room he could do his writing and studies at the table in there for all the scribbling he does at it and if he wants to read in bed in the morning like me as hes making the breakfast for I he can make it for 2 Im sure Im not going to take in lodgers off the street for him if he takes a gesabo of a house like this Id love to have a long talk with an intelligent welleducated person Id have to get a nice pair of red slippers like those Turks with the fez used to sell or yellow and a nice semitransparent morning gown that I badly want or a peachblossom dressing jacket like the one long ago in Walpoles only 8/6 or 18/6 Ill just give him one more chance Ill get up early in the morning Im sick of Cohens old bed in any case I might go over to the markets to see all the vegetables and cabbages and tomatoes and carrots and all kinds of splendid fruits all coming in lovely and fresh who knows whod be the 1st man Id meet theyre out looking for it in the morning Mamy Dillon used to say they are and the night too that was her massgoing Id love a big juicy pear now to melt in your mouth like when I used to be in the longing way then Ill throw him up his eggs and tea in the moustachecup she gave him to make his mouth bigger I suppose hed like my nice cream too I know what Ill do Ill go about rather gay not too much singing a bit now and then mi fa pieta Masetto then Ill start dressing myself to go out presto non son piu forte Ill put on my best shift and drawers let him have a good eyeful out of that to make his micky stand for him Ill let him know if thats what he wanted that his wife is I s l o fucked yes and damn well fucked too up to my neck nearly not by him 5 or 6 times handrunning theres the mark of his spunk on the clean sheet I wouldnt bother to even iron it out that ought to satisfy him if you dont believe me feel my belly unless I made him stand there and put him into me Ive a mind to tell him every scrap and make him do it out in front of me serve him right its all his own fault if I am an adulteress as the thing in the gallery said O much about it if thats all the harm ever we did in this vale of tears God knows its not much doesnt everybody only they hide it I suppose thats what a woman is supposed to be there for or He wouldnt have made us the way He did so attractive to men then if he wants to kiss my bottom Ill drag open my drawers and bulge it right out in his face as large as life he can stick his tongue 7 miles up my hole as hes there my brown part then Ill tell him I want £ 1 or perhaps 30/- Ill tell him I want to buy underclothes then if he gives me that well he wont be too bad I dont want to soak it all out of him like other women do I could often have written out a fine cheque for myself and write his name on it for a couple of pounds a few times he forgot to lock it up besides he wont spend it Ill let him do it off on me behind provided he doesnt smear all my good drawers O I suppose that cant be helped Ill do the indifferent I or 2 questions Ill know by the answers when hes like that he cant keep a thing back I know every turn in him Ill tighten my bottom well and let out a few smutty words smellrump or lick my shit or the first mad thing comes into my head then Ill suggest about yes O wait now sonny my turn is coming Ill be quite gay and friendly over it O but I was forgetting this bloody pest of a thing pfooh you wouldnt know which to laugh or cry were such a mixture of plum and apple no Ill have to wear the old things so much the better itll be more pointed hell never know whether he did it or not there thats good enough for you any old thing at all then Ill wipe him off me just like a business his omission then Ill go out Ill have him eying up at the ceiling where is she gone now make him want me thats the only way a quarter after what an unearthly hour I suppose theyre just getting up in China now combing out their pigtails for the day well soon have the nuns ringing the angelus theyve nobody coming in to spoil their sleep except an odd priest or two for his night office or the alarmclock next door at cockshout clattering the brains out of itself let me see if I can doze off 1 2 3 4 5 what kind of flowers are those they invented like the stars the wallpaper in Lombard street was much nicer the apron he gave me was like that something only I only wore it twice better lower this lamp and try again so as I can get up early Ill go to Lambes there beside Findlaters and get them to send us some flowers to put about the place in case he brings him home tomorrow today I mean no no Fridays an unlucky day first I want to do the place up someway the dust grows in it I think while Im asleep then we can have music and cigarettes I can accompany him first I must clean the keys of the piano with milk whatll I wear shall I wear a white rose or those fairy cakes in Liptons I love the smell of a rich big shop at 7 1/2d a lb or the other ones with the cherries in them and the pinky sugar I ld a couple of lbs of those a nice plant for the middle of the table Id get that cheaper in wait wheres this I saw them not long ago I love flowers Id love to have the whole place swimming in roses God of heaven theres nothing like nature the wild mountains then the sea and the waves rushing then the beautiful country with the fields of oats and wheat and all kinds of things and all the fine cattle going about that would do your heart good to see rivers and lakes and flowers all sorts of shapes and smells and colours springing up even out of the ditches primroses and violets nature it is as for them saying theres no God I wouldnt give a snap of my two fingers for all their learning why dont they go and create something I often asked him atheists or whatever they call themselves go and wash the cobbles off themselves first then they go howling for the priest and they dying and why why because theyre afraid of hell on account of their bad conscience ah yes I know them well who was the first person in the universe before there was anybody that made it all who ah that they dont know neither do I so there you are they might as well try to stop the sun from rising tomorrow the sun shines for you he said the day we were lying among the rhododendrons on Howth head in the grey tweed suit and his straw hat the day I got him to propose to me yes first I gave him the bit of seedcake out of my mouth and it was leapyear like now yes 16 years ago my God after that long kiss I near lost my breath yes he said I was a flower of the mountain yes so we are flowers all a womans body yes that was one true thing he said in his life and the sun shines for you today yes that was why I liked him because I saw he understood or felt what a woman is and I knew I could always get round him and I gave him all the pleasure I could leading him on till he asked me to say yes and I wouldnt answer first only looked out over the sea and the sky I was thinking of so many things he didnt know of Mulvey and Mr Stanhope and Hester and father and old captain Groves and the sailors playing all birds fly and I say stoop and washing up dishes they called it on the pier and the sentry in front of the governors house with the thing round his white helmet poor devil half roasted and the Spanish girls laughing in their shawls and their tall combs and the auctions in the morning the Greeks and the jews and the Arabs and the devil knows who else from all the ends of Europe and Duke street and the fowl market all clucking outside Larby Sharons and the poor donkeys slipping half asleep and the vague fellows in the cloaks asleep in the shade on the steps and the big wheels of the carts of the bulls and the old castle thousands of years old yes and those handsome Moors all in white and turbans like kings asking you to sit down in their little bit of a shop and Ronda with the old windows of the posadas 2 glancing eyes a lattice hid for her lover to kiss the iron and the wineshops half open at night and the castanets and the night we missed the boat at Algeciras the watchman going about serene with his lamp and O that awful deepdown torrent O and the sea the sea crimson sometimes like fire and the glorious sunsets and the figtrees in the Alameda gardens yes and all the queer little streets and the pink and blue and yellow houses and the rosegardens and the jessamine and geraniums and cactuses and Gibraltar as a girl where I was a Flower of the mountain yes when I put the rose in my hair like the Andalusian girls used or shall I wear a red yes and how he kissed me under the Moorish wall and I thought well as well him as another and then I asked him with my eyes to ask again yes and then he asked me would I yes to say yes my mountain flower and first I put my arms around him yes and drew him down to me so he could feel my breasts all perfume yes and his heart was going like mad and yes I said yes I will Yes.

Trieste-Zurich-Paris
1914-1921

THE END

www.ingramcontent.com/pod-product-compliance
Lightning Source LLC
Chambersburg PA
CBHW020916310726
48980CB00011B/915/J

* 9 7 8 1 8 3 4 1 2 4 2 7 8 *